leader Pittsburgh

Pittsburgh Leader Almanac

and compendium of facts

leader Pittsburgh

Pittsburgh Leader Almanac
and compendium of facts

ISBN/EAN: 9783337343590

Printed in Europe, USA, Canada, Australia, Japan

Cover: Foto ©Andreas Hilbeck / pixelio.de

More available books at **www.hansebooks.com**

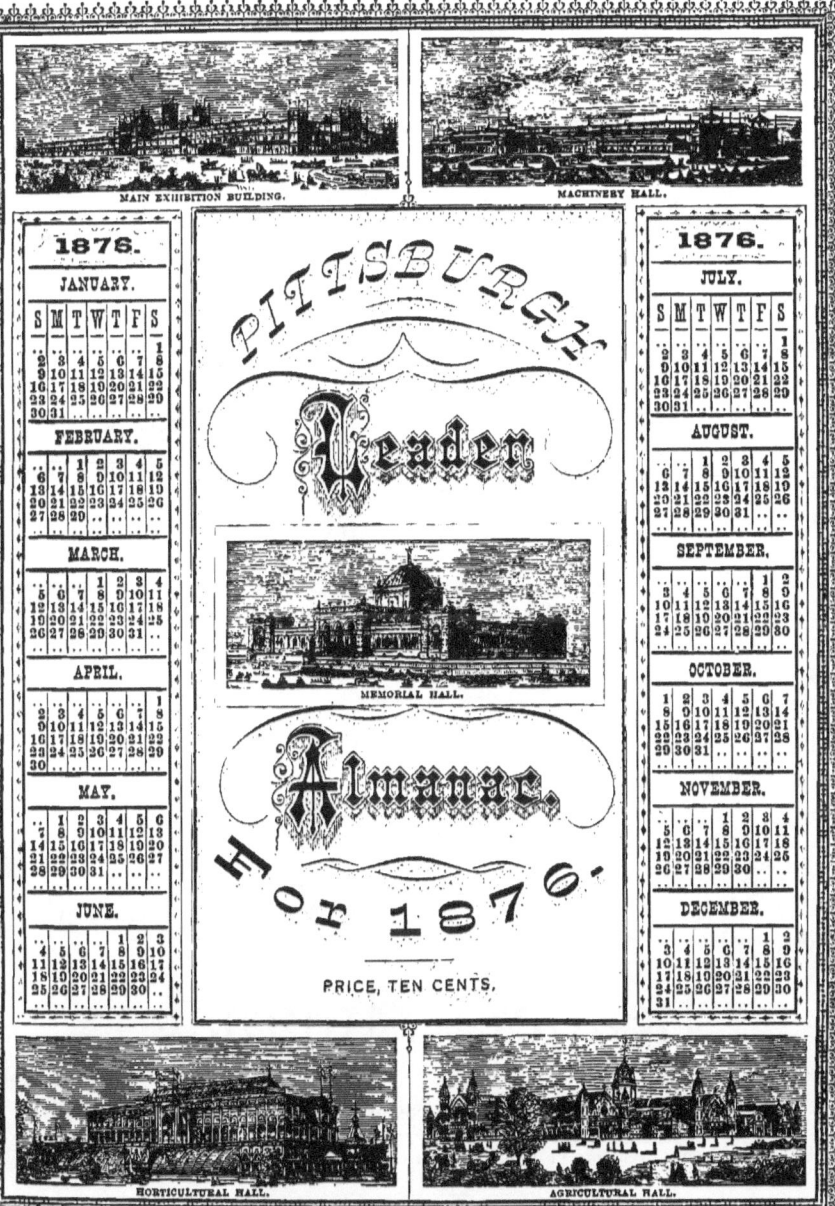

MAIN EXHIBITION BUILDING.

MACHINERY HALL.

1876.

JANUARY.

S	M	T	W	T	F	S
..	..	..	..	..	..	1
2	3	4	5	6	7	8
9	10	11	12	13	14	15
16	17	18	19	20	21	22
23	24	25	26	27	28	29
30	31	..	..	..	..	..

FEBRUARY.

S	M	T	W	T	F	S
..	..	1	2	3	4	5
6	7	8	9	10	11	12
13	14	15	16	17	18	19
20	21	22	23	24	25	26
27	28	29	..	..	..	..

MARCH.

S	M	T	W	T	F	S
..	..	..	1	2	3	4
5	6	7	8	9	10	11
12	13	14	15	16	17	18
19	20	21	22	23	24	25
26	27	28	29	30	31	..

APRIL.

S	M	T	W	T	F	S
..	..	..	..	..	..	1
2	3	4	5	6	7	8
9	10	11	12	13	14	15
16	17	18	19	20	21	22
23	24	25	26	27	28	29
30	..	..	..	..	..	..

MAY.

S	M	T	W	T	F	S
..	1	2	3	4	5	6
7	8	9	10	11	12	13
14	15	16	17	18	19	20
21	22	23	24	25	26	27
28	29	30	31	..	..	..

JUNE.

S	M	T	W	T	F	S
..	..	..	..	1	2	3
4	5	6	7	8	9	10
11	12	13	14	15	16	17
18	19	20	21	22	23	24
25	26	27	28	29	30	..

PITTSBURGH Leader

MEMORIAL HALL.

Almanac. For 1876.

PRICE, TEN CENTS.

1876.

JULY.

S	M	T	W	T	F	S
..	..	..	..	..	..	1
2	3	4	5	6	7	8
9	10	11	12	13	14	15
16	17	18	19	20	21	22
23	24	25	26	27	28	29
30	31	..	..	..	..	..

AUGUST.

S	M	T	W	T	F	S
..	..	1	2	3	4	5
6	7	8	9	10	11	12
13	14	15	16	17	18	19
20	21	22	23	24	25	26
27	28	29	30	31	..	..

SEPTEMBER.

S	M	T	W	T	F	S
..	..	..	..	..	1	2
3	4	5	6	7	8	9
10	11	12	13	14	15	16
17	18	19	20	21	22	23
24	25	26	27	28	29	30

OCTOBER.

S	M	T	W	T	F	S
1	2	3	4	5	6	7
8	9	10	11	12	13	14
15	16	17	18	19	20	21
22	23	24	25	26	27	28
29	30	31	..	..	..	..

NOVEMBER.

S	M	T	W	T	F	S
..	..	..	1	2	3	4
5	6	7	8	9	10	11
12	13	14	15	16	17	18
19	20	21	22	23	24	25
26	27	28	29	30	..	..

DECEMBER.

S	M	T	W	T	F	S
..	..	..	..	..	1	2
3	4	5	6	7	8	9
10	11	12	13	14	15	16
17	18	19	20	21	22	23
24	25	26	27	28	29	30
31	..	..	..	..	..	..

HORTICULTURAL HALL.

AGRICULTURAL HALL.

PRESS OF NEVIN, GRIFFIN & Co., cor. Fifth Ave. and Smithfield St.

LAWFUL WEIGHT PER BUSHEL OF GRAIN, Etc.

Wheat..............60	Buckwheat..........48	Blue Grass Seed......;14	Onion Sets..............35
Rye...................56	Clover Seed.........62	Hungarian.............50	Beans.................60
Ear Corn...........70	Timothy Seed........45	Apples, Dried.........25	Peas................63
Shell Corn.........56	Flax Seed.............56	Peaches, Dried........33	Bran.................20
Oats.................32	Hemp Seed...........42	Potatoes..............60	Hominy................60
Barley..............48	Millet Seed..........50	Onions.................50	

JEFFRIES, KIMBALL & CO.

No. 177 LIBERTY STREET, PITTSBURGH,

(Three doors above Sixth Street.)

GENERAL COMMISSION MERCHANTS,

—BUY, SHIP AND SELL—

FLOUR,	BUTTER,	SEEDS,	FEATHERS,
FEED,	EGGS,	POTATOES,	WOOL
GRAIN,	POULTRY,	TURNIPS,	STRAW,
FRUIT,	GAME,	NUTS,	HAY.

——And all kinds of Produce——

Shippers may rely unreservedly upon our securing the most immediate sales possible, as well as the first prices.

We invariably make returns and remit proceeds on day of sale, upon all sales effected, whether the whole or only part of goods are disposed of.

Advances will be made upon consignments, if goods are not perishable, to the amount of two-thirds of the value of consignment, at ruling prices.

We make NO CHARGE FOR STORAGE, having ample room in our warehouse to accommodate all our patrons without expense to them.

We solicit consignments from you, and pledge our personal attention to the sale of your goods.

REFERENCES:

By permission we refer to the following prominent business men of Pittsburgh.

Leader Publishing Co.   A. H. Bauman.   Maj. Y. Derr.   K. L. Laffer & Co.   J. L. Styne.

Nevin, Gribbin & Co.   Houck, McCague & Co.   John W. Pittock & Co.

PRESS NOTICES:

Messrs. JEFFRIES, KIMBALL & Co. start out with every reason to anticipate ample success. Mr. H. B. Jeffries, the senior member of the firm, has been on the LEADER for the past four years or so; he is a gentleman of energy and integrity, and goods consigned to him will be in reliable hands. Mr. Chas. Kimball, one of the partners, is an old commission man, acknowledged to be one of the finest salesmen in the city, and possesses a thorough knowledge of the business. Parties consigning goods to the firm will be certain of the quickest and largest returns possible.—*Evening Leader. Nov.* 18, 1875.

"MR. JEFFRIES has long been connected with the business department of the LEADER, of this city, and is well known as a gentleman of strict integrity and uprightness; Mr. Kimball is one of the best commission men in Pittsburgh, thoroughly acquainted with the trade, and a splendid salesman. Those consigning goods to the firm may rely upon fair dealings and quick returns, at the best prices to be had."—*Presbyterian Banner, Nov.* 23, 1875.

"MR. JEFFRIES is well known in Pittsburgh, having been connected with the LEADER for some years. He is a gentleman of established integrity, and will look closely after the interests of those entrusting goods to his firm for sale. Mr. Kimball has been in the commission business with different houses in this city, as buyer and salesman, for a long time, and is one of the most successful salesmen we have. Shippers will be honestly dealt with by the firm, and receive the largest and quickest returns to be obtained in this market."—*Christian Advance, Nov.* 20, 1875.

"MR. H. B. JEFFRIES, for several years connected with the LEADER, as journalist and in the business department, has taken a new departure. He will be found at the head of a general commission firm at 177 Liberty street. The gentlemen's well known integrity, energy and capacity for the new work should result in success, and we known that those who consign to the new house will be well satisfied that the qualities we attribute to Mr. Jeffries are nothing more than his merits deserve."—*Critic, Nov.* 28, 1875.

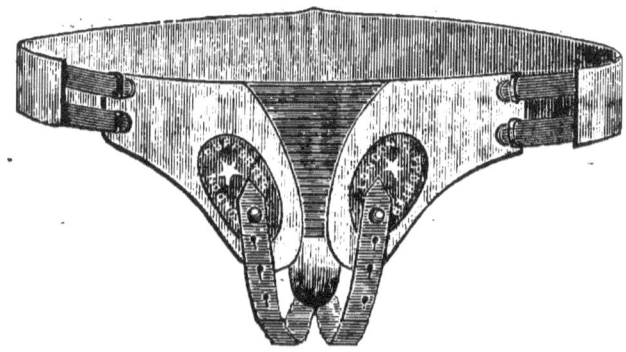
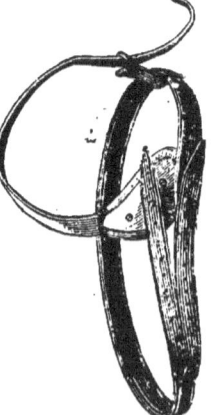

PITTSBURGH

LEADER ALMANAC

—— AND ——

COMPENDIUM OF FACTS.

1876.

CONTAINING, BESIDES ALL THE USEFUL INFORMATION USUALLY FOUND IN AN
ORDINARY ALMANAC, THE

PRINCIPAL EVENTS

Which have Occurred in Pittsburgh and Vicinity from 1750 to 1876.

PITTSBURGH, PA.:
LEADER PUBLISHING COMPANY.
1876.

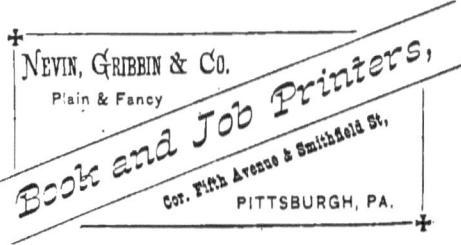

NEVIN, GRIBBIN & CO.

Plain & Fancy

Book and Job Printers,

Cor. Fifth Avenue & Smithfield St,

PITTSBURGH, PA.

LEADER BUILDING,
Pittsburgh, January, 1876.

The present volume makes the Fifth in the regular Annual Series of the LEADER ALMANAC. The usual array of statistical and other information which has made the book an indispensable one to the community, will be found as general and comprehensive in this as in the numbers which have preceded it. Great care has been exercised in the compilation of its pages, and they can be depended upon as reliable.

Leader Publishing Co.

| 1st Month. | | JANUARY, 1876. | | 31 Days. |

| DAYS OF MONTH. | DAYS OF WEEK. | CHRONOLOGICAL RECORD OF REMARKABLE EVENTS IN THE CITIES OF PITTSBURGH, ALLEGHENY AND VICINITY. | LUNATIONS. | PITTSBURGH. |

LUNATIONS.

	D.	H.	M.	
FIRST QUARTER				
FULL MOON......	4	10	3	Morning.
LAST QUARTER.	11	1	2	Morning.
NEW MOON.......	18	3	29	Morning.
	26	8	21	Morning.

		Chronological Record	SUN RISES. H. M.	SUN SETS. H. M.	MOON SETS. H. M.
1	Sa	1790...Population of Pittsburgh given 1,013.			
2	S	1793...Gen. Wayne's army arrives in Pittsburgh.			
3	Mo	1871...Abolition of corporal punishment in All'y schools.	7 24	4 45	10 51
4	Tu	1861...The guns from the arsenal for the south stopped.	7 24	4 46	11 40
5	We	1804...First iron foundry established in Pittsburgh.	7 24	4 46	Morn
6	Th	1868...Mayor Blackmore installed first term.	7 24	4 47	12 51
7	Fr	1873...Trouble at Beaver Falls with the Chinamen.	7 24	4 48	1 59
8	Sa	1873...Governor Geary delivers his last message.	7 24	4 49	3 0
9	S	1871...James McAuley, president select council, died.	7 24	4 50	4 12
10	Mo	1871...Hon. John Covode died.	7 24	4 51	5 22
11	Tu	1804...Total vote of the county for Governor 2,036.	7 24	4 52	6 19
12	We	1873...4,000 barrels of oil burned at Petrolia.	7 23	4 53	Rises
13	Th	1857...Henry A. Weaver elected Mayor of Pittsburgh.	7 23	4 54	6 26
14	Fr	1897...Slaves in Pittsburgh numbered 94.	7 23	4 55	7 31
15	Sa	1871...School House at Millvale burned; loss $10,000.	7 23	4 56	8 46
16	S	1873...Great rise in both rivers.	7 22	4 58	9 39
17	Mo	1856...Rev. C. Avery died leaving $700,000 for col'd schools.	7 22	4 59	10 29
18	Tu	1873....Ambrose Lynch sentenced to death.	7 21	5 0	11 27
19	We	1866...Martha Grinder, the poisoner, hung.	7 21	5 1	Morn
20	Th	1798...The first paper mill started in Pittsburgh.	7 20	5 2	12 24
21	Fr	1878...Explosion of molten iron at Garrison's Foundry.	7 20	5 3	1 25
22	Sa	1872...Edwin Forrest's last engage't in the city begins.	7 19	5 4	2 27
23	Su	1871...Death of Hon. Jasper E. Brady.	7 18	5 6	3 30
24	Mo	1852...Kossuth arrives in the city.	7 18	5 7	4 31
25	Tu	1872...Dedication of the new Trinity Church.	7 17	5 8	5 31
26	We	1851...Mechanic street bridge destroyed by fire.	7 16	5 9	6 24
27	Th	1850...Suspension of iron mills; many men out of work.	7 16	5 10	Sets
28	Fr	1863...Artemus Ward lectured before the Printer's Union	7 15	5 12	6 12
29	Sa	1841...President Harrison arrives by steamboat.	7 14	5 13	7 10
30	S	1873...Excelsior coffin factory burned.	7 13	5 14	8 9
31	Mo	1800...Population of Pittsburgh 1,569.	7 12	5 15	9 2
			7 11	5 16	10 1

PITTSBURGH.

WARDS AND BOUNDARIES.

FIRST WARD....Beginning at the city line, at the confluence of the Allegheny and Monongahela rivers; thence up the latter to a point opposite the middle of Wood street, thence up the middle of said street to a point opposite the middle of Diamond street, thence along Diamond to Market street, thence along Market street to the middle of Liberty street, thence down the middle of Liberty street to a point opposite the middle of Third street, thence along the middle of Third street to the city line of the Allegheny river, thence down the same to the place of beginning.

SECOND WARD....Beginning at a point in the city line opposite the middle of Wood street, thence up the middle of said street to a point opposite the middle of Diamond street, thence along the middle thereof to Old avenue, thence along the middle of said avenue to the old city line, thence along said line to the middle of the Monongahela river, thence down the same to the place of beginning.

THIRD WARD....Beginning at the middle of Liberty street opposite the end of Market street, thence up Liberty street to Grant street, thence along the same to Diamond street, thence along the same to the middle of Market street, thence along the same to the place of beginning.

FOURTH WARD....So much of the city as lies between the First and Third wards, the Allegheny river, and Eleventh street, shall be the Fourth ward.

FIFTH WARD....Beginning on Liberty street, thence up Washington street to Wylie, thence along Wylie to Chatham street, thence along Chatham to the junction of Fifth and Old avenues, thence along Old avenue to Diamond street, thence along Diamond street to Grant street, thence along Grant street to the place of beginning.

SIXTH WARD....Beginning on the Monongahela river where the old city line joins the same, thence up said river to a point opposite the middle of Miltenberger street, thence in a straight line and along the middle of said street to Fifth avenue, thence along the middle of said avenue to the old city line, thence along said line to the place of beginning.

SEVENTH WARD....Beginning on Washington street, opposite the center of Faber street, along Washington street to Wylie avenue, along Wylie avenue to Chatham, along Chatham to Fifth avenue, along Fifth avenue to Logan street, along Logan street and extension thereof to the line of Logan street, along the line of Faber street to the place of beginning.

EIGHTH WARD....Beginning on Fifth avenue at Logan street, along Logan street and extension thereof to Faber street, along the line of Faber street to Gum street, along Gum to Webster avenue, along Webster to Vine street, along Vine street to Fifth avenue, along Fifth avenue to the place of beginning.

NINTH WARD....Beginning on the Allegheny river at Eleventh street, thence up said river to Fifteenth street, thence along Fifteenth street to the line of Faber street, thence along the same to Washington street, thence along the same to Liberty street, thence along the same

2d Month.		FEBRUARY, 1876.		29 Days.

| | | CHRONOLOGICAL RECORD OF REMARKABLE EVENTS IN THE CITIES OF PITTSBURGH, ALLEGHENY AND VICINITY. | LUNATIONS. | PITTSBURGH. |

				D.	H.	M.	
			NEW MOON.........	2	8	33	Evening.
			FIRST QUARTER...	9	12	26	Evening.
			FULL MOON.........	16	11	35	Evening.
			LAST QUARTER....	25	12	59	Morning.

DAY OF MONTH.	DAY OF WEEK.		SUN RISES. H. M.	SUN SETS. H. M.	MOON SETS H. M.
1	Tu	1874—Lizzie Killien acquitted of the Brauenline murder.	7 10	5 18	11 0
2	We	1820—Population of Pittsburgh, 7,497.	7 9	5 19	Morn
3	Th	1875—Penn avenue freight depot hands strike.	7 8	5 20	12 54
4	Fr	1874—Thos. Nast lectures at Library Hall.	7 7	5 21	2 12
5	Sa	1854—Jewell, the murderer, attempts to break jail.	7 6	5 23	3 14
6	S	1869—The barber Kanfuan commits murder.	7 5	5 24	4 18
7	Mo	1873—Death of J. Woods, of Lloyd, Black & Co.	7 4	5 26	5 19
8	Tu	1873—Death of Governor John W. Geary.	7 3	5 27	6 23
9	We	1796—The number of houses in Pittsburgh, 98.	7 2	5 29	Rises
10	Th	1773—First court ever held in Pittsburgh in session.	7 1	5 30	6 20
11	Fr	1872—Mrs. Lopert burned to death.	7 0	5 31	7 22
12	Sa	1873—National Stove Manufacturers in council.	6 58	5 32	8 24
13	S	1815—News of conclusion of peace with England. Rejoic'g.	6 57	5 34	9 27
14	Mo	1861—Pres. Lincoln arrives on his way to Washington.	6 56	5 35	10 29
15	Tu	1865—Last lecture here by Artemus Ward.	6 55	5 36	11 32
16	We	1866—Bitter cold day ; thermometer ten deg. below zero.	6 53	5 37	Morn
17	Th	1873—Flood in the Monongahela river.	6 52	5 38	12 18
18	Fr	1872—Death of Alderman McMullin.	6 51	5 39	1 17
19	Sa	1872—South Improvement Company looms up.	6 50	5 41	2 10
20	S	1820—First St. Clair street bridge opened for travel.	6 48	5 42	3 4
21	Mo	1816—Bayardstown laid out by Geo. Bayard.	6 47	5 43	3 44
22	Tu	1855—13 deaths among German families from cold, &c.	6 45	5 44	4 23
23	We	1856—The Republican party organized here.	6 44	5 45	5 21
24	Th	1857—Lola Montez at the old theatre.	6 42	5 46	6 19
25	Fr	1850—City councils vote money for street preaching.	6 41	5 47	Sets
26	Sa	1873—Commencement of the season of Lent.	6 39	5 48	7 12
27	S	1830—Pittsburgh illuminated with gas.	6 37	5 49	8 10
28	Mo	1872—Arrival of the Japanese Embassy,	6 35	5 50	9 5
29	Tu	1872—First Rep. Club of campaign organizes.	6 34	5 51	9 54

PITTSBURGH.

WARDS AND BOUNDARIES.

to Eleventh street, thence along the same to the place of beginning.

TENTH WARD....Beginning on the Allegheny river at Fifteenth street to the line of Faber street, thence along the same to a point opposite Nineteenth street, thence along the same to the Allegheny river, thence down the same to Fifteenth street, the place of beginning.

ELEVENTH WARD....Beginning on Pennsylvania avenue at Vine street, along the said avenue to Jumonville street, along Jumonville street to De Villiers street, along De Villiers street to Centre avenue, along said avenue to Kirkpatrick street, along Kirkpatrick street to Webster avenue, along Webster avenue to Erin street, along Erin street to Fisk street, along Fisk street to southeast corner of the Tenth ward, thence along the line of the said ward to the north eastwardly corner of the Eighth ward, and thence along the line of the said ward to the place of beginning.

TWELFTH WARD....Beginning on the Allegheny river at Nineteenth street, thence up said river to Thirty-first street, thence along Thirty-first street to Penn avenue, thence along Thirtieth street to Arch street, thence along Arch to Gum street, thence along the line of Nineteenth street to the place of beginning.

THIRTEENTH WARD....To comprise all of Pitt township, except that part lying north of the Pennsylvania railroad.

FOURTEENTH WARD....All of Oakland township.

FIFTEENTH WARD....Beginning at Thirty-first street and Allegheny river, thence along Thirty-first to Penn avenue, Penn avenue to Butler, and along Butler to Greensburg turnpike, along turnpike to Arsenal street, thence along Arsenal street to Allegheny river, and thence down the Allegheny river to the place of beginning.

SIXTEENTH WARD.....Beginning at the intersection of Penn and Thirty-first streets, along Penn to Butler, along Butler to Greensburg turnpike, along turnpike to Pearl, along Pearl to Main, and along Main to the line of Jonas Roup's property, along said line to the Pennsylvania railroad, near Millvale, thence along the railroad to Thirtieth street, and along Thirtieth street to Penn, and along Penn to the place of beginning.

SEVENTEENTH WARD....The Second ward of Lawrenceville, together with the Allegheny cemetery.

EIGHTEENTH WARD....To begin at the Allegheny river, thence along Croghan street and the east line of the cemetery to the Morning Side road, along said road to its intersection with East Liberty road, thence by a straight line running west of the house of John R. Negley to Shuck's run, and down said run to Allegheny river, along the river to the place of beginning.

NINETEENTH WARD....To be bounded by the Allegheny river on the north, the Greensburg pike on the south, by Negley's run on the east, (the run crossing the pike east of the Episcopal church, East Liberty,) and on the west by the Eighteenth ward.

| 3d Month. | | MARCH, 1876. | | | 31 Days. |

| | | CHRONOLOGICAL RECORD OF REMARKABLE EVENTS IN THE CITIES OF PITTSBURGH, ALLEGHENY AND VICINITY. | LUNATIONS. | PITTSBURGH. |

LUNATIONS.
	D.	H.	M.
First Quarter....	3	4	26 Morning.
Full Moon........	10	12	51 Morning.
Last Quarter....	17	8	3 Evening.
New Moon.........	25	2	51 Evening.

DAY OF MONTH.	DAY OF WEEK.	CHRONOLOGICAL RECORD OF REMARKABLE EVENTS	SUN RISES.	SUN SET.	MOON SETS.
			H. M.	H. M. H.	M.
1	We	1872—Olympia Brown lectures on Women's Rights.	6 33	5 52	11 11
2	Th	1872—Josiah Welden dies.	6 32	6 53	Morn
3	Fr	1863—Neville B. Craig, prominent citizen, died.	6 31	5 54	12 33
4	Sa	1873—Hicken & Cambell's prize fight.	6 29	5 55	1 44
5	S	1873—Death of Colonel William Hopkins.	6 27	5 56	2 40
6	Mo	1851—The Fifth Presbyterian Church burned.	6 26	5 58	3 21
7	Tu	1873—Death of Judge Warner.	6 24	5 59	4 10
8	We	1863—The panic in pennies commenced.	6 28	6 0	5 6
9	Tr	1858—Monroe Stewart, the murderer, died of small-pox.	6 21	6 1	5 59
10	Fr	1865—Simon Loomis died.	6 20	6 2	Rises
11	Sa	1872—Meeting at Beaver Falls adverse to Chinamen	6 19	6 3	7 22
12	S	1873—Wholesale Grocers' Board organized.	6 18	6 4	8 24
13	Mo	1851—A fugitive slave case in the Courts.	6 16	6 5	9 26
14	Tu	1873—Suicide of Cashier Anderson, of Franklin.	8 14	6 6	10 29
15	We	1850—Dr. Morris opens a museum in Apolo Hall.	6 13	6 7	11 33
16	Th	1863—Reese C. Fleeson. a journalist, died.	6 11	6 8	Morn
17	Fr	1874—Garrison & Co's. foundry burned.	6 10	6 9	12 37
18	Sa	1816—The city of Pittsburgh incorporated.	6 8	6 11	1 21
19	S	1861—R. Jones, murderer of Mary Delaney, pardoned.	6 6	6 12	2 11
20	Mo	1874—Trans-Allegheny Canal Convention held.	6 4	6 13	2 59
21	Tu	1872—Theo. Tilton's lecture on "Marriage and Divorce."	6 3	6 14	3 42
22	We	1848—Henry Clay arrives in the city; much enthusiasm.	6 1	6 15	4 19
23	Th	1829—Select Council election consisting of three persons.	6 0	6 16	5 51
24	Fr	1854—David Jewell hung in the jail yard.	5 58	6 17	5 16
25	Sa	1874—Kittanning Woolen Mills burned	5 56	6 18	Sets
26	S	1873—Death of James McCully, well-known citizen.	5 55	6 19	7 20
27	Mo	1873—The Mahoning Valley miners strike.	5 53	6 20	8 28
28	Tu	1865—T. B. Keenan sentenced to hang for Obey murder.	5 51	6 21	9 56
29	We	1872—Consolidation of the South Side with Pitts.	5 49	6 22	11 10
30	Th	1867—Lockout of puddlers ended and work resumed.	5 47	6 23	Morn
31	Fr	1838—First malleable iron foundry established.	5 45	6 24	12 23

PITTSBURGH.

WARDS AND BOUNDARIES.

TWENTIETH WARD....Beginning at Pearl street and the Greensburg turnpike, along said pike to its intersection with Pennsylvania avenue or Fourth street road, thence along said avenue to the old line of Pitt township, thence along said line to the Pennsylvania railroad to Roup's line near Millvale, thence along the east line to the Sixteenth ward to the place of beginning.

TWENTY-FIRST WARD....To consist of all that part of the city between the Nineteenth ward and the eastern line of the consolidated city, and between the Allegheny river and the Greensburg turnpike.

TWENTY-SECOND WARD....Beginning at the intersection of the old Oakland township line and Pennsylvania avenue, thence along said township line to the Four Mile run road, thence along said road to the Nine Mile run at Salt Works and to the Monongahela river, thence along the river to the east line of the city, along said line to the Greensburg pike, and along said pike to Pennsylvania avenue, thence along the avenue to the place of beginning.

TWENTY-THIRD WARD....To comprise all of Peebles township between the Monongahela river and the south line of the Twenty-second ward.

PITTSBURGH...SOUTH SIDE.

TWENTY-FOURTH WARD....This ward is comprised of the territory contained in Ormsby borough. It begins at the foot of Twenty-seventh streeth, thence up the Monongahela river to the line of Lower St. Clair township, thence southerly to the line of St. Clair borough, thence westerly to the center of Twenty-seventh street, thence along Twenty-seventh street to the place of beginning.

TWENTY-FIFTH WARD....Late the Second ward of East Birmingham. It begins at Twenty-first street, thence along the Monongahela river to Twenty-seventh street, thence along Twenty-seventh street to a point sixty feet south of Josephine street, thence by a line parallel with Josephine street to the middle of Twenty-first street, thence by Twenty-first street to place of beginning.

TWENTY-SIXTH WARD....Late the First ward of East Birmingham. Begins at Seventeenth street, thence along the Monongahela river to Twenty-first street, thence along Twenty-first street to Josephine street, thence by a line parallel with Josephine street to Seventeenth street, thence along Seventeenth street to the place of beginning.

TWENTY-SEVENTH WARD....Comprises the borough of St. Clair, and is bounded on the north by Josephine and Manor streets and Ormsby borough, on the east by Lower St. Clair township, on the south by Lower St. Clair township and Allentown, and on the west by the borough of South Pittsburgh.

TWENTY-EIGHTH WARD....Late the Second precinct of Birmingham. Begins at the foot of Twelfth street, thence along the Monongahela river to Seventeenth street, thence along Seventeenth to Manor street, thence along Manor to Twelfth street, thence along Twelfth street to the place of beginning.

4th Month.		APRIL, 1876.		30 Days.

		CHRONOLOGICAL RECORD OF REMARKABE EVENTS IN THE CITIES OF PITTSBURGH, ALLEGHENY AND VICINITY.	LUNATIONS.	PITTSBURGH.

DAYS OF MONTH.	DAYS OF WEEK.	CHRONOLOGICAL RECORD OF REMARKABE EVENTS	LUNATIONS	PITTSBURGH

LUNATIONS.

	D	H.	M.	
FIRST QUARTER..	1	10	50	Morning.
FULL MOON........	8	2	17	Evening.
LAST QUARTER...	16	3	16	Evening.
NEW MOON........	24	1	42	Morning.
FIRST QUARTER..	30	5	5	Evening.

Days of Month	Days of Week	Record	Sun rises	Sun sets.	Moon Sets
			H. M.	H. M.	H. M.
1	Sa	1874—Jno. Shuettler acquitted of Brauenline murder.	5 43	6 25	1 34
2	S	1826—Population of Pittsburgh 10,315.	5 42	6 26	2 30
3	Mo	1872—W. J. Totten, a prominent manufacturer, died.	5 40	6 27	3 11
4	Tu	1873—Destructive fire at Oil City.	5 38	6 28	3 44
5	We	1873—Graff & Co.'s tube works destroyed by fire.	5 37	6 29	4 15
6	Th	1818—Mechanics Bank robbed of over $100,000.	5 35	6 30	4 46
7	Fr	1853—Bishop O'Connor lectured before the Y. M. C. A.	5 34	6 31	5 16
8	Sa	1871—St. Bridget's Catholic Church destroyed by fire.	5 32	6 32	Rises.
9	S	1872—Great freshet in the Monongahela.	5 30	6 33	7 35
10	Mo	1845—Great fire in Pittsburgh ; 56 acres devastated.	5 29	6 34	8 40
11	Tu	1853—Ohio and Penn'a Railroad opened to Crestline.	5 27	6 35	9 49
12	We	1873—Safe Deposit box recovered.	5 26	6 36	10 58
13	Th	1863—3,000 barrels of oil burned at the point.	5 24	6 37	11 57
14	Fr	1869—Great fire at Forsyth Bros.' oil works. Loss, $298,000.	5 23	6 38	Morn.
15	Sa	1870—Benjamin Trimble, founder Varieties Theater, died.	5 21	6 39	12 50
16	S	1814—The Allegheny Arsenal completed.	5 20	6 41	1 31
17	Mo	1873—President Grant arrives in the city.	5 18	6 42	2 9
18	Tu	1855—Strike of the nail-cutters for higher wages.	5 17	6 43	2 39
19	We	1873—Wholesale jail escape at Washington, Pa.	5 15	6 44	2 59
20	Th	1850—Bishop O'Connor recovers $4,000 against the city.	5 14	6 45	3 29
21	Fr	1873—Hampton, the bond robber, arrested.	5 12	6 46	3 59
22	Sa	1850—Charter of the House of Refuge obtained.	5 11	6 47	4 29
23	S	1861—The Greys mustered into the U. S. service.	5 9	6 48	4 55
24	Mo	1850—Death of Alexander Franklin, member of the bar.	5 8	6 49	Sets.
25	Tu	1873—Briceland, the murderer, recaptured.	5 6	6 50	8 39
26	We	1804—County Treasurer's salary increased to $125 per an.	5 5	6 51	9 20
27	Th	1801—Flour sold for $1.50 per 100 weight.	5 4	6 52	10 16
28	Fr	1873—Lizzie Moss murdered at Port Perry.	5 2	6 53	11 12
29	Sa	1869—The negro, Lane, hung in the jail yard.	5 1	6 54	Morn.
30	S	1873—Mount Pleasant Railroad war renewed.	5 0	6 55	12 39

PITTSBURGH.

WARDS AND BOUNDARIES.

TWENTY-NINTH WARD.—Late the First precinct of Birmingham. It begins at Sixth street, thence along the Monongahela river to Twelfth street, thence along Twelfth to Manor street, thence along Manor to Sixth street, thence along Sixth street to place of beginning.

THIRTIETH WARD.—Late South Pittsburgh. It has its beginning at the Suspension bridge, Thence along the Monongahela river to Sixth street, thence along Sixth to Manor and the line of St. Clair borough to Allentown, thence by Allentown and Mt. Washington to the Monongahela borough line, thence by the line of Monongahela borough to the place of beginning.

THIRTY-FIRST WARD.—This ward comprises the territory embraced in the borough of Allentown.

THIRTY-SECOND WARD—This ward comprises all the territory embraced in the borough of Mt. Washington.

THIRTY-THIRD WARD—Begins at the Suspension bridge, thence along the Monongahela river to West Pittsburgh, thence by the line of West Pittsburgh to High street, thence by High street to the line of South Pittsburgh, thence by this line to the place of beginning.

THIRTY-FOURTH WARD.—Late West Pittsburgh. Begins at Temperanceville, thence along the river to the line of Monongahela borough, thence by the line of this borough to High street, thence by High street to Temperanceville, thence by line of Temperanceville to the place of beginning.

THIRTY-FIFTH WARD.—This ward comprises all the territory embraced in Union borough.

THIRTY-SIXTH WARD.—This ward is comprised of the territory embraced in what was called Temperanceville.

THIRTY-SEVENTH WARD, Wilkins township, has been ruled out of the city by a decree of court, an error having been discovered in the count of the votes making it a part of the city, the number being insufficient.

CITY GOVERNMENT.

PITTSBURGH, 1876.

MAYOR.—WM. C. McCARTHY.
DEPUTY MAYORS.—WM. KING.
W. LOWRY.
P. HOERR.
J. M. SHAEFFER.
JNO. FITZSIMMONS.
MARTIN GEIER.
TREASURER.—CHRISTOPHER H MAGEE.
CONTROLER.—ROBT. M. SNODGRASS.

PITTSBURGH COUNCILS,

SELECT COUNCILS, 1876.

First Ward.—William B. Hunter, F. Schild.
Second Ward.—Benj. Singerly, Benjamin Darlington.
Third Ward.—Gus. L. Braun, John Shipton.
Fourth Ward.—H. Darlington, W. A. Herron.
Fifth Ward.—John O'Neil, A. B. Hayden.

5th Month.		MAY, 1876.		31 Days.

DAYS OF MONTH.	DAYS OF WEEK.	CHRONOLOGICAL RECORD *OF REMARKABLE EVENTS* IN THE CITIES OF PITTSBURGH, ALLE-GHENY AND VICINITY.	LUNATIONS.	PITTSBURGH.		
			FULL MOON.......... D. H. M. LAST QUARTER... 8 4 31 Morning. NEW MOON......... 16 8 5 Morning. FIRST QUARTER... 23 10 4 Morning. 30 12 27 Morning.	Sun rises. H. M.	Sun sets. H. M.	Moon sets H. M.
1	Mo	1874—Ortwein, the Hamnett murderer, arrested.		4 59	6 56	1 15
2	Tu	1851—Site for present Post Office selected.		4 57	6 57	1 46
3	We	1873—Last appearance here of Laura Keene.		4 56	6 58	2 12
4	Th	1832—Act of Assembly passed creating Duquesne Greys.		4 55	6 59	2 46
5	Fr	1864—Gen. Alex. Hays killed at battle of Wilderness.		4 54	7 0	3 5
6	Sa	1807—Pittsburgh contained 627 houses.		4 52	7 1	3 29
7	S	1859—Ten steamboats burned at the Monongahela wharf.		4 51	7 2	4 0
8	Mo	1872—County Agricultural and Mechanics Institute org'zd		4 50	7 3	Rises.
9	Tu	1873—The Novelty Works destroyed by fire.		4 49	7 4	8 57
10	We	1814—The Bank of Pittsburgh established.		4 48	7 6	9 50
11	Th	1874—Crusaders petition Councils to continue work.		4 47	7 7	10 32
12	Fr	1845—Aqueduct over the Allegheny river finished.		4 46	7 8	11 16
13	Sa	1814—Sailors depart to join the fleet on Lake Erie.		4 45	7 9	11 56
14	S	1874—Oil train burned at Stewart station, A. V. R. R.		4 44	7 10	Morn.
15	Mo	1840—A safe manufactory started in Pittsburgh.		4 43	7 11	12 38
16	Tu	1873—First Postal cards distributed.		4 42	7 12	1 11
17	We	1821—Flour sells at one dollar per barrel.		4 41	7 13	1 39
18	Th	1874—Edward Treacy shot and killed by Jno. Callahan.		4 40	7 14	2 4
19	Fr	1866—Grant house, Franklin, Pa., burned; two lives lost.		4 39	7 14	2 29
20	Sa	1860—Evans and Jacoby, wife murderers, hung.		4 39	7 15	2 55
21	S	1872—Red Cloud and party of Sioux arrive in city.		4 38	7 16	3 18
22	Mo	1873—Destructive fire in New Castle.		4 37	7 17	3 49
23	Tu	1873—Two children burned to death by an oil explosion.		4 36	7 18	Sets.
24	We	1871—Postmaster McClelland died.		4 36	7 19	8 31
25	Th	1837—Shinplasters in circulation here.		4 35	7 20	9 10
26	Fr	1866—Oil City almost destroyed by fire. Loss, $1,000,000.		4 34	7 20	10 16
27	Sa	1819—The U. S. Laboratory destroyed by fire.		4 34	7 21	11 22
28	S	1867—Manufactory for queensware established.		4 33	7 22	Morn.
29	Mo	1874—Bitner's car works destroyed by fire.		4 33	7 23	12 22
30	Tu	1870—Three boys drowned in Allegheny river.		4 32	7 23	12 49
31	We	1871—Knights Templars leave for Europe.		4 32	7 24	1 12

Sixth Ward.—Jacob Keebler, H. F. Dannals.
Seventh Ward.—John Musgrave, Chas. Jeremy.
Eighth Ward.—J. G. McCandless, John .W. McGimpsey.
Ninth Ward.—Jno. Froelich, A. L. Ricmaur.

CITY GOVERNMENT.

(CONCLUDED.)

Tenth Ward.—Jas. Lappan, J. Ahl.
Eleventh Ward.—William Moore, S. Barclay.
Twelfth Ward.—T. W. Welsh, R. N. Ray.
Thirteenth Ward.—C. L. Powers, Henry Metzger.
Fourteenth Ward.—Jas. B. Glass, R. S. Waring.
Fifteenth Ward.—S. Dietrich, J. G. Weldon.
Sixteenth Ward.—Samuel McKinley, J. B. Epping.
Seventeenth Ward.—Geo. Fox, W. T. Taylor.
Eighteenth Ward.—N. P. Sawyer, H. Lagerman.
Nineteenth Ward.—R. H. Negley, J. G. McConnell.
Twentieth Ward.—David Aiken, Jr., A. H. Gross.
Twenty-first Ward.—Jno. F. Denniston, James Littell.
Twenty-second Ward.—D. D. Bruce, James B. Murray.
Twenty-third Ward.—Sam'l. S. Brown, C. Evans.
Twenty-fourth Ward.—Wm. McClurg, Jas. S. Atkinson.
Twenty-fifth Ward.—M. M. Felker, R. B. Brown.
Twenty-sixth Ward.—Jno. H. Sorg, Dr. Arnholdt.
Twenty-seventh Ward.—P. Carr, Jacob Nusser.
Twenty-eighth Ward.—J. K. P. Duff, Dr. Kerr.
Twenty-ninth Ward.—Jos. Miller, Wm. Doyle.
Thirtieth Ward.—Wm. M. McCombs, H. D. Rolfe.
Thirty-first Ward.—Jacob Schwarm, John T. Bates.
Thirty-second Ward.—Henry Meyer, S. H. Goldthorpe.
Thirty-third Ward.—Thomas Kernan, Richard Perry.
Thirty-fourth Ward.—Alex. Foster, J. D. Buckley.
Thirty-fifth Ward.—George Holiday, *——.
Thirty-sixth Ward.—M. W. Rodgers, J. P. Vierheller.

Those marked * denote vacancies which have occurred either by reason of death, or by resignation.

COMMON COUNCIL.

First Ward.—J. F. Roth.
Second Ward.—John Torrence.
Third Ward.—Jno. N. Neeb.
Fourth Ward.—W. W. Thomson.
Fifth Ward.—P. Clark.
Sixth Ward.—Wm. J. Flinn, Otto Helmold.
Seventh Ward.—Samuel Mears.
Eighth Ward.—Wm. Moore, Wm. Keir.
Ninth Ward.—Geo. W. Kettenberg.
Tenth Ward.—Wm. J. Powers.

CITY GOVERNMENT.

(CONCLUDED.)

Eleventh Ward.—Henry Voscamp.
Twelfth Ward.—Chris. Roth, Jas. M. Acheson.
Thirteenth Ward.—T. H. Dixon.
Fourteenth Ward.—Jas. Reynolds, W. H. Dauler.
Fifteenth Ward.—John. A. Fox.
Sixteenth Ward.—B. F. Coll, W. J. Fennerty.
Seventeenth Ward.—Jos. G. Wainwright, W. S. Robeson.
Eighteenth Ward.—Neil C. McCafferty.
Nineteenth Ward.—Jas. L. Ferson.
Twentieth Ward.—W. B. Negley.
Twenty-first Ward.—W. F. Aull.
Twenty-second Ward.—D. B. Morrison.
Twenty-third Ward.—Jno. Fritz.
Twenty-fourth Ward.—C. P. Hagan.
Twenty-fifth Ward.—G. G. Rahauser.
Twenty-sixth Ward.—J. Hughes, Leonard Hahn.
Twenty-seventh Ward.—F. S. Hogle.
Twenty-eighth Ward.—Wm. Kirchner.
Twenty-ninth Ward.—R. H. Conway.
Thirtieth Ward.—W. H. Nantken.
Thirty-first Ward.—W. W. Nisbet.
Thirty-second Ward.—C. A. Boucher.
Thirty-third Ward.—P. Laughran.
Thirty-fourth Ward.—P. Foley.
Thirty-fifth Ward.—W. M. Bell.
Thirty-sixth Ward.—Jos. Lemmer.

ELECTION OF MEMBERS OF COUNCILS.

Members of both branches of the City Councils are elected on the third Tuesday of each February, but are not sworn in, nor do they assume the duties of their positions until the succeeding January, thus, under the new arrangement of things, members of Councils are chosen one year previous to the organization of the Councils to which they are elected.

ORGANIZATION OF COUNCILS.

The new Councils for 1876, meet for organization January 3, at 2 P. M. Each branch organizes separately. The election returns are at first presented and read by the old Clerk. The Council elect then elect a president and clerk, who are then sworn in. The president then administers the oath of office to the members; upon the completion of the organization of each branch, a joint meeting is held, when the returns for Mayor, Controller and Treasurer are received, and the persons elected to these offices are sworn in, the president of Select Councils administering the oath in presence of the members.

Councils, on the second Monday next succeeding organization, will again meet in joint session to elect city officers, and hear the reports from the presidents of the standing committees. Stated meetings of Councils are held on the second and last Mondays of every month, at 2 o'clock P. M.

6th Month.	JUNE, 1876.	30 Days.

DAY OF MONTH.	DAY OF WEEK.	CHRONOLOGICAL RECORD *OF REMARKABLE EVENTS* IN THE CITIES OF PITTSBURGH, ALLE-GHENY AND VICINITY.	LUNATIONS.		PITTSBURGH.		

LUNATIONS.

	D.	H.	M.	
FULL MOON	6	7	16	Evening.
LAST QUARTER	14	9	54	Evening.
NEW MOON	21	4	54	Evening.
FIRST QUARTER	28	9	51	Morning.

DAY OF MONTH	DAY OF WEEK	EVENTS	SUN RISES H. M.	SUN SETS H. M.	MOON SETS H. M.
1	Th	1868—News of the death of Ex-Pres. Buchanan received.	4 31	7 25	1 34
2	Fr	1871—Brooks, Ballantine & Co's oil refinery burned.	4 31	7 26	1 57
3	Sa	1871—N. P. Fetterman, of Pittsburgh Bar, dies.	4 30	7 26	3 16
4	S	1848—Western Pennsylvania Hospital commenced.	4 30	7 27	2 37
5	Mo	1865—The One Hundred and Fifty-fifth regiment arrives.	4 30	7 28	3 9
6	Tu	1871—Mrs. Swisshelm addresses the Woman Suffragists.	4 20	7 28	Rises
7	We	1850—Corner-stone of Poor House laid.	4 29	7 29	8 40
8	Th	1871—Corner-stone of Pennsylvania Female College laid.	4 29	7 29	9 33
9	Fr	1868—Erection of the New Municipal Hall commenced.	4 29	7 30	10 13
10	Sa	1871—The delinquent County Com., Neely & Magee, sen.	4 29	7 30	10 46
11	S	1872—William Hatfield murdered by Ambrose Lynch.	4 29	7 31	11 16
12	Mo	1841—Court House removed to its present site.	4 29	7 31	11 39
13	Tu	1873—Manus Patton, a desperado, killed at Gallitzen.	4 28	7 32	Morn
14	We	1865—Convention Supts. Insane Asylums of America.	4 28	7 32	12 21
15	Th	1852—Corner-stone of St. Paul's Catholic Cathedral laid.	4 28	7 33	12 46
16	Fr	1872—Glass and Iron Bank robbed of $28,000 in bonds.	4 29	7 33	1 14
17	Sa	1872—Celebration of Freedom's Day by the negroes.	4 29	7 33	1 40
18	S	1873—Ohio River Improvement Committee meet.	4 29	7 33	2 5
19	Mo	1792—Auction sale of slaves in Pittsburgh.	4 29	7 34	2 31
20	Tu	1873—First case of sun-stroke reported.	4 29	7 34	2 56
21	We	1873—Committee on Industrial Exposition appointed.	4 30	7 24	Sets
22	Th	1863—Large fire among warehouses at old canal basin.	4 30	7 34	8 49
23	Fr	1873—Cholera proclamation issued.	4 30	7 34	9 30
24	Sa	1855—St. Paul's Cathedral dedicated.	4 30	7 34	10 12
25	S	1875—Boat race bet. Scharff and Ten Eyck ; won by latter.	4 30	7 34	10 42
26	Mo	1871—The Baltimore excursionists arrive here.	4 31	7 34	11 4
27	Tu	1862—Col. Sam Black killed at battle Gains' Mills.	4 31	7 34	11 27
28	We	1870—Great petroleum fire ; Sharpsburgh bridge burned.	4 31	7 34	11 45
29	Th	1871—East Liberty lighted with gas for the first time.	4 32	7 34	Morn
30	Fr	1851—Opening of Ohio and Pa. railroad to New Brighton.	4 32	7 34	12 4

GENERAL STATISTICS.

VOTE FOR MAYOR—1874, 1871, 1868, 1867.
The following are the complete official returns for Mayor of the City of Pittsburgh, at the regular election, held the 17th day of February, 1874:

WARDS.	McCarthy, R.	Guthrie, D.	Hershberger, T.
First	288	139	5
Second	229	215	12
Third	157	141	1
Fourth	170	205	10
Fifth	99	382	.....
Sixth	405	236	5
Seventh	338	196	12
Eighth	428	151	10
Ninth	259	248	.....
Tenth	140	170	4
Eleventh	400	196	62
Twelfth, first precinct	171	149	8
Twelfth, second precinct	160	155	2
Thirteenth, first precinct	235	110	.....
Thirteenth, second precinct	50	29	6
Fourteenth	322	252	6
Fifteenth	281	194	12
Sixteenth, first precinct	82	126	3
Sixteenth, second precinct	128	135	14
Seventeenth, first precinct	188	207	9
Seventeenth, second precinct	131	196	23
Eighteenth	49	91	2
Nineteenth	140	182	25
Twentieth	64	200	5
Twenty-first, first precinct	221	172	14
Twenty-first, second precinct	12	9	.....
Twenty-second, first precinct	34	64	4
Twenty-second, second precinct	14	36	1
Twenty-third	189	168	2
Twenty-fourth	256	75	2
Twenty-fifth	248	198	26
Twenty-sixth	405	271	111
Twenty-seventh, first precinct	44	166	.....
Twenty-seventh, second precinct	75	2	2
Twenty-eighth	265	200	25
Twenty-ninth	224	142	11
Thirtieth	189	104	5
Thirty-first	100	32	3
Thirty-second	162	92	31
Thirty-third	43	85	1
Thirty-fourth	81	67	5
Thirty-fifth	39	40	17
Thirty-sixth	43	147	193
Thirty-seventh	107	70	15
Total	7515	6445	704

RECAPITULATION.

1874.—Whole vote cast, 14,664. William C., McCarthy, R., majority over Mr. Guthrie, D. 1,070.

1871.—Whole vote cast, 10,995. James Blackmore's, Independent, majority over Benjamin W. Morgan, Republican, 1,336.

GENERAL STATISTICS.

CONTINUED.

1868.—Whole vote cast, 12,997. Jared M. Brush, Republican, majority over James Blackmore, Independent, 1,553.

1867.—Whole vote cast, 8,449. James Blackmore's Independent, majority over John W. Riddell, Republican, 2,777.

VOTE FOR CITY TREASURER AND CONTROLLER.

The following are the complete official returns for Treasurer and Controller of the City of Pittsburgh, at the regular election, held on the 17th day of February, 1874:

WARDS.	TREASU'R			CONTR'R		
	McGee, R.	Ihnsen, D.	McGaw, T.	Snodgrass, Jr.	Elder, D.	Morgan, T.
First	230	200	1	212	218	1
Second	277	171	3	267	176	3
Third	184	119	.....	182	114	.....
Fourth	199	164	6	201	164	.....
Fifth	109	370	.....	103	376	.....
Sixth	409	233	.....	422	227	.....
Seventh	394	151	9	440	108	10
Eighth	451	125	7	457	127	7
Ninth	249	258	.....	249	258	.....
Tenth	158	150	1	124	183	1
Eleventh	397	197	3	409	187	3
Twelfth, 1st p	177	148	8	147	145	8
Twelfth, 2d p	167	149	1	162	149	-1
Thirteenth, 1st p	237	93	.....	245	93	.....
Thirteenth 2d p	52	29	4	52	29	4
Fourteenth	391	187	2	377	203	2
Fifteenth	229	190	8	229	193	8
Sixteenth, 1st p	82	120	3	88	115	3
Sixteenth, 2d p	141	126	.....	142	124	.....
Seventeenth, 1st p	179	167	4	160	185	4
Seventeenth, 2d p	159	173	.....	156	175	.....
Eighteenth	74	66	2	73	66	2
Nineteenth	226	112	14	226	111	13
Twentieth	209	58	.....	205	62	.....
Twenty-first, 1st p	265	135	6	271	133	7
Twenty-first, 2d p	15	6	.....	15	6	.....
Twenty-second,1st p	91	6	4	91	9	4
Twenty-second, 2d p	39	11	.....	33	17	1
Twenty-third	173	134	.....	180	126	.....
Twenty-fourth	260	68	.....	265	53	.....
Twenty-fifth	235	212	22	378	70	22
Twenty-sixth	419	265	4	432	246	7
Twenty-seventh,1st p	35	175	.....	35	176	.....
Twenty-seventh,2d p	75	3	1	75	3	1
Twenty-eighth	209	251	23	234	232	19
Twenty-ninth	221	143	9	229	139	9
Thirtieth	219	70	5	199	93	5
Thirty-first	106	28	1	100	28	1
Thirty-second	186	56	31	188	68	38
Thirty-third	43	85	.....	43	84	.....
Thirty-fourth	37	113	3	37	113	2
Thirty-fifth	44	40	13	43	39	9
Thirty-sixth	150	53	68	149	54	66
Thirty-seventh	130	55	8	132	52	8
Total	8332	5665	274	8462	5334	266

| 7th Month. | | JULY, 1876. | | | 31 Days. |

DAYS OF MONTH.	DAYS OF WEEK.	CHRONOLOGICAL RECORD OF REMARKABLE EVENTS IN THE CITIES OF PITTSBURGH, ALLEGHENY AND VICINITY.	LUNATIONS.	PITTSBURGH.		

		LUNATIONS.	D. H. M.
FULL MOON........	6 10 16 Morning.
LAST QUARTER....	14 8 34 Morning.
NEW MOON........	20 11 31 Evening.
FIRST QUARTER...	27 9 56 Evening.

Days	Day	Event	Sun rises.	Sun sets.	Moon sets.
			H. M.	H. M.	H. M.
1	Sa	1873...Prohibitionists Convention held.	4 33	7 34	12 30
2	S	1871...Wood's rolling-mills, McKeesport, burned.	4 33	7 34	1 1
3	Mo	1851...Running of the first locomotive in Allegheny City.	4 34	7 34	1 35
4	Tu	1874...Great fire in Allegheny City.	4 35	7 33	2 15
5	We	1865...Hamill, the oarsman, defeated in England by Kelly.	4 35	7 33	3 2
6	Th	1866...Pittsburgh divided into twenty-three wards.	4 36	7 33	Rises.
7	Fr	1874...Great wind storm. Hand street bridge roof blown off.	4 36	7 33	8 48
8	Sa	1873...Barbers agree to shave no more on Sunday.	4 37	7 32	9 20
9	S	1755...Gen. Braddock defeated by the French and Indians.	4 38	7 32	9 46
10	Mo	1815...Lawrenceville laid out by Wm. D. Foster.	4 38	7 31	10 10
11	Tu	1871...Patrick Barry murders his wife in South Pittsburgh	4 39	7 31	10 35
12	We	1853...Corner-stone of Christ M. E. Church laid.	4 40	7 30	10 56
13	Th	1847...Mercantile Library opened.	4 41	7 30	11 22
14	Fr	1851...Father Matthew, great temperance advocate, in city.	4 41	7 29	11 53
15	Sa	1781...The Duquesne Greys organized.	4 42	7 29	Morn.
16	S	1794...Line of boats started bet. this city and Cincinnati.	4 43	7 28	12 31
17	Mo	1794...The great whisky insurrection.	4 44	7 28	1 19
18	Tu	1855...Six fugitive slaves pass through to Canada.	4 45	7 27	2 23
19	We	1859...Corner-stone of Dixmont insane hospital laid.	4 46	7 26	3 32
20	Th	1878...A case of cholera reported at Union Depot.	4 46	7 25	Sets.
21	Fr	1870...The Great Council of Red Men closes.	4 47	7 25	8 4
22	Sa	1822...The W. Penitentiary finished; a prisoner received.	4 48	7 24	8 28
23	S	1818...Stages run from Washington, Pa., to Baltimore.	4 49	7 23	9 2
24	Mo	1859...Mary Delancy shot and killed.	4 50	7 22	9 34
25	Tu	1861...Gen. McClellan arrived on way to command the army	4 50	7 21	9 56
26	We	1873...Luther and Denmarsh race on the Monongahela.	4 51	7 20	10 20
27	Th	1873...Zirhurt arrives in Cincinnati in a shell boat.	4 52	7 19	10 46
28	Fr	1861...Much rejoicing over the return of the 13th regiment.	4 53	7 18	11 16
29	Sa	1870...Chas. B. Taylor, an eccentric character, died.	4 54	7 17	11 52
30	S	1861...Destruction of the Duquesne depot by fire.	4 55	7 16	Morn.
31	Mo	1868...One hundred buildings destroyed by fire in Oil City	4 56	7 15	12 34

GENERAL STATISTICS.

(CONTINUED.)

RECAPITULATION.

1874.—Whole vote cast for Treasurer, 14,271, Christopher L. Magee, R.; majority over Mr. Ihmsen, D., 2,667.
1871.—Whole vote cast, 10,806. Christopher L. Magee's, Republican, majority over J. F. Stark, Reform, 1,116.

1874.—CONTROLLER.

Whole vote cast, 14,082. Robert M. Snodgrass', R., majority over John A. Elder, D., 3,128.

CITY TAXES.

CITY TREASURER'S OFFICE, MUNICIPAL HALL.

The following are the provisions of the ordinance authorizing the levying of taxes in the City, for 1874, and with some slight changes, will be adopted by Councils for 1875:
1. Upon all property taxable for state and county purposes, four mills upon each dollar of valuation.
2. Upon all property taxable for state and county purposes, within the limits of the City of Pittsburgh, as it existed prior to the consolidation under the Act of April, 1867, one-half mill upon each dollar of valuation, as a special tax for the separate indebtedness of said district.
3. Upon all property taxable for state and county purposes within the limits of the former borough of Lawrenceville, one mill upon each dollar of valuation, as a special tax for the separate indebtedness of said district.
4. Upon all goods, wares and merchandise, and upon all articles of trade and commerce sold in said city in any manner not herein otherwise provided for, two mills upon each dollar of said sales.
5. Upon sales of goods, wares and merchandise, and articles of trade or commerce, sold by commission merchants in said city, two mills on each dollar of said sales.
6. Upon the actual yearly sales of each and every person or firm engaged in the trade, business, or occupation of retailing for his, her or their benefit, vinous, fermented or distilled liquors, fifteen mills upon each dollar of said sales.
7. Upon the actual yearly sales of each and every person or firm engaged in business or occupation of an auctioneer, two mills on each dollar of said sales.
8. Upon the commissions or brokerage of all merchandise brokers, forwarding and commission merchants, not including commissions on sales, fifteen mills on each dollar of said commissions.
9. Upon the average line of discounts of brokers, banks and banking institutions, one mill on each dollar.
10. Upon the gross receipts of insurance companies, insurance agencies, express companies and telegraph companies, three mills on each dollar of said receipts.

GENERAL STATISTICS.

(CONTINUED.)

11. Upon the gross receipts of persons, engaged in the business of keeping billiard tables, ten-pin alleys or bagatelle tables for public use, twelve mills on each dollar of said receipts.
12. Upon all property taxable for state or county purposes, one mill on each dollar of valuation; also upon the yearly receipts of all fire, life and marine insurance companies, or their agents, three and one-half mills upon the dollar of said receipts, to be used for maintaining and extending the fire department.
13. Water Works interest and sinking fund tax, one and one-half mills upon each dollar of valuation.

SEC. II. And at the above rates the City Assessor shall assess said taxes.

SEC. III. That the amount necessary to pay the interest on the separate indebtedness of the old city and the borough of Lawrenceville, shall be taken from receipts from the special taxes of the districts aforesaid, and placed in appropriation No. 1, on which warrants shall be drawn for all interest accruing or accrued on the debts of said districts respectively.

SEC. IV. That the balance of said receipts from said special taxes (after payment of interest), shall be paid into a sinking fund for the district from which it is collected, and shall be used for the payment of the special debt of said district.

Taxes are payable at the City Treasurer's office, Municipal Hall, Smithfield street: City tax on property, business and occupations and water rents, from June 1st to August 1st, with 5 per cent. discount. After this date the accounts are placed in the hands of a collector, to whom they are paid with 10 per cent. added.

Vehicle licences are payable March 1st of each year, at the following rates: One-horse vehicle, $7 50; two-horse vehicle, $12 00, four-horse vehicle, $15 00, two-horse hack, $15 00, and $1 00 for each extra horse that may be used over the number provided for above.

ASSESSMENTS.

The assessments by the City Assessor are made on city property, in November; on business and water rents, in April of each year.

City taxes are levied and collected for a period extending over twelve months from the following dates: City, business and water rents, April 1; property and occupation—which includes school, fire, special, city building, etc.—January 1; vehicle license February 1; State mercantile license, May 1.

The State mercantile license is assessed as follows: A fee of one dollar over and above the sums mentioned being collected on each, wherewith to remunerate the appraiser and treasurer

State mercantile license, assessed within the city limits, payable at the City Treasurer's office, between June 1st and July 1st; after July 1st, placed in the hands of city aldermen for collection.

| 8th Month. | AUGUST, 1876. | 31 Days. |

| | CHRONOLOGICAL RECORD | LUNATIONS. | PITTSBURGH. |

CHRONOLOGICAL RECORD			
OF REMARKABLE EVENTS		LUNATIONS.	PITTSBURGH.
	IN THE		
	CITIES OF PITTSBURGH, ALLE-GHENY AND VICINITY.		

LUNATIONS.

	D.	H.	M.	
FULL MOON	5	5	16	Morning.
LAST QUARTER	12	4	37	Evening.
NEW MOOK	19	7	3	Morning.
FIRST QUARTER	27	42	59	Evening.

Day of Month.	Day of Week.	Event	Sun Rises. H. M.	Sun Sets. H. M.	Moon Sets. H. M.
1	Tu	1871—Murder of Mrs. Alexander, col., in Alle. by her husb.	4 57	7 14	
2	We	1862—Joseph Barker, ex-Mayor of Pittsburgh, killed.	4 58	7 18	1 22
3	Th	1861—Death of Bishop Bowman.	4 59	7 12	2 2
4	Fr	1815—Neptune fire company organized.	5 0	7 11	2 40
5	Sa	1873—Arrival of Joseph Cloud, the oarsman.	5 1	7 10	3 19
6	S	1829—Gen. Jackson visits the city.	5 2	7 9	Rises.
7	Mo	1869—The Duquesne Greys reorganized.	5 3	7 7	7 59
8	Tu	1864—The Sixty-second regiment mustered out of service.	5 4	7 6	8 22
9	We	1814—Pittsburgh Blues leave to join the Nor'wn army.	5 5	7 5	8 45
10	Th	1852—National Free Soil convention held.	5 6	7 4	9 9
11	Fr	1872—Thos. Reese, Fire Commissioner, died.	5 7	7 2	9 34
12	Sa	1872—Suspension of the oil firm of Fisher Bros.	5 8	7 1	10 2
13	S	1873—Father Ferris' church struck by lightning.	5 8	7 0	10 37
14	Mo	1873—Great land slide on P. R. R., at Altoona.	5 9	6 58	11 22
15	Tu	1868—Jared M. Brush nom. for Mayor of Pittsburgh.	5 10	6 57	Morn.
16	We	1872—Meeting to protest against Coolie labor.	5 11	6 56	12 26
17	Th	1862—Excitement over the news of Gen. Pope's retreat.	5 12	6 54	1 38
18	Fr	1866—Ardesco oil refining works destroyed by fire.	5 13	6 53	9 39
19	Sa	1869—Hamill def. by Coulter on Monon.; time, 37:51½.	5 14	6 51	3 42
20	S	1861—Col. Sam Black's regiment leaves for the war.	5 15	6 50	Sets.
21	Mo	1857—McKim hung at Hollidaysburgh for murder.	5 16	6 48	7 32
22	Tu	1870—The Pearl flouring mill burned. Loss, $120,000.	5 17	6 47	7 55
23	We	1865—The body of the murdered Forrester found.	5 18	6 45	8 15
24	Th	1820—News of the death of George III. rec'd in the city.	5 16	6 44	8 38
25	Fr	1852—House of Refuge building commenced.	5 20	6 42	9 2
26	Sa	1874—Dem. State Con. held at Library Hall.	5 21	6 41	9 28
27	S	1866—Work of erecting fire alarm commenced.	5 22	6 39	10 16
28	Mo	1861—Rejoicing over Union victories at Cape Hatteras.	5 23	7 38	11 6
29	Tu	1873—Revolt of prisoners in the Penitentiary.	5 24	6 36	Morn.
30	We	1873—The Columbia Regatta on the Allegheny river.	5 25	6 35	12 2
31	Th	1865—Mrs. Grinder, the poisoner, arrested.	5 26	6 33	1 46

GENERAL STATISTICS.

CONTINUED.

MERCANTILE LICENSE.

Class.	Sales.	License.
14	$ 1,000 to 5,000	$ 7 00
13	5,000 to 10,000	10 00
12	10,000 to 15,000	10 00
11	15,000 to 20,000	15 00
10	20,000 to 30,000	20 00
9	30,000 to 40,000	25 00
8	40,000 to 50,000	30 00
7	50,000 to 60,000	40 00
6	60,000 to 75,000	50 00
5	75,000 to 85,000	60 00
4	85,000 to 100,000	80 00
3	100,000 to 200,000	100 00
2	200,000 to 300,000	150 00
1	all above 300,000	200 00

In addition to the present classification of licenses of vendors of merchandise, all dealers who are esteemed and taken to effect annual sales to the amount of $500,000, shall constitute class A, and pay $350; those to the amount of one million of dollars, class B, and pay $450; those to the amount of two millions of dollars, class, C, and pay $600; those to the amount of three millions of dollars, class D, and pay $800 00; those to the amount of four millions of dollars, class E, and pay $900 00; those to the amount of five millions of dollars, class F, and pay $1,000.

RATES OF WATER RENTS.

SMALL DWELLINGS.

Fronting on courts or alleys, or small tenement houses, occupied exclusively as dwellings, for the use of hydrant water of convenient access, whether on the premises or not, charge for

One room	$ 2 50
Two rooms	5 94
Three rooms	7 50
Four rooms	9 06
For each additional room	1 55

DWELLINGS.

Fronting on public streets, occupied exclusively as dwellings, for each family occupying the premises, charge for

Four rooms,	$11 87
Five rooms	13 44
Six rooms	15 00
Seven rooms	16 56
Eight rooms	18 12
Nine or ten rooms	21 25
Each additional room	2 00
Baths supplied with cold water, each	2 50
Baths supplied with cold and hot water, each	5 00
Baths supplied with cold and hot water, by separate ferrule, from main pipe each	9 87
Baths supplied with cold and hot water, additional, each	6 25
Water closets, self-closing, each	4 37
Water closets, self-closing, for each additional one	2 50

GENERAL STATISTICS.

CONTINUED.

Wash basins and urinals in chambers, same rate.	
Wash pavements, of every description, without hose	6 25
Wash pavements, of every description, without hose, used by more than one family, each	3 12
Street hose, for sprinkling in front of one building	from $6 25 to 18 75
Street hose, for sprinkling in front of each additional building	from $3 75 to 6 25
All additional fixtures and extra attachments for the use of city water, extra rates.	

STORES, OFFICES AND WORK SHOPS.

Wholesale and retail store and shop, from	$4 69 to $25 00
Warehouses, each	12 50
Offices of professional men, Companies, &c.	from $ 4 69 to 31 25
Sleeping room, each	4 69
Druggists, barbers, and bakeries, special rates.	
Water closets, self-closing, each	4 37
Water closets, other descriptions	6 25
Urinals, self-closing	6 25
Urinals, other descriptions	8 75
Each tenant in the building charged according to the nature of business; families, dwelling rates.	

HOTELS, RESTAURANTS, AND BOARDING HOUSES.

For families keeping boarders, the house dwelling rates.

Boarders, 10 persons or under	$ 9 76
Boarders, over 10 and under 25	19 53
Boarders, every 25 persons additional	9 76
Bar, with water fixtures inside	$18 75 to 29 25
Bar, without water fixtures inside	10 00 to 18 75
Wash basins and slop sinks, each	6 25
Water closets and urinals, self-closing, each	7 50
Water closets and urinals, other descriptions	10 00
Baths for use of boarders, each	12 50
Wash tubs, according, each	
Kitchens according to capacity and No.	
of draw cocks	from $10 00 to 60 00
Outside hydrants for watering horses, no trough allowed	6 25
Hotels, for each additional room above dwelling house rates, each	2 00

PUBLIC BUILDINGS.

Hydrants, each	$10 00
Basins or slop sinks, each	6 25
Water closets and urinals, self-closing	7 50
Water closets and urinals, other descriptions	10 00
Billiard hall, from one to three tables, each	1 25
Billiard hall, additional tables, each	62
Public baths, each tub	12 50

PUBLIC SCHOOLS.

For each one hundred children .... $ 6 25
All arrangements for use of water same as public buildings.

9th Month.	SEPTEMBER, 1876.	30 Days.

DAY OF MONTH.	DAY OF WEEK.	CHRONOLOGICAL RECORD *OF REMARKABLE EVENTS* IN THE CITIES OF PITTSBURGH, ALLEGHENY AND VICINITY.	LUNATIONS.			PITTSBURGH.		
						D. H. M.		
			FULL MOON.........			3 8 52 Evening.		
			LAST QUARTER.....			10 10 59 Evening.		
			NEW MOON.........			17 4 33 Evening.		
			FIRST QUARTER...			25 6 42 Morning.		
						Sun rises.	Sun sets.	Moon sets.
						H. M.	H. M.	H. M.
1	Fr	1870...Col. Jas. Duncan, of 102 Regiment, died.				5 27	6 31	2 44
2	Sa	1840...Allegheny chartered, making it a city.				5 28	6 30	3 40
3	S	1866...Death of John Thaw, an old citizen.				5 29	6 28	Rises.
4	Mo	1871...Murder of Jacob Duffield, in West Pittsburgh.				5 30	6 26	7 24
5	Tu	1873...French parade in honor of the Republic.				5 31	6 25	7 48
6	We	1873...Coulter and Morris row at Toronto.				5 32	6 23	8 16
7	Th	1850...Sharpsburg's population, 1,229.				5 33	6 22	8 47
8	Fr	1873...Two boys drowned at Herr's Island.				5 34	6 20	9 33
9	Sa	1873...Trans-Allegheny canal convention held.				5 35	6 18	11 20
10	S	1844...Aqueduct over the Allegheny river torn down.				5 36	6 17	11 52
11	Mo	1853...Meeting to supress omnibus travel on Sunday.				5 37	6 15	Morn.
12	Tu	1855...Connellsville railroad opened to Connellsville.				5 38	6 13	12 50
13	We	1866...Pres't Johnson, Gen. Grant & Adm'l Farragut here.				5 39	6 12	1 46
14	Th	1856...W. W. Irwin, ex-Mayor of Pittsburgh, died.				5 40	6 10	2 36
15	Fr	1871...Campaign opens with a mass meeting at City Hall.				5 41	6 8	3 39
16	Sa	1813...Late Charles Shaler admitted to the bar.				5 42	6 7	4 54
17	8	1873...Reunion of the Army of the Cumberland.				5 43	6 5	Sets.
18	Mo	1873...Failure of Jay Cook & Co. announced.				5 44	6 3	6 34
19	Tu	1872...Horace Greely arrives in Pittsburgh.				5 45	6 2	7 11
20	We	1859...Opening of Trimble's Varieties Theater.				5 46	6 0	7 34
21	Th	1854...This day there were eighty-eight deaths from cholera				5 47	5 58	8 4
22	Fr	1873...James T. Brady & Co., bankers, suspended.				5 48	5 57	8 38
23	Sa	1850...One hundred fugitive slaves leave here for Canada.				5 49	5 55	9 18
24	S	1853...Laughlin murdered by Duff, near McKeesport.				5 50	5 53	10 6
25	Mo	1855...The Central High School opened.				5 51	5 52	11 2
26	Tu	1841...The Court House removed to its present site.				5 52	5 50	Morn.
27	We	1813...Proposition to supply city with water by steam pwr.				5 53	5 48	12 15
28	Th	1850...Meeting in opposition to the Fugitive Slave Law.				5 54	5 47	1 13
29	Fr	1873...Two men drowned in the Allegheny at Verona.				5 55	5 45	2 10
30	Sa	1872...Great industrial strike in the oil regions.				5 56	5 43	2 56

GENERAL STATISTICS.

CONTINUED.

STABLES.

Livery, per stall, counting all stalls........	$ 2 50
County stables...	1 25
Horses not in livery stables......................	2 50
Cows...	1 87
Each four-wheeled vehicle, (except ordinary rough wagons).............................	2 50
Each two-wheeled vehicle........................	1 25

STEAM ENGINES.

Each horse power, ten hours per day......$ 3 75
Distilleries, rectifiers, breweries and manufacturing establishments rated according to capacity and size of supply pipe, granted by special agreement.

FOUNTAINS.

Flowing ten hours per day for six months of the year, from a half-inch ferrule.

For the first jet of 1-16 of an inch...........	$12 50
For each additional jet of 1-16 of an inch,	2 50
For the first jet of ⅛ of an inch............	15 00
For each additional jet of ⅛ of an inch...	5 00
For the first jet of ¼ of an inch.............	37 50
For each additional jet of ¼ of an inch....	17 81
For each jet of ½ of an inch...................	62 50

BUILDING PURPOSES.

For each perch of stone...........................	$ 6¼
For each thousand brick...........................	10
For each hundred yards of plaster...........	62½

All dwellings & establishments of whatsoever kind, the owners of which neglect or refuse to use water fronting on streets, where water mains containing water are laid, charge one-third of rates charged similar dwellings or establishments that use water and in dwellings or establishments not otherwise subject to tax, and within one thousand feet of fire plug, one-sixth of full rates.

ESTIMATED EXPENDITURES AND REVENUES FOR THE YEAR 1875.

APPROPRIATIONS FOR 1875.

No.		Amount.
1,	Interest, premium and tax on City loan...	$157,000 00
2,	Salaries..	30,000 00
3,	Printing..	20,000 00
4,	Fire Department..................................	133,000 00
5,	Police..	207,000 00
6,	Water Works..	100,000 00
7,	Streets...	110,000 00
8,	Pittsburgh Gas Company....................	34,500 00
9,	Diamond Markets................................	6,000 00
10,	Monongahela Wharf............................	3,500 00
11,	Allegheny Wharf..................................	1,000 00
12,	Weigh Scales.......................................	1,000 00
13,	Contingent Fund..................................	50,000 00
14,	Board of Health...................................	18,000 00
15,	East End Gas Company.......................	20,000 00
16,	City Property.......................................	10,000 00
18,	Finance Fund.......................................	20,000 00
19,	Sinking Fund..	28,732 00
20,	Fifth Ward Market..............................	400 00
21,	City Hall Furnishing, Cleaning and Repairing...............................	7,960 00
22,	Roads..	30,000 00
23,	Surveys...	10,000 00
24,	Water Extension.................................	143,874 63

GENERAL STATISTICS.

CONTINUED.

25, Water Extension Loan Interest...	257,000 00
26, Water Extension Loan Sinking Fund..	88.268 00
27, Fifth Avenue Market.........................	15,00 00
28, Special Sinking Fund.........................	7,000 00
29, Lawrenceville Sinking Fund..............	3,250 00
31, South Side Market............................	2,300 00
32, South Side Wharf..............................	1,500 00
34, Equalization......................................	20,000 00
35, South Side Gas Company..................	16,000 00
36, Fire Department Loan Interest and Sinking Fund...........................	24,000 00
38, West Pittsburgh Gas Company...	8,000 00
	$1,669,824 63

ESTIMATED RECEIPTS FOR 1875.

City Tax.........................3½ mills...$	444,000 00
Fire Tax............................1 " ...	127,000 00
Old City Special Tax........¾ " ...	32,000 00
Lawrenceville Spec'l Tax..1 " ...	9,000 00
Water Works Int............1⅓ " ...	175,000 00
Sinking Fund Tax...........1 " ...	127,000 00
Business Tax...................1¼ " ...	149,000 00
Water Rents...................................	267,000 00
Monongahela Wharf.........................	10,000 00
Allegheny Wharf..............................	2,500 00
Mayor's Office..................................	40,000 00
Diamond Markets.............................	45,000 00
Fifth Avenue Market........................	2,500 00
City Gauger.....................................	3,000 00
Vehicle Licenses..............................	31,574 63
Street Railroads..............................	3,750 00
Building Inspector...........................	2,500 00
Interest on Bank Balances................	10,000 00
Streets..	12,000 00
South Side Market...........................	4,500 00
South Side Wharf,...........................	3,500 00
Weigh Scales...................................	5,000 00
Appropriation No. 30, Street and Sewer Assessments in excess of amount due Contractors..............	50,000 00
City Building Commission, balance on hand....................................	14,000 00
	$1,569,824 63

SOUTH SIDE SEPARATE INDEBTEDNESS.

24th ward, Borough of Ormsby.........$	2,250 99
25th and 26th wards, Borough of East Birmingham......................	19,510 84
27th ward, Borough of St. Clair...........	2,125 68
28th and 29th wards, Borough of Birmingham (Special)..................	4,300 00
31st ward, Borough of Allentown.......	501 82
32d ward, Borough of Mt. Washington	2,306 96
35th ward, Borough of Union.............	172 86
36th ward, Borough of Temperanceville................................	3,881 25
36th ward, Borough of Temperanceville, Special for Main Street...........	4,500 00
	$39,550 40

The debt of the City of Pittsburgh, February 1st, 1873, was $5,138,394; thus it will be seen the increase in the municiapal debt for one year was $2,388,907.15.

10th Month.   **OCTOBER, 1876.**   **31 Days.**

		CHRONOLOGICAL RECORD	LUNATIONS.			PITTSBURGH.		
DAY OF MONTH.	DAY OF WEEK.	*OF REMARKABLE EVENTS* IN THE CITIES OF PITTSBURGH, ALLE- GHENY AND VICINITY.			D. H. M. FULL MOON......... 3 5 35 Morning. LAST QUARTER.... 10 4 59 Morning. NEW MOON......... 17 3 36 Morning. FIRST QUARTER... 25 2 33 Morning.			
					Sun Rises	Sun Sets.	Moon Sets.	
					H. M.	H. M.	H. M.	
1	S	1860—Prince of Wales arrives in city.			5 57	5 42	3 44	
2	Mo	1866—Calling of the hour by police discontinued.			5 58	5 40	4 52	
3	Tu	1868—The Old Pittsburgh Theater sold for $90,000.			5 59	5 38	Rises.	
4	We	1860—Lady Franklin arrives in Pittsburgh.			6 0	5 37	9 36	
5	Th	1855—Iron City College opens.			6 1	5 35	6 49	
6	Fr	1873—Meeting to aid the Memphis Sufferers			6 2	5 33	7 39	
7	Sa	1826—James Sharp settles at Sharpsburg.			6 3	5 39	8 26	
8	S	1873—Case of murderer Lynch before the Supreme Court.			6 4	5 28	9 25	
9	Mo	1873—Semi-Indian girl lays claim to Mowry estate.			6 5	5 26	10 24	
10	Tu	1870—New Library Hall opened by Cantata Society.			6 6	5 24	11 39	
11	We	1870—Negroes of Allegheny county cast their first vote.			6 7	5 22	Morn.	
12	Th	1874—E. N. Ladley estab's Soc. to sup. cruelty to animals			6 8	5 21	12 49	
13	Fr	1871—The High School building dedicated.			6 9	5 19	1 50	
14	Sa	1865—Nine persons killed on Pa. R. R., near Lancaster.			6 10	5 18	3 5	
15	S	1865—John G. Saxe lectures before the Tennyson club			6 11	5 16	4 9	
16	Mo	1855—Barnum holds a baby show at City Hall.			6 12	5 15	5 11	
17	Tu	1865—St. Patrick's Catholic Church dedicated....			6 13	5 14	Sets.	
18	We	1870—First number of EVENING LEADER appeared.			6 15	5 12	5 56	
19	Th	1873—Rev. N. Sheshadri preaches at Library Hall.			6 16	5 11	6 22	
20	Fr	1874—Oakland races commence.			6 17	5 9	6 55	
21	Sa	1873—Corner-stone laid of the new Washington College.			6 18	5 9	7 32	
22	S	1873—Lizzie Schuetler conf. the murder of Mrs. Brauenlein			6 19	5 8	8 16	
23	Mo	1855—Opening of the Valley R. R. to the Kiskiminitas.			6 20	5 7	9 8	
24	Tu	1871—Inquest on body of Dr. Murdoch.			6 21	5 5	10 6	
25	We	1850—Rev. J. Black, pastor for fifty years, died in city.			6 22	5 4	11 4	
26	Th	1790—Termination of the great whisky insurrection.			6 24	5 3	Morn.	
27	Fr	1855—Trial of the first steam fire engine in the city.			6 25	5 1	12 12	
28	Sa	1850—Remains of President Taylor arrive in a canal boat.			6 26	5 0	1 22	
29	S	1871—Corner-stone of the Turner Hall laid.			6 27	4 59	2 32	
30	Mo	1826—A market house opened on the South Side.			6 28	4 58	3 46	
31	Tu	1870—City Councils auth. the purchase of plank roads.			6 29	4 57	4 59	

CITY OFFICERS.
PITTSBURGH.

ELECTED BY COUNCILS.

City Attorney.—Office Municipal hall; term three years.

City Assessor.—Office Municipal hall; term three years.

Superintendent of Markets.—Office Diamond market; term three years,

Clerk of Markets.—Office Diamond market; term three years.

Clerk of Markets.—Office South Pittsburgh market.

Building Inspector.—Office Municipal hall; term three years.

Meat Inspector.—Office Diamond market; term three years.

Assessor of Water Rents.—Office Municipal hall; term three years.

Wharfmaster.—Office Monongahela Wharfboat; term three years.

Wharfmaster.—South Side, office, Tenth street; term three years.

City Engineer.—Office Municipal hall; term three years.

City Gauger.—Office corner Penn and Ninth streets; term three years.

Clerk of the City.—Office Municipal hall; term three years.

Assistant Clerk of City.—Office Municipal hall; term three years.

Messenger to Councils and Committees.—Office Municipal hall; term three years.

Street Commissioner.—First and second districts—Office Municipal hall; term three years.

Street Commissioner.—Third district—Office Thirty-eighth street; term three years.

Street Commissioner.—Fifth district—Office Carson street, South Side; term three years.

Street Commissioner.—Sixth district—Office No. 725 Carson street, South Side; term three years.

Street Commissioner.—Seventh district—Office Pike street, near Carson street, South Side; term three years.

Road Commissioner—First district—Office Herron avenue, Thirteenth ward; term three years.

Road Commissioner—Second district—Office Penn avenue, Twentieth ward; term three years.

Road Commissioner—Third district—Office Fifth avenue, Twenty-second ward; term three years.

Superintendent of Water Works—Office, Municipal Hall; term three years.

BOARD OF HEALTH.

Office Municipal Hall.

J. F. Slagle, President; John D. Fleming, Secretary; Addison Arthurs. M. D. Treasurer; T. P. Graham, M. D., J. D. Thomas, M. D., George W. Backoffen, James McCann, M. D., W. J. Asdale, M. D., Thos. S. Mitchel, J. F. Slagle, M. D., J. D. Thomas, M. D., James McCann, M. D., Finance Committee; Thos. S. Mitchel, T. P. Graham, M. D., George W. Baackoffen, John D. Fleming, W. J. Asdale, M. D.,

Sanitary Committee; Addison Arthurs, M. D. Sohn D. Fleming, T. P. Graham, M. D., James McCann, M. D., W. J. Asdale, Sanitary Committee; Addison Arthurs, M. D., John D. Fleming, T. Graham, James McCann, M. D., W. Asdale, M. D. Hospital Committee; George W. Backoffen, J. D. Thomas, M. D., Addison Arthurs, M. D., Printing Committee.

WATER COMMITTEE.

T. S. Mitchell, Chairman; R. L. Hamilton, Secretary. Members—R. B. Brown, J. D. Scully, S. H. Goldthorpe, W. B. Hunter, Wm. McClurg, Gregor Fox, John Harrison, Charles Meyran, W. W. Thompson, J. C. Reilly, Samuel Mears, P. Foley, P. D. Perchment, W. F. Aull, D. B. Morrison.

BOARD OF REVISION.

Office Municipal Hall.

B. F. Kennedy, President; Thomas H. Phelps, Clerk. The Board consists of one member from each ward in the city. Term of office three years.

PUBLIC CHARITIES, PITTSBURGH.

Western Pennsylvania Hospital.—City General Hospital building, Twelfth ward. Incorporated 1848. Built by contributions of citizens. Open for the reception of the sick, afflicted and infirm. Insane department, under State patronage, at Dixmont.

Home for Aged Protestant Woman—Near Wilkinsburg.

House for Destitute Women—No. 45 Chatham street.

Young Men's Home, Bethel and Home for Destitute Men—Duquesne Way, near Ninth street.

Homeopathic Hospital and Dispensary—No. 146 Second avenue. Chartered 1866. Dispensary department is open for the treatment of the poor, gratuitously, every day, except Sunday, from 11 to 12 A. M., and from 2 to 3 P. M.. No contagious diseases admitted. Persons suffering from injuries from accident are admitted at any hour, if brought to the hospital within twenty-four hours after the casualty occurs. Both private and charity patients admitted.

PUBLIC CHARITIES....Continued.

Mercy Hospital.—Stevenson street, Sixth ward. In charge of Sisters of Mercy. Incorporated 1847. Persons afflicted with any disease admitted without distinction on account of creed or color. Those whose circumstances admit of it are charged a nominal sum, while the poor are cared for gratuitously. Friends of private patients may visit them from 9 to 11 A. M., and 2 to 5 P. M. Friends of free patients on Mondays and Thursdays, at the same hours.

Pittsburgh Infirmary.—Roberts and Reed streets, Eleventh ward. Under the direction of Rev. W. A. Passavant. Established 1848. Derives its support chiefly from voluntary contributions. Indigent persons are cared for free of charge on the presentation of an entrance permit from one of the attending physicians. All others pay from $5 to $10 per week. Contagious and other diseases admitted.

| 11th MONTH. | NOVEMBER, 1876. | 30 Days. |

DAY OF MONTH.	DAY OF WEEK.	CHRONOLOGICAL RECORD OF REMARKABLE EVENTS IN THE CITIES OF PITTSBURGH, ALLEGHENY AND VICINITY.	LUNATIONS.	PITTSBURGH.		

LUNATIONS.

	D.	H.	M.	
FULL MOON..........	1	6	9	Evening.
LAST QUARTER......	8	11	55	Evening.
NEW MOON..........	15	7	26	Evening.
FIRST QUARTER...	23	11	5	Evening.

Day of Month	Day of Week	Event	Sun Rises. H. M.	Sun Sets. H. M.	Moon Rises. H. M.
1	We	1870—First negro jury in county sworn in on an inquest.	6 30	4 56	
2	Th	1870—Pittsburgh gas works destroyed by fire.	6 32	4 55	
3	Fr	1868—Hockinberry murd. Miss. McCandless, near Butler.	6 33	4 54	6 16
4	Sa	1785—Allegheny contained but two houses, log.	6 34	4 53	7 10
5	S	1870—Drs. Hartung and Hewitt sentenced to Pententiary.	6 35	4 52	8 20
6	Mo	1807—First cotton mill in Alleghenytown in operation.	6 36	4 51	9 30
7	Tu	1873—A terrible tragedy at Monongahela City.	6 38	4 50	10 41
8	We	1867—Explosion at the rolling mill of Reese, Graff & Dull.	6 39	4 49	11 50
9	Th	1870—Dedication of the Penitentiary chapel.	6 40	4 48	Morn.
10	Fr	1829—First canal boat arrives in Pittsburgh.	6 41	4 47	12 59
11	Sa	1862—Dixmont Asylum for the insane opened.	6 42	4 46	2 11
12	S	1873—Mechanic's Saving Bank suspended.	6 43	4 45	3 26
13	Mo	1851—Jenny Lind gives a concert in the city.	6 44	4 44	4 32
14	Tu	1859—Work on railway to Manchester commenced.	6 46	4 43	5 51
15	We	1868—Death of James A. Herron.	6 47	4 42	Sets.
16	Th	1808—Mr. O'Hara builds glasshouse on South Side.	6 48	4 42	5 22
17	Fr	1794—Old jail and Court House, Diamond square, comp'd.	6 49	4 41	6 8
18	Sa	1873—The Nation Trust Company closes its doors.	6 50	4 40	6 56
19	S	1851—Henry Clay arrives in Pittsburgh.	6 52	4 39	7 55
20	Mo	1873—Thos. Fleming kills Henry Keesch at McKeesport.	6 53	4 39	9 59
21	Tu	1868—Hon. Judge Kirkpatrick takes his seat in D. C.	6 54	4 38	10 5
22	We	1873—Hampton, bond robber, sentenced to Penitentiary.	6 55	4 37	11 11
23	Th	1850—Hon. Thos. Benton visits the city.	6 56	4 37	Morn.
24	Fr	1873—$500,000 of water bonds missing.	6 57	4 36	12 12
25	Sa	1858—100th anniversary Ft. Duquesne's evac. by French.	6 58	4 36	1 13
26	S	1859—Rutherford, Sup't. House Refuge, sentenced to jail.	6 59	4 35	2 14
27	Mo	1874—Rev. J. Scarborough ac. call as Bishop to diocese N. J.	7 1	4 35	3 16
28	Tu	1873—Alexander McClintock died.	7 2	4 35	4 20
29	We	1874—Riot bet. Italian and Amer. miners at Buena Vista.	7 3	4 34	5 22
30	Th	1873—Murder of old John C. Kerr by Samuel Beightly.	7 4	4 34	6 26

PUBLIC CHARITIES—Continued.

*Roman Catholic Orphan Asylum....*Tannehill street. Established 1838. Under charge of the Sisters of Mercy. Object, to support and educate orphan children.

Convent of the Sisters of Mercy. Webster avenue and Chatham street. Established 1845. Object, to educate the youth and to visit the sick and the poor. This was the first convent of the order instituted in America.

*St. Mary's Hospital....*Forty-fifth street. Connected with St. Mary's Convent.

PUBLIC SCHOOLS.

*City Superintendent....*PRO. GEO. J. LUCKEY, Office High School building.

*County Supt....*PRO. JAMES DICKSON. Pittsburgh High School, Fulton street and Bedford avenue.

Duquesne District, (First ward) First and Second avenues, and Short street.

South District, (Second ward) Ross and Diamond streets.

Grant District, (Third ward) Grant street and Strawberry alley.

North District, (Fourth ward) Penn street and Cecil alley.

Hancock District, (Fifth ward) Webster, head of Seventh avenue.

Forbes District, (Sixth ward) Ann, between Magee and Stevenson; also Second, near Brewery street.

Franklin District, (Seventh and Eighth wards) Franklin, between Elm and Logan streets.

Ralston District, (Ninth and Tenth wards) Penn and Fifteenth streets.

Moorhead District, (Eleventh ward) Granville and Enoch streets.

O'Hara District, (First precinct, Twelfth ward) Twenty-fifth and Smallman streets; Springfield District, (Second precinct, Twelfth ward) Smallman and Thirty-first streets.

Minersville District, (Thirteenth ward) Center avenue and Morgan street; also on Ridge street.

Oakland District, (Fourteenth ward) Fifth avenue and Denny; also, Fifth avenue, near Brady street.

Lawrence District, (Fifteenth ward) Thirty-seventh and Charlotte streets.

Howard District, (Sixteenth ward) Liberty street; also, Bloomfield.

Washington District, (Seventeenth ward) Fortieth street; also, Hatfield.

Mount Albion District, (Eighteenth ward) Fiftieth street.

Highland District, (Nineteenth ward) near Hiland avenue.

Liberty District, (Twentieth ward) near Roup's station.

Lincoln District, (Twenty-first ward) three school houses—Frankstown road, Riverside, Remington.

Colfax District, (Twenty-second ward) Squirrel Hill.

Peebles District, (Twenty-third ward) three school houses—Hazlewood, Brown's station, Squirrel Hill.

Mute school, Grant District, Grant street and Strawberry alley.

St. Michael's school, Pius street, Twenty-seventh ward, South Side.

MISCELLANEOUS.

Custom House.—Fifth avenue and Smithfield street.

Court House and Jail.—Fifth avenue, Grant, Diamond and Ross streets.

Municipal Hall.—Smithfield street and Virgin alley.

Diamond Markets.—Diamond, Market street, between Fourth and Fifth avenues.

South Side Market.—Twelfth street, South Pittsburgh.

Fifth Avenue Market.—Fifth avenue and Miltenberger street.

Lower Water Works.—Twelfth and Etna streets.

Upper Water Works.—Bedford avenue, near Fulton street.

THEATERS AND HALLS.

Pittsburgh Opera House.—Entrance 62 Fifth avenue.

Fifth Avenue Opera House.—Fifth avenue, between Smithfield and Wood streets.

Varieties Theater.—Penn street, near Sixth.

Academy of Music.—Liberty street and Strawberry alley.

Library Hall.—Penn street, near Sixth.

Liberty Hall.—Penn and Centre avenues, East Liberty.

Masonic Hall.—Fifth avenue, between Wood and Smithfield streets.

Martin's Variety Theater.—Fourth avenue.

Wilkins Hall.—Fourth avenue, between Wood and Smithfield streets.

Mozart Hall.—Seventh avenue, between Grant and Smithfield streets.

Lafayette Hall.—Wood street, near Fourth avenue.

Philo Hall.—Third avenue and Market street.

Neville Hall.—Fourth avenue and Liberty street.

City Hall.—Over East Diamond Market-house.

Ashland Hall.—Wylie, near Fifth avenue.

Turner Hall.—Sixth avenue, between Grant street and Cherry alley.

Bracken Hall.—Butler street, Lawrenceville.

Odd Fellows'.—Sarah and Eighteenth streets, South Side.

Turners'.—Jane, between Seventeenth and Eighteenth streets, South Side.

Ormond's.—Carson, between Nineteenth and Twentieth streets, South Side.

Salisbury Hall.—New Market building, South Side.

| 12th Month. | | DECEMBER, 1876. | | 3I Days. |

| CHRONOLOGICAL RECORD | LUNATIONS. | PITTSBURGH. |

OF REMARKABLE EVENTS

IN THE

CITIES OF PITTSBURGH, ALLE-

GHENY AND VICINITY.

FULL MOON	1	5	42	Morning.
LAST QUARTER	7	9	3	Evening.
NEW MOON	15	12	53	Evening.
FIRST QUARTER	23	6	21	Evening.
FULL MOON	30	4	88	Evening.

Days of Month	Days of Week	Event	Sun rises.	Sun sets.	Moon rises.
1	Fr	1870—State debt, $31,111,661.90.	7 5	4 34	Rises.
2	Sa	1754—The foundation of Fort Duquesne laid.	7 6	4 34	5 45
3	S	1872—Old John Allingham murdered.	7 7	4 34	6 59
4	Mo	1874—Jos. Trex and Geo. Hill escape from penitentiary.	7 8	4 34	8 19
5	Tu	1871—James Blackmore elected Mayor second term.	7 9	4 33	9 36
6	We	1872—Briceland arrested for murder.	7 10	4 43	10 58
7	Th	1802—Ice-gorge at Oil City; 40,000 barrels of oil destroyed.	7 11	4 43	Morn.
8	Fr	1872—Dennis Leonard dies.	7 12	4 43	12 0
9	Sa	1869—Right Rev. Domenec consecrated a bishop.	7 13	4 43	1 2
10	S	1851—Penn'a R. R. opened to Turtle Creek; much rejoicing.	7 13	4 43	4
11	Mo	1864—The first number of the SUNDAY LEADER issued.	7 14	4 34	2 6
12	Tu	1873—The House of Refuge dedicated.	7 15	4 34	3 10
13	We	1872—Edmund Yates lectures at Library Hall;	7 15	4 34	4 15
14	Th	1871—Philip Winebiddle, a millionaire, died, aged 92.	7 16	4 34	6 16
15	Fr	1868—The Hon. Walter Lowrie died.	7 17	4 34	Sets.
16	Sa	1819—Col. James O'Hara died, aged 66.	7 18	4 35	5 18
17	S	1865—St. Patrick Catholic Church dedicated.	7 18	4 35	6 20
18	Mo	1872—U. S. Marshall Murdock resigns.	7 19	4 36	7 23
19	Tu	1753—George Washington camps on Wainwright's Island.	7 19	4 36	8 26
20	We	1845—Building of Iron Works at Sharpsburg commenced.	7 20	4 36	9 22
21	Th	1874—The Cub-you-quit case closes.	7 20	4 37	10 20
22	Fr	1854—Cornelius Darragh, U. S. Minister, died.	7 21	4 37	11 18
23	Sa	1859—The great "Floyd" gun successfully cast in the city.	7 21	4 38	Morn.
24	S	1869—Edwin M. Stanton's death announced in the courts.	7 22	4 38	12 10
25	Mo	1870—George Weyman died, aged 71 years.	7 22	4 39	1 22
26	Tu	1787—Presbyterian Congregation of Pittsburgh incorpor'd.	7 22	4 40	2 34
27	We	1861—Death of Judge McClure, in the 55 year of his age.	7 23	4 41	3 54
28	Th	1871—First rail Pittsb'gh, Virginia & Charleston road laid.	7 23	4 41	5 10
29	Fr	1872—N. Buntline admitted to practice law in these courts.	7 23	4 42	6 12
30	Sa	1870—Wire bridge at Franklin falls, killing num. persons.	7 24	4 43	Rises.
31	S	1818—First bridge across Mononga'la opened for pedest'ns.	7 24	4 44	5 33

FIRE DEPARTMENT.

PITTSBURGH.

Organization, Location of Engines, &c.

COMMISSIONERS.

GEORGE W. Wilson, - - - - - - - - - PRESIDENT

JAMES A. CHAMBERS,	THOMAS PENDER,
WILLIAM B. HAYS,	JOHN LARIMER,
ALEX. PITCAIRN,	JOHN H. McELROY,
JOHN J. TORLEY,	JENKINS JONES.

Chief Engineer, - - - - - - - JOHN HAMILL,
Assistant Engineer, - - - - - - - SAMUEL V. EVANS.
Secretary, - - - - - - - - FRANK P. CASE.

ENGINE COMPANIES AND LOCATION.

No. 1, Fourth avenue, near Liberty street.
No. 2, Smithfield street, near Second avenue.
No. 3. Seventh avenue, between Smithfield and Grant streets.
No. 4, Fifth avenue, between Van Braam and Miltenberger streets.
No. 5, Centre avenue, near Kirkpatrick street.
No. 6, Corner Forty-fourth and Calvert streets.
No. 7, Penn avenue, between Twenty-second and Twenty-third streets.
No. 8, Corner Hiland avenue and Broad street.

SOUTH SIDE.

No. 10, Chestnut street, Thirty-sixth ward.
No. 11, Corner Ninth and Bingham streets.
No. 12, Sarah street, between Twentieth and Twenty-first streets.

HOSE AND HOOK AND LADDER COMPANIES:

No. 1, Penn avenue, between Fourteenth and Fifteenth streets.
Hook and Ladder Company A, Seventh ave. between Smithfield and Grant streets.
Hook and Ladder Company B, Corner Hiland avenue and Broad street.

SOUTH SIDE.

Hook and Ladder Company C, Sarah street, bet. Twentieth and Twenty-first sts.

Extra Engines...Vigilant and Eagle.

FIRE AND POLICE TELEGRAPH.

Sup't....S. L. FULLWOOD. *As'ts.* GEO. WILSON, GEO. E. McLAIN, RICH'D. McCLATCHEY.

INSTRUCTIONS.

The following instructions are officially promulgated by the Fire Commissioners, for the instruction of those whom it may concern:

Upon positive information of a fire *near* your Signal-box, unlock the door and pull the hook all the way down; then let go and shut the door.

Never open the box, except in case of fire.

Never give an Alarm, except from the Box nearest the fire.

Be sure the Box is locked before leaving it.

Never let the key go out of your possession, unless to some responsible person, for the purpose of giving an Alarm, or when called for by the Superintendent.

Alarms are sounded by striking the *Number of the Box* upon the *Alarm Bell*, upon the *Gongs* in the Engine-house, and upon the small bells in the Signal-boxes.

For instance; An alarm is given from Box 16, which is at the Duquesne Engine-house...the Gongs and bells will strike simultaneously one blow, and pause; then six blows...1...6...16, and so repeat until sufficient alarm has been given.

Complaints concerning the Telegraph, (irregular striking of the Bells or tapping of the Boxes broken wires, etc.,) should in all cases be made at the Fire-Alarm office.

PITTSBURGH.

Locations of Signal Boxes.

2 Penn avenue and Second street.
3 Short and Water streets,
4 Second avenue and Ferry street.
5 Eagle E. H., Fourth avenue, near Liberty.
6 Penn avenue and Cecil alley.
7 Market and Water streets.
10 Central Station, City Hall.
.12 Liberty and Sixth street.
13 Third avenue and Market street.
14 Wood street and Diamond alley.
15 Duquesne way and Fourth avenue.
16 Duquesne E. H., Smithfield street.
17 Sixth avenue and Wood street.
18 Second avenue and Canton street.
19 Stevenson street, near Mercy Hospital.
21 Seventh street and Duquesne way.
23 Penn avenue and Ninth street.
24 Fifth avenue and Smithfield street.
25 Third avenue and Grant street.
26 Grant and Diamond streets.
27 Webster avenue and Grant street.
31 Hook and Ladder house, Seventh avenue.
32 Penn avenue and Tenth street.
34 Liberty and Eleventh streets.
35 Washington and Wylie streets.
36 Fifth avenue and High street.
37 Second avenue and Try street.
41 Second avenue and Brewery street.
42 Fifth avenue and Federal street.
43 Fifth avenue and Elm street.
45 Logan and Franklin streets.
46 Thirteenth and Pike streets.
47 Niagara E. H., 554 Penn avenue.
51 Wylie avenue and Fulton street.
52 Fifth avenue and Pride street.
53 Relief E. H., 316 Fifth avenue.
54 Centre avenue and Arthurs street.
56 Webster avenue and Arthurs street.
57 Green street and Centre Avenue.
61 Penn avenue and Seventeenth street.
62 Independence E. H., 833 Penn avenue.
63 Penn avenue and Twenty-sixth street.
64 Penn avenue and Twenty-eighth street.
65 Thirty-first and Railroad streets.
67 Penn avenue and Thirty-second street.
71 Penn avenue and Butler street.
72 Thirty-sixth and Butler streets.
73 Forty-first and Butler streets.
74 Forty-fourth and Butler streets.
75 Forty-eighth and Butler streets.
76 Fifth avenue and Brady street.
81 No. 5 Engine house.
82 Central Passenger stables, Herron avenue.
83 A. V. R. R. shops.
84 Fifty-fifth and Butler street.
85 Butler street, above Sharpsburg bridge.
86 Fifth and Craft avenues.
87 Fifth avenue and Charlotte street, Oakland
91 Second avenue and Morehead's Mills.
92 Second avenue, Keystone iron works.
93 Second avenue, Eliza Furnace.

94 Second avenue, Frankstown.
95 Second avenue, Hazlewood station.
96 Second avenue, Marion station.

SOUTH SIDE.

112 Walnut street, Temperanceville.
113 Corner Main and Walnut streets.
114 Engine-house, Temperanceville.
115 Mouth of Saw-mill Run.
116 Pittsburgh ferry landing.
117 Lorenz & Wightman's glass works.
123 Clinton rolling mill.
124 Pan-handle railroad depot, Carson street.
125 First and Carson streets.
126 Fourth and Carson streets.
127 Seventh and Carson streets.
128 Tenth and Bradford streets.
132 Tenth and Neville streets.
134 Eleventh and Carson streets.
135 Twelfth and Frederick streets.
136 Thirteenth and Neville streets.
137 Fourteenth and Washington streets.
138 Fifteenth and Manor streets.
142 Seventeenth and Neville streets.
143 Eighteenth and Sarah streets.
145 Eighteenth and Josephine streets.
146 Nineteenth and Sidney streets.
147 Twentieth and Mary streets.
148 Engine-house, Sarah st., bet. 20th & 21st.
152 Twenty-third and Jane street.
153 Twenty-fifth and Sarah streets.
154 Twenty-sixth and Sidney streets.
156 Twenty-seventh and Jane streets.
157 Twenty-seventh and Carson streets.
158 Thirtieth and Carson streets.

EAST END.

213 Penn avenue and Thirty-eighth street.
214 Penn avenue and Winebiddle street
215 Liberty and Pearl streets, Bloomfield.
216 Penn avenue and Pearl street.
217 Penn avenue and Rebecca street.
218 Penn avenue and Euclid street.
219 Engine-house, Highland ave, & Broad st.
231 Fifth ave and Neville street.
234 Aiken and Ellsworth aves., Shadyside.
235 Fifth avenue and Roup street.
236 Shady avenue and Walnut street.
237 Penn and Center aves., Liberty Hall,
238 Penn and Dennison avenues.
241 Hiland avenue and Stewart street.
243 Larimer avenue and Meadow street.
245 Frankstown and Lincoln avenues.
246 Penn and Fifth avenues, Point Breeze.
247 Dallas station, P. R. R.
251 Penn and Homewood avenues.
253 Homewood station, P. R. R.
254 Penn and Brushton avenues.

ALLEGHENY CITY.
WARDS AND BOUNDARIES.

ALLEGHENY CITY, 1876.

First Ward—On the north by Ohio street and Western avenue, on the south by the Allegheny river, on the east by Federal street, on the west by Allegheny avenue.

Second Ward—On the north by city line, on the south by Ohio street and Western avenue, on the east by Federal street, on the west by Allegheny avenue, and the line of the same prolonged to city line on the north.

Third Ward—On the north by old city line, on the south by Ohio street, on the west by Federal street, on the east by old city line.

Fourth Ward—On the north by Ohio street, on the south by Allegheny river, on the west by Federal street, on the east by old city line.

Fifth Ward—On the north by Locust street, on the south by Ohio river, on the east by Allegheny avenue, on the west by Ohio river.

Sixth Ward—On the north by Strawberry lane, on the south by Locust street, on the east by Allegheny avenue, and same prolonged to city line on the north, and on the west by the Ohio river.

Seventh Ward—On the north by new city line, on south by old city line, and Troy Hill road and Lowrie street, on the east by new city line, on the west by Federal street and old city line.

Eighth Ward—On the north by Troy Hill road and Lowrie street, on the south by Allegheny river, on the west by old city line, on the east by new city line.

Ninth Ward—On the north and east by Ft. Wayne railroad, on the west by Ohio river, on the south by Strawberry lane.

Tenth Ward—On the east by East street and Evergreen plank-road, on the north by the line of Ross township, on the west by the Eleventh ward, Woods' Run road and the New Brighton road, and on the south by the old city line.

Eleventh Ward—On the east by New Brighton road, Woods' Run and Tenth ward line, on the north by Ross township, Bellevue borough and Jack's Run to the track of the Pittsburgh, Ft. Wayne and Chicago Railway, on the west by the track of the Pittsburgh, Ft. Wayne and Chicago Railway, to Strawberry lane, and on the south by Strawberry lane.

CITY GOVERNMENT.

ALLEGHENY CITY, 1876.

	TERM.
Mayor	O. Phillips, 3 yrs
Comptroller	James Brown, 1 yr
Treasurer	D. Macferron, 1 yr
Solicitor	Wm. B. Rodgers, 1 yr
City Engineer	Chas. Davis, 1 yr
Sup't of Water Works	H. C. Richmond, 1 yr
Street Com. East Dist.	W. W. Tyson, 1 yr
Street Com. Western Dist.	Alex. Hanna, 1 yr
Assessor of Water Rents	James Nichol, 1 yr
City Assessor	Thomas Ward, 1 yr
Clerk of Markets	D. Hastings, 1 yr
Chief Engineer Fire Dep't	James E. Crow, 1 yr
Sup't Fire Alarm Tel	Geo. W. Winn, 1 yr
Weighmaster Dia'd Scales, Geo. B. McNulty,1 yr	

ALLEGHENY CITY—Continued.

Weighmaster Second Ward Scales	D. J. Boden
Weighmaster Fourth Ward Scales	Victor Paulin
Clerk of Select Councils	R. T. White
Clerk of Committees	R. T. White
Clerk of Common Councils	Rob't Dilworth
Bark Measurer	Wm. Greenawald
Wharfmaster, Eastern Dist.	Aug. Duffner
Wharfmaster, Western Dist.	S. R. Davis
Meat Inspector	Jos. A. Drexler
Physician to Tombs	Dr. W. R. Thorn
Messenger	J. R. Lupton
Health Officer	C. Hoch

The above officers are elected by Councils for the term of one year each.

SELECT COUNCIL, 1876.

First Ward—Thos. M. Bayne, D. E. McKelvey
Second Ward—Simon Drum, Alfred Slack.
Third Ward—N. H. Voegtley, John Huckestein.
Fourth Ward—James Callery, Josiah C. Patterson.
Fifth Ward—Jas. H. Lindsay, Wm. Heagy.
Sixth Ward—John A. Cochran, G. M. D. Knox.
Seventh Ward—Wm. Eberhardt, C. C. Hax.
Eighth Ward—G. P. Wilhelm, Simon McRoberts.
Ninth Ward—Chas. Weaver, David Davis, Jr.
Tenth Ward—Chas. B. Welfe, Henry Kreiling.
Eleventh Ward—Walton Woolsey, C. H. Hartman.

COMMON COUNCIL, 1876.

First Ward—Thomas Neeley, W. P. Bidell.
Second Ward—Samuel Sholes, James Hunter, James Wilson, Archibald Alston.
Third Ward—A. W. Kredel, Wm. Swindel, C. Lingenfelter, Raymond Mueller, J. S. Kerr.
Fourth Ward—Louis Moul, Hiram Loudes, Hugh McGuire, A. D. Armstrong.
Fifth Ward—Wm. C. Cooke, Leon Long.
Sixth Ward—George A. Cochran, L. F. Stone, J. Parkhill.
Seventh Ward—Anton Schmidt, G. R. Riber, Frank Hopf.
Eighth Ward—Christian Klicker, Smith Walker.
Ninth Ward—John Hughes, Patrick Wall.
Tenth Ward—J. O. S. Golden, George W. Schumaker.
Eleventh Ward—Thomas Kerr, John Selling.

CEREAL DISCOVERY.—A new cereal has been grown in the State of Oregon, and thus far no one has been able to classify it; for while it bears a general resemblance to wheat, yet its stalk, mode of growth, and heavy filaments cause it to be taken for rye or barley by the most experienced farmers. The grain was originally discovered in the stomach of a wild goose, by a farmer. From seven to ten stalks spring from one root, and attain a height, when ripe, of four and a half to five feet. They are very thin, compact, of a bright straw color, and extremely hard, as if they contained a large quantity of silex.

GENERAL STATISTICS.

ALLEGHENY CITY, 1876.

VOTE FOR MAYOR, 1874.

ALLEGHENY.

The election for Mayor takes place on the third Tuesday of February of every third year. The following are the returns at the election held February 17th, 1874.

WARDS.	Phillips, I.	Fairly, D.	Smith, R.	Shellaby, I.
First	397	171	68	5
Second	445	205	197	13
Third, 1st precinct	296	101	296	12
Third, 2d precinct	26	302	286	9
Fourth, 1st precinct	304	275	119	4
Fourth, 2d precinct	75	145	104	
Fifth	379	152	111	2
Sixth	335	401	97	7
Seventh	51	317	214	20
Eighth	62	153	53	4
Ninth	80	145	22	33
Tenth	41	73	37	17
Eleventh	108	103	22	4
Total	2599	2553	1626	130

TOTAL VOTE.

Phillips 2,599
Fairley 2,553
Smith 1,626
Shellaby 130

Phillips' majority over Fairley 46

Vote for Mayor, 1871.

Alex P. Callow 4,499
Mr. Dickson 573

POPULATION OF ALLEGHENY CITY.

The last census shows the population of the city June 1st.

1870.

Wards		Wards	
1	4,739	6	4,693
2	9,010	7	5,300
3	12,507	8	2,182
4	10,302	9	3,570
5	4,449	10	1,213
		11	1,403

Total 59,368

CITY TAXES.

Yearly taxes are assessed for one year, commencing at the following dates: Water, April 1st; all others January 1st. Assessments of county taxes are made, commencing in December; city and poor in January; city taxes are paid to City Treasurer, school taxes also.

GENERAL STATISTICS.

(CONTINUED.)

SCHEDULE OF THE RATES OF TAXES.

Mills.

City tax 4
Business tax (on gross amount of sales) 1
Poor 1
School 2

Public Park Tax.

1st class	5 mills per superficial foot.
2d class	2	" " "
3d class	1	" " "
4th class	¾	" " "
5th class	½	" " "
6th class	⅓	" " "

Sewer Tax.

1½ mills on valuation of grounds alone.

Water Tax.

One room and one person $2 50
Two rooms and two persons 4 00
Three rooms and three persons .. 5 75
Four rooms and four persons 7 25
Five rooms and five persons 8 75
Six rooms and six persons 10 25
Each additional room over six .. 1 50
Each additional person over ten. 1 00
Rooms over halls, attic rooms, etc. 1 00
Public baths, each 10 00
Private baths. (cold water.) each. 2 00
Private baths, (hot water,) each.. 3 00
Water closets, public and private,
  from .... 2 00 to $10 00
Plug, basing each 1 50
Carriages, buggies, etc., from ... 2 50 to 10 00
Horses, each 1 50
Fountain in yard, one jet 5 00
Each additional jet 2 00
Churches .... 3 00 to 7 00
Schools .... 3 00 to 6 00
Cows, each 75
Slaughtering houses, from .... 3 00 to 5 00
Store rooms, from .... 2 50 to 6 00
Pavement hydrants, from .... 3 00 to 6 00
Garden hose, from .... 2 50 to 12 00
Barber shops, 1st chair 5 00
  " " each additional 3 00
Blacksmith's forges, each 2 00
Street sprinklers, from .... 5 00 to 15 00

Regulations Governing the Payment of Taxes.

If paid in the month of June, a deduction of 5 per cent. allowed.
If paid in the month of July, a deduction of 4 per cent. allowed.
If paid in the month of August, a deduction of 2 per cent. allowed.
If paid in the month of September, no deduction allowed.
If not paid until the month of October, 5 per cent. is added.
In the month of November the taxes pass into the hands of the collector, with 5 per cent. added and subject to the costs which may accrue thereon.

GENERAL STATISTICS.

(CONTINUED.)

APPROPRIATIONS.

The following were the amounts estimated to meet the expenses of the various departments of Allegheny City, for the year 1875:

No. 1, Salaries	$ 38,128 00
No. 2, Interest	43,560 00
No. 3, Fire Department	68,707 46
No. 4, Printing	10,000 00
No. 5, Streets	40,000 00
No. 6, Wharves and landings	2,000 00
No. 7, Surveys	4,000 00
No. 8, Police	46,411 75
No. 9, Contingent fund	47,569 88
No. 11, Water works	30,000 00
No. 12, Outstanding warrants	2,428 51
No. 13, Gas	25,000 00
No. 14, Sinking fund	20,000 00
No. 15, Interest on wharf bonds	1,960 00
No. 16, City property	5,000 00
No. 17, Sanitary	2,000 00
No. 18, Bills payable	50,000 00
No. 19, Markets	500 00
Park Commission	13,000 00
Sinking fund, redemption of water bonds	7,500 50
Sinking fund for the redemption of city property bonds	3,000 00
Total	$460,760 60

THE ESTIMATED RECEIPTS.

from all sources for the year were as follows:

City taxes	$224,000 00
Business tax	14,780 64
Water tax	110,000 00
Weigh scales	7,739 61
Wood and bark	1,513 48
Vehicle license	11,000 00
Proceeds from sale of ferrules	1,500 00
Fines and forfeitures	4,500 00
Lot regulations	1,318 50
Markets	20,066 70
Sewer permits	299 00
Ground Rents	1,749 92
Interest on daily balances	3,980 30
U. S. Postoffice department rent	1,600 00
Switch licenses	75 00
Pleasant Valley R. W. Co	847 00
Street opening permits	871 00
Collection of school taxes	1,500 00
Sundry sources	653 44
Board of health	265 00
Wharves and landings	2,500 00
Pittsburgh, Fort Wayne & Chicago R. W. Co	3,400 00
P. & M. Railway Co	1,600 00
Delinquent taxes	45,000 00
Total	$460,760 60

PHILADELPHIA manufacturers have introduced improvements in their machinery for punching cold iron, by which they are able to punch a half-inch hole through an inch and three-quarters of wrought iron cold, making a perfectly smooth perforation.

CITY OFFICERS.
ALLEGHENY.

DIRECTORS OF THE POOR.

Office, City Building.

Members: Jos. F. Neely, Abraham Dickson, Wm. Walker, Leonard Walter, W. W Speer, Henry Faulkner, Martin Ley, A. Jackson, Wm. Trimble, Dr. E. M. Riggs, T. F. Grubbs. J. Q. Workman, Secretary; R. D. McGunnigle, Clerk; T. F. Grubbs, Steward of the House; Dr. B. B. Smith, Physician.

BOARD OF HEALTH.

Office, City Building.

Messrs. Reed, Heagy, Ober, Day, Cochran, Burton, Wachob, Brown, Wilson. Dr. C. Cole, Physician ; C. Hoch, Health officer.

POSTOFFICE.

City Building.

John A. Myler, Postmaster ; Theo. Myler, Assistant Postmaster.

PUBLIC BUILDINGS,
ALLEGHENY CITY.

Western Penitentiary—Sherman avenue and West Ohio street.
Water Works—River avenue Eighth Ward.
City Hall—Diamond Square.
Market House—Diamond Square.
Observatory—Observatory Hill.
House of Refuge—Ninth ward.

HALLS.

Turners' Hall—South Canal and Cherry sts.
Templars' Hall—Lacock and Federal streets.
Odd Fellows' Hall—North Diamond and East Diamond streets.
Masonic Hall—Madison avenue and Washington street.
Masonic Hall—South Diamond and East Diamond streets.
Pythian Hall—Corner of Park way and Pine alley.

PUBLIC CHARITIES, ETC.

Home for the Friendless—Washington street, near East Park.
Allegheny Widows' Home Association—Webster street.
House of Industry—Washington street, near East Park.
Allegheny Orphan Asylum—Ridge street,

PUBLIC BUILDINGS.

CONTINUED.

PUBLIC SCHOOLS.

First Ward—Rebecca and School streets.
Second Ward—Palo Alto street and North avenue; also, Washington and Irwin streets.
Third Ward—North avenue and Esplanade street; also, cor. Chestnut and Perry streets.
Fourth Ward—Liberty, near East Park; also, Liberty, below Madison avenue and Chestnut street.
Fifth Ward—Fulton and Page streets.
Sixth Ward—Chartiers and Juniata streets.
Seventh Ward—Spring Garden avenue, near city line; also, Madison avenue extension.
Eighth Ward—River avenue, near Herr's Island.
Ninth Ward—Wilkins street, near Western avenue.

The public schools are under the management of a board of control, composed of the directors of all the wards.

FIRE DEPARTMENT.

ALLEGHENY CITY.

FIRE COMMITTEE.

S. Sholes, Chairman. H. McGuire, George Wittmer, John A. Cochran, George Ober, Jacob Born, Wm. Twindle, S. Drum, R. McKelvey, H, Phillips. Paul Gschwend.

OFFICERS.

Chief Engineer, - - James E. Crow.
Sup't of Fire Alarm. - - George Weinn.

STEAMERS AND LOCATION.

No.
1. Hope, Martin and Corry streets.
2. Grant, Madison, near Pike street.
3. Friendship, Arch and Jackson streets.
4. Good Will, Franklin and Manhattan sts.
5. Lincoln. Kerr and Refuge streets.
6. Columbia, Sandusky and Water streets.
7. Ellsworth Hose, River avenue.
8. Allegheny Hose, Forest and Lowrie sts.

LOCATION OF SIGNAL BOXES.

No.
2 Beaver avenue and Strawberry lane.
3 Beaver and Washington avenues.
4 Beaver avenue and Greenwood street.
5 Rebecca street and Western avenue.
6 Rebecca street and Ridge avenue.
7 Fulton and Fayette streets.
8 Taggart street and Washington avenue.
9 Taggart and Charles streets.
12 Good Will E. H., Franklin & Manhattan sts
13 Bidwell and Western avenues.
14 Bidwell street and Pennsylvania avenue.
15 Gas works, Rebecca street.
16 Rebecca street and Grant avenue.

17 Irwin avenue and Western avenue.
21 Irwin and Taylor avenues.
23 Palo Alto street and Taylor avenue.
24 Hope E. H., Martin street.
25 Robinson and Craig streets.
26 Arch street and Park way.
27 Arch street and North alley.
31 Friendship E. H., Arch and Jackson sts.
32 Federal street and North avenue.
34 Central Station, City Hall.
35 Federal street and Church avenue.
36 Federal and Isabella streets.
37 Anderson and Lacock streets.
41 Columbia E. H., Central Bell.
42 Sandusky street and North alley.
43 Sandusky and Hemlock streets.
45 Third and West streets.
46 Ohio street and Cedar avenue.
47 Goodrich and Robinson streets.
51 North and Washington streets.
52 Grant E. H., Madison avenue.
53 Third and Chestnut streets.
54 Main and Walnut streets.
56 Sycamore and South Canal streets.
57 East street and Madison avenue.
58 East street.
59 Vinal and Troy Hill avenues.
61 Spring Garden avenue.
62 Spring Garden avenue and Overhill.
63 Ellsworth E. H., River avenue, 8th ward
64 River avenue and Ridge street.
65 Gardner and Lowrie streets.
67 Forest and Lowrie streets.
71 Preble avenue, 9th ward.
72 Lewis, Oliver & Phillips.
73 Verner Station.

PROPERTY VALUATION OF ALLEGHENY CITY, 1875.

	1875.	1874.
First ward	$ 7,227,125	$6,881,141
Second ward	10,888,426	9,985,250
Third ward	7,904,537	7,905,480
Fourth ward	8,778,485	8,655,449
Fifth ward	5,872,468	4,884,058
Sixth ward	4,722,377	4,536,670
Seventh ward	8,412,710	2,608,402
Eighth ward	1,238,966	1,083,290
Ninth ward	1,841,600	1,501,885
Tenth ward	1,800,172	1,919,115
Eleventh ward	1,834,000	1,620,611
Total	$55,020,811	$50,981,200

TAX, 1875.

COUNTY.	STATE.
$ 9,638,42	$ 516,05
18,657,83	727,19
10,544,81	401,66
11,700,84	392,32
7,528,74	817,23
6,299,72	255,48
4,554,84	181,09
1,652.27	127.36
2,456,08	54,07
2,401,23	119,60
2,446,78	222,70
78,390,61	3,905,95

RECAPITULATION.

Valuation—$55,020,811

County Tax— 78,390.61
State— 3,905.95

Total Tax—$77,296,56

ELECTION RETURNS, 1875.

The following are the official returns of the Allegheny county election for Governor and State Treasurer, held on the first Tuesday of November, 1875, Browne and Pennypacker being the Prohibitionist candidates.

DISTRICTS.	GOVERNOR			STATE TREASURER.		
	Hartranft, R.	Pershing, D.	Browne, P.	Rawle, R.	Piollet, D.	Pennypacker, P.
PITTSBURGH.						
First, 1st district.....	21	131	.....	20	131	.....
First, 2d d.............	100	67	2	100	68	1
First, 3d d.............	96	65	5	90	70	5
Second, 1st d.........	90	27	8	88	30	2
Second, 2d d..........	122	67	2	117	71	2
Second, 3d d..........	89	60	6	84	66	6
Third, 1st d............	82	28	1	77	33	1
Third, 2d d.............	103	79	3	97	82	3
Fourth, 1st d..........	104	54	3	106	53	3
Fourth, 2d d..........	88	96	1	88	98	.....
Fourth, 3d d..........	91	55	6	91	55	6
Fifth, 1st d............	48	70	1	48	70	1
Fifth, 2d d............	46	128	5	51	129	.....
Fifth, 3d d............	53	119	5	52	120	5
Sixth, 1st d...........	98	103	5	100	108	3
Sixth, 2d d...........	106	57	6	104	58	6
Sixth, 3d d...........	143	72	2	141	74	2
Sixth, 4th d..........	44	32	4	48	32	4
Seventh, 1st d........	127	71	6	123	75	5
Seventh, 2d d........	121	61	9	122	60	9
Seventh, 3d d........	85	58	1	83	61	1
Eighth, 1st d.........	62	78	2	61	78	.....
Eighth, 2d d.........	113	28	.....	111	31	.....
Eighth, 3d d.........	121	45	1	120	46	1
Eighth, 4th d.........	124	27	11	124	27	12
Ninth, 1st d..........	69	81	1	66	85	1
Ninth, 2d d..........	105	83	.....	101	91	.....
Ninth, 3d d..........	81	113	.....	26	117	1
Tenth, 1st d..........	66	156	.....	61	161	.....
Tenth, 2d d..........	54	79	1	52	82	1
Eleventh, 1st d......	99	49	2	96	52	2
Eleventh, 2d d......	174	90	13	169	96	13
Eleventh, 3d d......	89	52	6	86	55	6
Eleventh, 4th d......	82	46	5	81	47	5
Twelfth, 1st d.......	85	72	3	82	74	3
Twelfth, 2d d.......	89	45	7	89	45	7
Twelfth, 3d d.......	58	81	1	53	81	1
Twelfth, 4th d.......	137	100	1	135	103	1
Thirteenth, 1st d.....	84	35	7	82	37	6
Thirteenth, 2d d.....	140	69	10	139	69	10
Thirteenth, 3d d.....	73	51	4	69	55	8
Fourteenth, 1st d.....	124	76	10	124	77	10
Fourteenth, 2d d.....	68	35	.....	60	38	.....
Fourteenth, 3d d.....	86	20	6	89	20	2
Fourteenth, 4th d.....	67	33	1	68	32	.....
Fourteenth, 5th d.....	91	57	2	89	58	2
Fifteenth, 1st d.......	60	60	2	58	62	2
Fifteenth, 2d d.......	83	64	3	82	66	3

ALLEGHENY COUNTY.

Allegheny county is bounded on the north and northwest by Butler and Beaver counties, on the east by Westmoreland county, and on the south and southwest by Washington county.

POPULATION OF ALLEGHENY COUNTY FROM 1800 TO 1870.

1870.................................262,204
1860................................178,831
1850................................138,290
1840.................................81,285
1830.................................50,552
1820.................................34,921
1810.................................25,317
1800.................................15,087

ALLEGHENY COUNTY OFFICERS.

1876.

COMMON PLEAS COURT No. 1.

PRESIDENT JUDGE.   COMMISSIONED.
James P. Sterrett.................................1862

ASSISTANT LAW JUDGE.
Fred'k H. Collier...............................1869

ASSOCIATE LAW JUDGE.
Edwin H. Stowe..............................1862

Term return days: First Monday of March, June, September and December; also, monthly return days first Monday of each month.

COMMON PLEAS COURT No. 2.

PRESIDENT JUDGE.   COMMISSIONED.
Thomas Ewing..............................1873

ASSISTANTS.
John M. Kirkpatrick.........................1869
J. W. F. White...............................1873

Term return days: Fourth Monday of January, April, July and November; also, monthly return days first Monday of each month.

JUDGE OF ORPHANS' COURT.

Office created under new Constitution.
    COMMISSIONED.
William G. Hawkins......................1874

No term return days as yet established.

DISTRICT ATTORNEY.

Edward A. Montooth........................1874

ASSISTANT DISTRICT ATTORNEY.
Morton Hunter............................1874

CLERK OF COURTS.

W. H. McCleary.............................1872

PROTHONOTARY.

F. B. Kennedy..............................1873

ELECTION RETURNS.

(CONTINUED.)

	H	P	B	R	P	P
Fifteenth, 3d d.......	87	90	1	81	95	1
Sixteenth, 1st d......	46	70	2	40	74	2
Sixteenth, 2d d	43	43	.....	37	47	.....
Sixteenth, 3d d......	48	85	1	48	35	1
Sixteenth, 4th d......	66	27	.....	63	30	.....
Sixteenth, 5th d......	58	52.....		57	53	.....
Seventeenth, 1st d..	131	54	6	125	60	6
Seventeenth, 2d d...	145	79	4	145	79	3
Seventeenth, 3d d...	102	106	3	101	107	3
Seventeenth, 4th d..	80	74	5	80	74	5
Eighteenth	61	100	4	58	108	4
Nineteenth, 1st d ...	94	36	12	98	31	10
Nineteenth, 2d d......	84	42	7	83	41	7
Nineteenth, 3d d.....	69	63	11	68	65	15
Twentieth, 1st d.....	82	39	4	80	42	4
Twentieth, 2d d......	117	32.....		113	37	.....
Twentieth, 3d d......	70	58	7	68	60	7
Twenty-first, 1st d..	166	108	23	167	109	21
Twenty-first, 2d d...	24	12	6	24	12	6
Twety-first, 3d d.....	104	32	4	104	31	4
Twenty-sec'd 1st d..	103	26	10	102	27	10
Twenty-sec'd, 2d d..	44	19.....		36	18	.....
Twenty-third, 1st d	48	41.....		48	41	.....
Twenty-third, 2d d..	112	74	4	112	74	4
Twenty-fourth,1st d	94	85.....		90	91	.....
Twenty-fourth, 2d d.	47	40	4	48	40	4
Twenty-fifth, 1st d..	73	81	3	72	83	3
Twenty-fifth, 2d d..	102	78	2	97	83	3
Twenty-fifth, 3d d..	92	81	3	82	92	5
Twenty-sixth, 1st d	109	52	2	108	52	2
Twenty-sixth, 2d d	114	135	2	110	140	1
Twenty-sixth, 3d d..	118	42	2	116	42	2
Twenty-sixth, 4th d	101	73.....		100	73	.....
Twenty-sev'th,1st d	44	190.....		43	191	.....
Twenty-sev'th 2d d	53	51	2	52	52	2
Twenty-eighth 1st d	104	70	3	103	70	3
Twenty-eighth, 2d d	69	63	0	68	65	0
Twenty-eighth 3d d	77	75	4	76	77	3
Twenty-ninth, 1st d	82	52	10	79	53	11
Twenty-ninth. 2d d	126	93	6	127	92	6
Thirtieth, 1st d	94	62	2	94	62	2
Thirtieth, 2d d.......	81	67	2	82	66	2
Thirty-first	79	45	10	79	46	9
Thirty-sec'd, 1st d...	127	67	8	126	68	8
Thirty-sec'd, 2d d...	114	40	14	119	55	15
Thirty-third	36	82.....		36	82	.....
Thirty-fourth.........	42	165	4	42	165	4
Thirty-fifth, 1st d...	66	28	2	64	29	2
Thirty-fifth, 2d d....	42	43	8	42	43	6
Thirty-sixth, 1st d..	64	94	12	64	95	12
Thirty-sixth, 2d d...	64	29	20	66	29	18
Thirty-sev'th, 1st d.	79	20	7	80	20	6
Thirty-sev'th, 2d d..	94	19	5	93	20	5
ALLEGHENY.						
First.....................	436	167	32	425	176	32
Second, 1st district..	123	52	23	221	54	25
Second, 2d d...........	216	79	31	215	83	30
Second, 3d d...........	228	95	28	2g8	86	26
Second, 4th d	122	62	13	122	62	13
Third, 1st d	152	47	19	153	47	17
Third, 2d d.............	197	61	27	200	60	23
Third, 3d d.............	120	43	9	119	45	7
Third, 4th d............	126	125	2	122	127	2
Third, 5th d............	137	109.....		135	110	.....
Fourth, 1st d...........	175	77	19	172	80	18
Fourth, 2d d	121	63	8	117	68	5
Fourth, 3d d	122	93	9	121	93	10
Fourth, 4th d	182	144	1	179	144	1

ALLEGHENY COUNTY.

(CONTINUED.)

SHERIFF.

Richard H. Fife.................................1875

RECORDER.

Ralph J. Richardson........................1872

REGISTER AND CLERK OF ORPHANS' COURT.

Joseph H. Gray.................................1872

TREASURER.

Samuel Kilgore.................................1873

CONTROLLER.

Henry Warner...................................1872

CORONER.

William McCallin..............................1873

COMMISSIONERS.

John McClelland...............................1873
James Irwin.......................................1874
August Beckert..................................1873

COUNTY SURVEYOR.

J. B. Stilley.......................................1874

GAS INSPECTOR.

R. H. Smith.......Appointed by Governor...3 yrs
SUPERINTENDENT PUBLIC SCHOOLS.
James Dickson................................3 yrs

FLOUR INSPECTOR.

Adam Weaver...Appointed by Governor...3 yrs.
SEALER OF WEIGHTS AND MEASURES.
David Lewis......Appointed by Governor...3 yrs

TAXES.

The tax levy for Allegheny county is made on or before the first day of March of each year, and the fiscal year commences on the first day of January. The books are placed in the hands of the County Treasurer on or about the first of May. All taxes enumerated in this article are payable to him directly, up to a certain date stated hereafter, after which they are transferred to the collectors of the respective districts for settlement.

TERMS OF PAYMENT.

From May 1st until August 1st the Treasurer is authorized to make a deduction of five per cent.
During August no deduction is made.
After September 1st ten per cent. additional is charged, and as soon after that date as possible, generally about October 1st, all unpaid levies are placed in the hands of the collectors.

VALUATION, MILEAGE, &c.

The valuation on which the county levy for 1874 was made, was $300,000,000.
The cities of Pittsburgh and Allegheny are exempt from the county poor tax, those corporations having provided independently for their paupers.
The millage for county purposes for 1875 was one and one-third mills on each dollar; for poor, one-third mill; State, on personal property only, three mills.

ELECTION RETURNS.

(CONTINUED.)

	H	P	B	R	P	P
Fifth, 1st d	82	57	13	81	58	13
Fifth, 2d d	212	96	17	209	108	14
Fifth, 3d d	96	62	6	99	61	4
Sixth, 1st d	175	110	25	170	115	25
Sixth, 2d d	111	77	14	114	77	11
Sixth, 3d d	84	87	11	85	86	11
Seventh, 1st d	61	129	6	61	129	.....
Seventh, 2d d	120	127	1	117	131	.....
Seventh, 3d d	90	56	4	88	63	-4
Eighth, 1st d	99	84	1	97	76	1
Eighth, 2d d	71	34	1	71	84	1
Ninth ....ʃ.........	104	167	3	95	177	3
Tenth	64	82	1	68	83	9
Eleventh	132	76	6	127	82	5
BOROUGHS.						
McKeesport, 1st w ..	134	152	4	135	150	4
McKeesport, 2d w ...	149	70	16	146	74	15
McKeesport, 3d w ...	70	69	1	69	72	1
Braddocks	87	85	37	88	33	37
Bellevue	95	15	14	96	17	11
Beltzhoover..	16	12	3	15	11	3
Chartiers	85	66	5	84	58	7
Etna.....................	172	57	1	173	57	.....
Elizabeth...............	92	60	35	94	61	32
Millvale	110	46	5	109	47	5
Mansfield	99	22	10	97	23	11
Sewickley	157	67	17	161	63	17
Sharpsburg	162	180	22	160	182	22
Tarentum	93	37	54	91	38	54
Verona, 1st ward ...	45	9	.....	45	9	.....
Verona, 2d ward.....	30	19	9	20	18	10
West Bellevue	21	12	3	20	12	3
West Elizabeth	67	37	9	67	37	9
TOWNSHIPS.						
Baldwin, 1st d	61	77	4	60	76	5
Baldwin, 2d d	102	101	1	94	107	3
Chartiers	101	107	9	152	106	9
Collier..................	61	58	4	61	58	4
Crescent................	27	32	.....	27	32	.....
Elizabeth, 1st d	72	56	12	73	56	11
Elizabeth, 2d d	50	31	2	51	31	1
Elizabeth, 3d d	32	18	20	30	18	21
Elizabeth, 4th d	91	32	4	90	32	4
East Deer, 1st d	80	38	19	89	33	19
East Deer, 2d d	50	38	15	50	37	16
Franklin	49	53	3	49	58	3
Fawn	74	11	7	75	11	7
Findley	93	120	5	93	120	5
Forward	88	56	7	92	56	4
Hampton	64	54	2	64	54	2
Harrison	107	88	40	108	89	39
Harmar	33	23	25	31	27	23
Indiana.................	79	45	5	79	45	5
Jefferson	136	102	25	137	102	24
Kilbuck, 1st d ...:..	62	26	8	62	26	8
Kilbuck, 2d d	84	36	7	85	37	3
Leet	80	14	8	83	14.	2
L. St. Clair 1st d ...	40	139	2	40	139	2
L. St. Clair, 2d d ...	37	40	2	37	41	2
L. St. Clair, 3d d ...	25	29	6	25	29	6
Lincoln.................	80	32	9	80	32	9
Mifflin, 1st d	29	109	9	29	108	10
Mifflin, 2d d	83	92	5	82	93	4
Mifflin, 3d d	66	33	27	67	32	27
Moon	94	87	17	97	87	13
Marshall................	35	53	.....	36	52	.....
McCandless.............	38	65	.....	37	66	.....
North Fayette.........	78	71	32	77	72	32

ALLEGHENY COUNTY. •

(CONTINUED.)

The total debt of the county January 1st, 1874, was $2,329,221,73. This debt was reduced during the year fully $75,000, as the Controller's report issued January, 1875, will show.

The following is a statement of personal property, etc., on which all the taxes above mentioned are levied:

All horses, mares, geldings, mules and meat cattle, over the age of four years.

Real estate is not now taxed for State purposes.

All shares of stock in any railroad, insurance company, building and loan association, incorporated by or in pursuance of any law of this Commonwealth, or any other State or Government, except such building or loan associations as make or declare no dividends.

All public loans or stocks whatsoever, except those issued by this Commonwealth, by the Government of the United States, by the city of Allegheny for city purposes since March 31st, 1870; also, excepting the bonds of said city of Allegheny, known as the renewal bonds of 1870; also, excepting the bonds of the city of Pittsburgh, known as the Water Extension Loan, and the bonds of said city issued for the purpose of retiring the matured and maturing indebtedness thereof, (under the act of April 12th, 1869.)

All monies loaned or invested on interest in any other state, together with the amount of said respective objects of taxation, and the amount per cent. of the dividend or profit annually accruing or received therefrom respectively.

All household furniture, including gold or silver plate, exceeding in value $300, owned by person or persons, corporation or corporations.

All salaries and emoluments of office; all offices and posts of profit, professions, trades and occupations.

On all pleasure-carriages, both of two and four wheels, a tax of one per cent.

The following are liable for State Tax alone:

All able-bodied white male citizens of the age of twenty-one years, and under the age of forty-five years, except persons having served nine months in the army, enlisted into volunteer companies or having served five years therein, idiots, lunatics, common drunkards, vagabonds, paupers and persons convicted of any infamous crime.

Gold lever watches, one dollar each; all other gold watches, seventy-five cents; silver lever watches, seventy-five cents; every other description of watch, being over $20 in value, fifty cents each.

All trades, occupations and professions (except the occupation of farmers) over and above $200.

All salaries and emoluments of office created by or held under the Constitution and Laws of this Commonwealth, or created by or held under any corporation, institution or company incorporated by the Commonwealth, wherein such salaries or emoluments exceed $200.

All annuities over $200, except those granted by this Commonwealth, or by the United States, and upon all property, real or personal, (not taxed under existing laws) held, owned, used or

• *ELECTION RETURNS.*

(CONTINUED.)

	H	P	B	R	P	P
Neville	25	6	4	26	6	3
North Versailles	106	132	4	107	132	4
Ohio	33	36	4	35	35	3
O'Hara, 1st d	65	30	1	60	35	1
O'Hara, 2d d	29	32	2	27	33	2
Plum	105	95	36	106	95	35
Penn	164	87	16	165	87	15
Pine	51	51	1	50	52	1
Patton, 1st d	32	29	18	35	27	18
Patton, 2d d	58	57	14	58	57	14
Robinson, 1st d	7	1	.....	7	1	.....
Robinson, 2d d	66	35	14	66	35	14
Ross, 1st d	62	23	3	65	23	.....
Ross, 2d d	48	55	5	48	55	5
Reserve	71	33	6	71	34	5
Richland	61	65	15	61	64	15
Shaler, 1st d	87	23	1	88	22	1
Shaler, 2d d	52	42	4	52	42	4
South Versailles	27	40	.....	28	40	.....
Snowden	119	47	14	119	47	14
South Fayette	100	25	14	100	25	14
Sewickley	33	12	.....	30	13	.....
Scott, 1st d	41	28	4	41	28	4
Scott, 2d d	43	29	1	44	29	.....
Stowe	39	43	3	41	43	3
Springdale	50	88	15	50	37	16
U. St. Clair, 1st d	33	29	3	33	29	3
U. St. Clair, 2d d	39	35	1	39	35	1
Union	155	36	6	154	38	5
Versailles	32	29	2	34	29	.....
Wilkins, 1st d	97	25	9	99	23	9
Wilkins, 2d d	56	64	8	57	65	6
West Deer	126	41	38	125	42	37

ECLIPSES FOR 1876.

In the year 1876 there will be four Eclipses: two of the Sun, and two of the Moon.

I. A partial eclipse of the Moon, March 9th and 10th, visible as the following table shows.

II. An annular eclipse of the Sun, March 25th, visible as the table shows.

III. A partial eclipse of the Moon, September 3d, invisible.

IV. A total eclipse of the sun, September 17th, invisible.

Eclipse of the Moon, March 9th and 10th.

	Beg.	Mid.	Ends.
	H. M.	M. H.	M.
Boston 10th	12 40	1 41	2 40 mo
New York, "	12 27	1 28	2 27 mo
Philadelphia, "	12 22	1 23	2 22 mo
Washington, "	12 16	1 17	2 16 mo
Pittsburgh, "	12 3	1 4	2 3 mo
St. Louis, Ev. & M. t9 &10	11 22	12 23	1 22 mo
New Orleans" " "	11 23	12 24	1 23 mo

Eclipse of the Sun. March 25th.

	Beg.	Mid.	Ends.
	H. M. H.	M. H.	M.
Boston	4 17	5 10	5 51 ev.
New York	4 4	4 57	5 88 ev.
Philadelphia	3 56	4 52	5 33 ev.
Washington	3 50	4 46	5 27 ev.
Pittsburgh	3 37	4 33	5 15 ev.
St. Louis	2 56	3 52	4 33 ev.
N. Orleans, small eclp. at		3 53	ev.

Venus (*) will be Evening Star till the 14th of July, then Morning Str to the end of the year.

ALLEGHENY COUNTY.

(CONTINUED.)

invested by any person, company or corporation, in trust for the use, benefit or advantage of any other person, company or corporation, excepting always such property as shall be held in trust for religious purposes.

All mortgages, judgments, recognizances and moneys owing upon articles of agreement for the sale of real estate, (except such as are given by corporations.)

ALLEGHENY COUNTY FINANCES.

Statement of finances of Allegheny county for 1875. In some instances the amounts are estimated, but will not vary much from actual figures.

ACTUAL RECEIPTS.

Cash in County Treasury, Jan. 1, '75	$110,958 46
Matured Debt	25,000 00
Interest	16,572 39
Fees and Salaries	108,646 51
Election Expenses	28 00
Printing and Stationery	17,032 10
Court House	17 00
County Jail	1,523 50
Court of Quarter Sessions	12,573 52
Courts of Common Pleas	1,692 00
Aldermen and Justices of the Peace	98 00
Gas Inspection	4,181 04
Bridges	69 60
Penn'a Reform School	3 90
Contingent Fund	10 00
Taxes 1873 and former years	450 92
" 1874	61,442 22
" 1875	322,038 70
Total	$682,332 86

ACTUAL EXPENDITURES.

Matured Debt	$ 25,150 00
Interest	119,091 33
Fees and Salaries	185,622 69
Commissioner's Officers	2,098 12
Assessment of Taxes	13,789 11
Election Expenses	14,199 35
Constables	5,097 51
Coroner's Office	3,994 81
Printing and Stationery	31,341 73
Court House	7,553 92
County Jail	8,257 92
Court House and Jail	8,424 64
Court of Quarter Sessions	56,519 38
Court of Common Pleas	40,987 03
Supreme Court	1,125 62
Aldermen and Justices of the Peace	2,187 17
Gas Inspector	4,180 95
Commonwealth of Pennsylvania	65,858 89
Sinking Fund	25,000 00
Bridges	25,140 62
Roads	2,292 35
Penn'a Reform School	20,739 85
Western Penitentiary	7,286 48
Western Penn'a Hospital	1,928 10
Law Library	8,534 72
Contingent Fund	4,814 62
Total	$636,171 86

ELECTION RETURNS.

(CONTINUED.)

The following are the official returns of the Allegheny County election for Sheriff, County Treasurer and Recorder, held on the first Tuesday of November, 1875.

Districts.	SHERIFF			TREASURER			RECORDER		
	Fife, R.	Patterson, D.	Hershberger, P	Murray, R.	English, D.	Gallagher, P.	Richardson, R.	Giles, D.	Butler, P.
PITTS'RGH.									
Wards.									
1st, 1st dist.....	16	126	.....	18	132	.....	17	134	....
1st, 2d d.........	71	72	1	102	65	2	104	62	2
1st, 3d d.........	61	79	5	93	68	1	89	71	6
2d, 1st d.........	73	39	3	88	32	3	83	31	3
2d, 2d d.........	82	105	5	113	77	2	18	74	1
2d, 3d d.........	44	94	3	88	58	6	87	65	4
3d, 1st d.........	35	69	.....	74	36	.....	70	40	....
3d, 2d d.........	77	101	1	99	79	1	104	74	2
4th, 1st d.........	86	71	1	109	45	4	111	44	3
4th, 2d d.........	66	112	5	90	92	1	92	91	....
4th, 3d d.........	64	80	2	91	57	4	90	49	4
5th, 1st d.........	53	61	1	49	67	1	42	74	1
5th, 2d d.........	31	144	.....	52	125	.....	25	155	.....
5th, 3d d.........	35	138	3	50	122	4	51	121	4
6th, 1st d.........	81	112	4	96	104	3	97	103	5
6th, 2d d.........	81	71	5	101	60	5	104	55	6
6th, 3d d.........	113	89	3	141	76	2	144	73	1
6th, 4th d.........	40	35	3	43	34	4	43	34	4
7th, 1st d.........	101	98	2	124	77	3	125	77	4
7th, 2d d.........	102	79	6	126	53	9	120	56	10
7th, 3d d.........	66	74	1	84	59	1	82	60	1
8th, 1st d.........	51	90	.....	57	82	1	57	82	1
8th, 2d d.........	95	44	.....	108	31	.....	108	33	....
8th, 3d d.........	113	56	2	127	42	1	123	44	1
8th, 4th d.........	97	52	9	121	30	11	120	30	11
9th, 1st d.........	43	101	1	65	83	1	96	51	1
9th, 2d d.........	96	95	2	107	87	.....	140	52	.....
9th, 3d d.........	25	117	.....	32	111	.....	62	81	....
10th, 1st d.....	46	174	.....	55	116	2	100	121	1
10th, 2d d.....	47	86	1	67	77	14	75	57	1
11th, 1st d.....	78	63	3	97	50	2	98	46	4
11th, 2d d.....	148	112	13	168	94	.....	167	94	14
11th, 3d d.....	86	59	2	87	51	5	90	50	5
11th, 4th d.....	69	42	4	84	35	3	81	35	2
12th, 1st d.....	68	87	2	82	74	2	89	67	4
12th, 2d d.....	78	55	7	89	44	8	101	32	7
12th, 3d d.....	39	87	10	56	80	1	57	80	1
12th, 4th d.....	90	147	1	138	100	1	151	87	1
13th, 1st d.....	78	44	4	84	37	4	81	37	6
13th, 2d d.....	142	74	5	143	70	6	144	71	7
13th, 3d d.....	53	62	4	78	48	4	74	49	3
14th, 1st d.....	110	86	7	126	76	7	126	79	7
14th, 2d d.....	54	41	.....	62	35	.....	64	34	.....
14th, 3d d.....	67	27	1	91	17	1	89	18	1
14th, 4th d.....	59	39	.....	72	28	.....	72	28	.....
14th, 5th d.....	58	61	2	66	63	2	68	64	2
15th, 1st d.....	40	64	3	55	62	2	61	56	2
15th, 2d d.....	66	70	3	62	63	4	91	61	3
15th, 3d d.....	59	89	2	83	96	.....	90	88	.....
16th, 1st d.....	35	73	1	46	70	1	50	67	1
16th, 2d d.....	30	58	5	48	46	.....	45	44	....
16th, 3d d.....	36	37	2	44	38	1	46	34	1

PUBLIC INSTITUTIONS.

WESTERN PENITENTIARY.

This institution was authorized by Act of the Legislature, dated March 8, 1818, and was finished ready for occupancy about nine years after. Was originally intended to be conducted on the solitary confinement principle, but recently the "congregate" system has been adopted. Situated at Ohio street, Sherman avenue and West Park, Allegheny City. Cost, nearly $520,000; area of site, six and one-half acres.

WESTERN PENNSYLVANIA HOSPITAL FOR THE INSANE.

Is an adjunct of the City General Hospital, Twelfth ward, the insane department of which was removed under the provisions of a supplement to its charter, passed in 1855. The site at Dixmont was purchased with funds privately contributed. State aid, to a very great extent, constructed the buildings, which are capable of accommodating 410 patients. Indigent insane have, by law, the preference of "paying" patients. Area of grounds, 350 acres; cost of buildings, $508,000.

REFORM SCHOOL OF WESTERN PENNSYLVANIA.

The new Reform School at Morganza, is situated on the Pittsburgh & Washington, Pa., Railroad, near Canonsburg. The new Reform School is one of the most complete and handsome institutions of the kind in the country.

ALLEGHENY CITY POOR HOUSE.

Situated at Claremont, about seven miles above the city, under the management of a board of guardians elected annually by City Councils.

CITY FARM FOR PITTSBURGH.

Situated on the left bank of the Monongahela, about two miles above the city limits. It contains 149 acres, and the buildings were erected in 1851, at a cost of $42,000. The grounds cost $14,900. Under the management of a board of twelve guardians elected by City Councils.

ALLEGHENY COUNTY HOME.

Situated near Chartiers Valley railway, about seven miles south of Pittsburgh. The farm, containing 205 acres, was purchased in 1853, at $90 per acre. The buildings cost $23,255.

ALLEGHENY COUNTY WORKHOUSE.

Situated on the right bank of the Allegheny, about seven miles above Allegheny City, at Claremont station, West Penn railway. The grounds are fifty acres in extent. Cost, about $500,000.

ELECTION RETURNS.—Continued.

	F	P	H	M	E	G	R	G	B
16th,4th d	50	41½	...	63	31	...	64	29	...
16th,5th d	40	62	...	54	56	...	58	52	...
17th,1st d	111	71	6	123	62	5	125	61	5
17th,2d d	116	99	8	140	84	3	142	81	2
17th,3d d	93	110	1	105	104	2	104	106	1
17th,4th d	77	74	4	81	74	3	81	73	3
18th	38	117	4	61	106	4	61	100	4
19th,1st d	81	54	4	99	32	8	105	31	5
19th,2d d	75	53	4	88	39	5	98	29	6
19th,3d d	55	76	7	66	69	10	87	48	9
20th,1st d	59	39	8	77	41	4	91	29	2
20th,2d d	91	57	...	117	31	...	120	30	...
20th,3d d	54	69	6	66	62	5	76	53	4
21st,1st d	118	148	20	165	113	16	168	111	18
21st,2d d	10	21	3	24	11	6	24	12	6
21st,3d d	97	44	3	107	34	3	103	35	6
22d,1st d	58	72	5	65	71	3	106	28	5
22d,2d d	34	30	1	38	27	1	44	20	1
23d,1st d	35	34	...	46	41	...	40	42	...
23d,2d d	93	81	3	113	71	5	98	91	5
24th,1st d	90	84	...	93	84	...	100	77	...
24th,2d d	46	38	4	50	37	4	51	35	4
25th,1st d	69	85	3	72	84	3	71	85	3
25th,2d d	93	87	2	102	80	2	104	78	2
25th,3d d	82	83	2	91	82	2	93	79	2
26th,1st d	63	53	2	110	52	2	108	52	2
26th,2d d	104	137	...	109	141	1	122	128	1
26th,3d d	118	40	2	115	43	2	118	41	2
26th,4th d	198	73	...	102	72	...	105	68	...
27th,1st d	42	186	...	44	185	...	46	187	...
27th,2d d	49	54	2	51	54	2	58	47	1
28th,1st d	90	75	5	104	70	6	100	68	6
28th,2d d	60	66	...	67	67	...	78	56	...
28th,3d d	68	75	4	78	76	3	81	73	3
29th,1st d	70	59	11	78	53	11	78	53	11
29th,2d d	16	98	5	132	88	6	133	87	5
30th,1st d	187	65	2	98	59	4	98	61	2
30th,2d d	73	68	2	76	69	2	76	69	2
31st	94	34	4	85	41	7	84	42	7
32d,1st d	12	82	6	123	69	8	122	73	8
32d,2d d	192	54	14	108	44	15	108	44	15
33d	33	75	1	38	84	...	93	83	...
34th:	17	159	8	40	165	5	43	164	3
35th,1st d	55	31	3	63	30	2	66	28	2
35th,6d d	16	50	18	40	48	9	40	43	9
36th,1st d	48	97	22	63	96	13	71	90	11
36th,2d d	53	27	31	64	29	20	67	29	17
37th,1st d	58	42	6	81	17	6	70	16	8
37th,2d d	79	29	6	91	19	6	103	11	5
ALLEGHE'Y.									
1st	352	242	27	436	158	34	439	166	27
2d,1st dist	101	80	18	122	52	23	126	53	20
2d,2d d	165	127	32	204	82	39	212	82	3?
2d,3d d	211	88	25	221	79	29	221	81	26
2d,4th d	109	73	8	117	61	12	119	60	9
3d,1st d	132	68	12	149	48	1	153	48	13
3d,2d d	174	86	22	198	55	25	198	54	25
3d,3d d	112	59	6	124	44	7	130	42	4
3d,4th d	108	138	2	119	132	2	119	132	2
3d,5th d	115	122	...	133	113	...	134	112	...
4th,1st d	136	117	11	177	75	16	178	78	16
4th,2d d	106	70	12	128	53	14	119	59	12
4th,3d d	105	106	6	122	93	8	122	95	6
4th,4th d	122	165	2	181	141	2	183	141	2
5th,1st d	70	65	11	77	57	16	81	57	10
5th,2d d	185	121	10	212	92	13	218	90	13
5th,3d d	65	87	8	90	64	9	99	59	8
6th,1st d	115	114	28	164	121	20	170	121	14
6th,2d d	105	82	10	116	74	14	119	76	9
6th,3d d	81	94	4	87	83	10	87	82	11
7th,1st d	49	135	...	58	131	...	59	131	...

Post Offices of Allegheny County.

Allegheny	Monroeville
Bakerstown	Moon
Beers	Mount Lebanon
Bennett	Mount Oliver
Boston	Mount Washington
Braddock's Fields	Natrona
Brinton	Negley
Bridgeville	New Texas
Brodhead	Noblestown
Buena Vista	North Star
Carrick	Oakdale Station
Castle Shannon	Obeyville
Chartiers	Palmersville
Clinton	Perrysville
Coal Valley	Pittsburgh
Culmerville	Port Perry
Dixmont	Remington
Dorseyville	Robella
Dravosburg	Rural Ridge
Duncan	Saint Elmo
Eakin	Sewickleyville
Elizabeth	Sharpsburg
Elkhorn	Shirland
Emsworth	Shousetown
Etna	Spring Dale
Ewing's Mills	Sunny Side
Fairhaven	Surgeon's Hall
Gamble's	Swissvale
Gill Hall	Tally Cavy
Green Tree	Tarentum
Harmarville	Thornhill
Herriottsville	Turtle Creek
Homestead	Upper Saint Clair
Hope Church	Vancefort
Houston	Walker's Mills
Hulton	West Elizabeth
Lebanon Church	West View
Leetsdale	Wexford
Library	White Ash
Logan's Ferry	Wilkinsburg
M'Keesport	Woodville.
Mansfield Valley	

PRINCIPAL CEMETERIES.

ALLEGHENY.

Situated in Pittsburgh, between Butler street, Seventeenth ward, and Penn avenue, Sixteenth ward. Citizens Passenger railway cars run to main entrance, on Butler street.

ST. MARY'S.

Situated immediately west of the Allegheny cemetery, entrances near Butler street, and on Penn avenue.

UNIONDALE.

Northwestern part of Allegheny, entrance on New Brighton pike. Formed of Mt. Union and Hilldale cemeteries.

CHARTIERS.

Situated in Chartiers township, near Mansfield.

GERMAN.

On hill between Oakland and Minersville.

ELECTION RETURNS.—Continued.

	F	P	H	M	E	G	R	G	B
7th, 2d d........	84	136	.....	110	136	.....	108	136	....
7th, 3d d........	101	42	3	90	60	3	90	60	3
8th, 1st d........	96	97	.....	99	77	.....	98	76	....
8th, 2d d........	65	36	1	71	33	1	72	32	1
9th...............	98	164	1	99	175	1	101	174	1
10th...............	64	35	4	62	32	10	63	33	7
11th...............	124	86	8	131	79	5	134	76	5
BOROUGHS.									
McKees't, 1 w	132	151	2	130	152	4	133	152	4
McKees't, 2 w	146	71	16	146	72	17	149	69	16
McKees't. 3 w	67	68	3	66	73	1	66	73	1
Braddocks......	81	67	38	87	85	38	89	84	37
Bellevue........	86	25	10	94	13	15	95	12	13
Beltzhoover...	13	15	.....	17	11	3	17	11	3
Chartiers	105	124	19	143	107	13	154	101	10
Etna...............	151	70	1	138	65	.....	167	59	....
Elizabeth	99	61	27	88	62	37	98	60	28
Millvale..........	103	55	4	109	49	4	109	49	4
Mansfield......	110	13	7	91	21	14	100	31	9
Sewickley......	151	71	17	156	61	19	155	62	21
Sharpsburg...	148	151	18	162	183	18	163	180	18
Tarentum......	93	42	50	34	40	60	94	41	49
Verona, 1st w	50	4	.....	44	8	.....	45	8	....
Verona, 2d w	24	20	13	27	17	13	28	17	11
WestBellevue	19	15	1	22	10	3	23	11	2
West Eliza'th	75	28	8	61	37	12	68	36	8
TOWNSHIPS.									
Baldwin, 1 d...	59	77	4	59	81	4	59	81	4
Baldwin, 2 d...	95	49	2	78	111	5	90	106	4
Chartiers	82	50	7	80	54	7	89	62	5
Collier..........	62	57	3	39	73	2	61	59	3
Crescent........	31	29	.....	6	32	.....	28	32	....
Elizabeth, 1 d	72	56	11	56	57	24	71	57	11
Elizabeth, 2 d	50	33	.....	50	33	.....	49	33	....
Elizabeth, 3 d	33	16	21	26	17	23	38	15	21
Elizabeth, 4 d	87	38	2	86	33	3	93	30	2
East Deer, 1 d	91	33	18	84	35	20	91	32	19
East Deer, 2 d	55	42	6	44	38	11	59	37	7
Franklin........	37	55	1	48	59	1	51	59	1
Fawn..............	66	10	6	64	9	6	78	9	5
Findley..........	93	120	3	91	122	4	93	121	8
Forward........	93	56	2	80	56	8	91	56	5
Hampton......	62	65	1	65	54	1	65	54	1
Harrison........	100	98	39	95	101	43	113	89	40
Harmar..........	46	32	1	48	29	3	50	27	4
Indiana..........	75	46	3	78	47	4	79	46	4
Jefferson......	176	85	19	36	126	93	139	99	21
Kilbuck, 1st d	48	45	6	56	23	15	59	21	14
Kilbuck, 2d d	65	40	2	84	37	4	82	37	4
Leet...............	62	21	3	77	15	3	79	15	3
L. St. Clair,1 d	43	131	1	43	134	2	40	137	2
L. St. Clair, 2d	32	39	2	41	36	1	38	41	1
L. St. Clair, 3 d	23	33	6	23	31	6	25	31	6
Lincoln..........	82	28	7	77	32	8	78	32	8
Mifflin, 1st d...	33	99	9	26	108	9	29	104	10
Mifflin, 2d d...	79	74	4	82	91	5	83	91	4
Mifflin, 3d d...	50	27	25	56	41	27	55	42	27
Moon	97	67	12	111	73	12	98	87	10
Marshall........	35	53	.....	24	57	.....	36	54	....
McCandless...	39	64	.....	38	64	.....	39	64	....
NorthFayette	80	69	32	77	69	31	80	70	29
Neville..........	23	9	3	25	5	4	29	1	3
N. Versailles..	83	158	1	114	125	3	108	133	2
Ohio..............	31	33	8	34	35	4	35	35	3
O'Hara, 1st d..	44	51	.....	58	35	.....	69	26	....
O'Hara, 2d d...	23	18	2	30	32	2	31	31	2
Plum.............	99	101	34	99	95	34	105	94	32
Penn..............	147	98	16	155	89	17	161	87	16
Pine..............	47	55	.....	50	52	.....	50	52	....
Patton, 1st d..	34	27	18	33	28	18	35	27	18
Patton, 2d d..	58	61	12	58	53	13	58	53	13

PRINCIPAL CEMETERIES.

(CONTINUED.)

BELLEVUE.

Situated in the borough of Bellevue, adjoin-ing the city of Allegheny.

SOUTH SIDE CEMETERY.

Located on the Brownsville road, one mile from Mt. Oliver, and fronts also on the Saw Mill Run road. It is but a few minutes walk from the city line, and is passed by the Castle Shannon Railroad.

BOARD OF PUBLIC CHARITIES.

George L. Harrison, of Philadelphia, President; G. Dawson Coleman, Lebanon; Heister Clymer, Berks; William Bakewell, Pittsburgh; A. C. Noyes, Clinton; George Bullock, Montgomery; Francis Wells, Philadelphia. Salary of Diller Luther, General Agent and Secretary, $3,000.

ELEVATION OF THE OHIO RIVER AT LOW WATER.

	FEET ABOVE TIDE.
Mouth of Ohio above high tide in Gulf of Mexico	275
Mouth of Wabash, (approximately)	297
Evansville, (approximately)	320
New Albany, below Falls	353
Louisville, above Falls	377
Cincinnati	432
Portsmouth	474
Mouth of Great Kanawha	522
Head of Le Tart's shoals	555
Marietta (mouth of Muskingum)	571
Wheeling	620
Pittsburgh	699
Franklin	960
Warren	1,187
Chatauqua Lake	1,306
Olean Point	1,403
Mouth of Osway	1,419
Smithport	1,480
Coudersport	1,649
Surface of Lake Erie	565
Town of Washington, Port Hempfeld, crossing of Main street	1,080

DESCENT OF THE ALLEGHENY, OHIO AND MISSISSIPPI RIVERS.

PLACES.	Dist. in Miles.	Fall in Feet	Fall per Mile. Ft. In
FROM			
Coudersport to Olean Point...	40	246	6 2
Olean Point to Warren..........	50	216	4 4
Warren to Franklin..............	70	227	3 3
Franklin to Pittsburgh..........	130	216	2 ......
Pittsburgh to Beaver............	26	30	1 1.85
Beaver to Wheeling..............	62	49	... 9.50
Wheeling to Marietta............	90	49	... 6.53
Marietta to Le Tart's shoals...	31	16	... 6.17
LeTart's shoals to m'h of Ken	55	33	... 7.20
M'th of Kenaw to Portsm'th..	94	48	... 6.13
Portsmouth to Cincinnati......	105	42	... 4.80
Cincinnati to Evansville........	328	112	... 4.10
Evansville to Gulf of Mexico	1356	810	... 2351
Coudersport to m'th of Miss..	2446	1649	....

ELECTION RETURNS.—Continued.

	F	P	H	M	E	G	R	G	B
Robinson, 1 d	7	1	.....	6	1	.....	7	1	....
Robinson, 2 d	67	33	11	64	36	15	67	36	12
Ross, 1st d	55	30	......	55	21	......	66	22	....
Ross, 2d d	31	61	7	41	53	10	46	51	7
Reserve	32	46	5	71	32	6	70	33	6
Richland	62	65	12	56	63	13	64	62	12
Shaler, 1st d	55	23	......	40	36	1	94	16	1
Shaler, 2d d	31	28	3	51	41	3	55	41	2
S. Versailles	14	54	......	29	38	......	30	38	....
Snowden	130	45	6	95	47	18	117	47	18
South Fayette	84	30	24	79	30	18	97	20	18
Sewickley	82	7	......	82	13	......	33	13	....
Scott, 1st d	29	35	4	27	30	3	43	28	2
Scott, 2d d	45	29	2	31	39	1	54	17	....
Stowe	33	45	3	32	45	5	40	44	3
U. St. Cl'r, 1 d	27	23	15	33	17	12	28	29	8
U. St. Cl'r, 2 d	47	27	1	42	28	1	40	34	1
Union	141	41	10	140	36	18	152	36	6
Versailles	33	30	......	37	20	......	29	29	....
Wilkins, 1 d	95	27	7	94	24	8	102	23	7
Wilkins, 2 d	51	67	7	57	65	7	55	65	7
West Deer	112	60	27	122	43	83	131	43	29

PENNSYLVANIA STATISTICS.

GOVERNOR AND HEADS OF DEPARTMENTS.

Governor—JOHN F. HARTRANFT, Montgomery county; salary, $10,000.

Lieutenant Governor—John Latta, of Westmoreland county; salary, $3,000.

Governor's Secretary—A. Wilson Norris, Philadelphia; salary, $2,500.

Secretary of the Commonwealth—Mathew S. Quay, Beaver county; salary, $4,000.

Deputy Secretary of the Commonwealth—John B. Linn, Centre county; salary, $2,500.

Chief Clerk—Thomas McCamant, Blair county; salary, $1,800.

Attorney General—George Lear, Bucks county; salary, $3,500.

Deputy Attorney General—Lyman D. Gilbert, Dauphin county; salary, $1,800.

Auditor General—Justus F. Temple, Green county; salary, $3,000.

Chief Clerk—G. W. G. Waddell, Green county; salary, $1,800.

State Treasurer—R. W. Mackey, Philadelphia; salary, $5,000.

Cashier—W. B. Hart, Mongomery county; salary, $2,000.

Secretary of Internal Affairs—William M'Candless, Philadelphia; salary, $8000.

Chief Clerk—J. Simpson Africa, Huntingdon county; salary, $1,800.

Superintendent of Common Schools and Supt. of Soldiers' Orphan Schools—J. P. Wickersham, Lancaster county; salary, $3,750.

Deputy Superintendent Common Schools—Henry Houck, Lebanon county; salary, $1,800.

Adjutant General—James W. Latta, Philadelphia; salary, $2,500.

Chief Clerk—Geo. C. Kelley, Union county; salary, $1,800.

Department of Insurance — J. Montgomery Forster, Harrisburg, Commissioner.

Deputy Commissioner—L. R. Boggs, Harrisburg.

Bureau of Statistics—W. Hays Grier, Commissioner, Lancaster county; salary, $2,500.

State Librarian — O. H. Miller, Allegheny county; salary, $1,800.

Superintendent of Public Printing — J. W. Jones, Dauphin county; salary, $1,600.

Superintendent of Public Buildings and Grounds—William H. Patterson, Dauphin county; salary, $1,400.

State Printer—B. F. Meyers, Dauphin county.

Printer of Journal—Chas. H. Bergner, Harrisburg.

EXPIRATION OF THE TERMS OF MEMBERS OF THE SENATE.

Geo. H. Smith, R...	1876	W. W. Watson, R...	1877
David A. Nagle, D...	1877	A. H. Dill, D...	1876
John Lamon, R...	1876	H. G. Bussey, D...	1877
H. G. Jones, R...	1877	O. P. Bechtel, D...	1876
E. W. Davis, R...	1877	J. P. Coolihan, D...	1877
A. K. Dunkel, R...	1877	J. B. Wareum, D...	1876
Hiram Horter, R...	1877	James Chestnut, D...	1877
Jacob Crouse, R...	1877	C. McKibben, D...	1877
Thos. V. Cooper, R...	1877	T. C. Boyer, D...	1877
Harman Yerkes, D...	1876	John Lamon, R...	1876
D. Ermentrout, D...	1876	E. D. Yutzy, R...	1877
W. A. Yeakle, R...	1876	R. C. Winslow, R...	1877
J. B. Warfel, R...	1876	D. P. Thomas, D...	1876
P. J. Roebuck, R...	1877	J. C. Clark, D...	1877
A. J. Herr, R...	1877	James W. Hayes, D...	1876
Edwin Albright, D...	1876	S. M. Jackson, R...	1877
J. G. Heilman, R...	1876	Hugh McNeill, R...	1876
S. C. Shimer, Ind. D...	1877	G. H. Anderson, R...	1876
R. L. McClellan, R...	1877	J. C. Newmyer, R...	1876
W. H. Stanton, R...	1877	E. A. Wood, D...	1877
H. B. Payne, R...	1877	G. V. Lawrence, R...	1876
Charlton Barrett, D...	1876	J. H. Briggers, D...	1876
Delos Rockwell, D...	1877	W. S. McMullen, R...	1877
R. P. Allen, D...	1876	H. Butterfield, R...	1876
B. B. Strang, R...	1877	G. K. Anderson, R...	1876

HOW ENGLAND IS SUPPLIED WITH FOOD.

The English food supply is an increasingly interesting subject for American Farmers, as it is likely to be more and more drawn from American sources. England is increasing her grain product by higher manuring and better methods of tillage; but aside from this, the tendency in ordinary times is to devote more and more land to stock growing and feeding. During the past year, as appears by statistics recently published, 1,068,166 animals of all kinds were imported into the United Kingdom. The animals are epitomised as follows: 119,808 oxen and bulls, 38,013 cows, 86,041 calves, 753,915 sheep and lambs, and 118,389 swine. The total quantity of dead meat imported into the United Kingdom was 968,921 cwt. as compared with 890,839 cwt. in 1873, and 853,255 cwt. in 1872.

Pennsylvania Statistics.
CONTINUED.

For Governor and State Treasurer.

The following are the official returns, by counties, of the Pennsylvania State election of Governor and State Treasurer, held on the first Tuesday of November, 1875:

| | Governor. | | | State Treasurer. | | |
COUNTIES.	Hartranft, R.	Pershing, D.	Browne, T.	Rawle, R.	Piollet, D.	Pennypacker, T.
Adams	2477	3008	22	2478	3005	20
Allegheny	18707	13246	1585	18492	13513	1514
Armstrong	3605	3121	196	3591	3164	154
Beaver	3086	2702	801	3139	2709	258
Bedford	2906	3099	27	2900	3100	26
Berks	6804	13433	24	6876	13363	28
Blair	3711	3166	264	3696	3169	260
Bradford	6526	4265	466	6356	4325	440
Bucks	6713	7000	280	6701	7011	276
Butler	3796	3891	503	3936	3986	407
Cambria	2325	3399	117	2359	3366	119
Cameron	552	476	18	545	482	19
Carbon	2347	2728	6	2351	2722	5
Center	2097	3504	590	2108	3458	587
Chester	7015	5005	739	6954	5035	750
Clarion	2196	3221	157	2207	3244	121
Clearfield	1819	3273	53	1826	3275	46
Clinton	1771	2593	91	1799	2568	87
Columbia	1643	3757	107	1623	3730	108
Crawford	6146	5526	131	6043	5637	108
Cumberland	3603	4309	66	3597	4266	48
Dauphin	6574	4704	53	6536	4781	54
Delaware	4075	2079	50	4076	2071	....
Elk	503	1055	8	503	1052	8
Erie	6609	4744	120	6809	4641	94
Fayette	3472	4299	98	3466	4321	91
Forrest	376	319	37	374	322	32
Franklin	4074	3954	95	4060	3955	97
Fulton	684	981	12	689	983	4
Greene	1517	2699	9	1512	696	8
Huntingdon	2546	2695	498	2553	2610	478
Indiana	3640	1795	400	3651	1788	373
Jefferson	1923	2248	458	2043	2268	305
Juniata	1198	1771	143	1200	1761	142
Lancaster	12725	7581	575	12687	7614	512
Lawrence	2335	1427	676	2391	1453	748
Lebanon	3858	2608	17	3860	2599	16
Lehigh	4630	6758	3	4612	6776	2
Luzerne	9899	11135	503	9514	11167	527
Lycoming	3488	4641	97	3489	4654	88
McKean	940	976	12	939	956	12
Mercer	4911	4267	502	5030	4203	463
Mifflin	1446	1586	50	1461	1540	46
Monroe	662	2630	6	588	2557	4
Montgom	8364	8330	244	8274	8382	268
Montour	1001	1322	35	1004	1307	31
Northampton	4364	7248	22	4292	7289	21
Northum'd	3691	4567	74	3734	4494	68
Perry	2429	2448	52	2429	2446	50
Philadelphia	65262	47980	647	64646	48574	638

Pennsylvania Statistics.
CONTINUED

	H	P	B	R	P	P
Pike	434	1056	4	420	1071	4
Potter	1223	1019	2	1222	1023	2
Schuylkill	7699	9037	58	7757	9053	63
Snyder	1701	1369	26	1692	1373	26
Somerset	2989	1689	53	2999	1684	46
Sullivan	336	749	49	343	694	50
Susquehanna	3517	2951	150	3525	2935	183
Tioga	3933	1909	113	3890	1965	109
Union	1784	1177	24	1769	1176	26
Venango	2953	2940	570	2900	3003	552
Warren	2057	1790	284	2027	1788	266
Washington	4917	4763	189	4936	4769	160
Wayne	1854	2135	88	1826	2161	88
Westmorel'd	4957	6242	199	4976	6273	157
Wyoming	1365	1610	164	1861	1551	147
York	5203	5223	92	5345	1314	79

RECAPITULATION.

The following is a summary of the vote, with the pluralities by which the Republican candidates are elected, and their minorities on the aggregate vote:

	Governor.	Treasurer.
Republican	304,175	302,875
Democratic	298,145	298,150
Temperance	13,244	12,468
	699,564	608,493
Plurality	12,030	9,825
Minority	1,214	2,743

Hartranft ahead of Rawle.......................1,309
Piollet ahead of Pershing...................1,005
Browne ahead of Penneypacker.............776

ELECTION RETURNS.

The following are the official returns of the Allegheny county election for County Commissioners held the first Tuesday of November, 1875.

DISTRICTS.	Becker, R.	McClelland, R.	Irvin, D.	O'Reilly, D.	O'Neil, P.	Humes, P.	Lashel, D.
PITTSBURGH. **Wards.**							
1st, 1st district	18	16	134	132			3
1st, 2d d	91	93	74	37	5	2	34
1st, 3d d	77	83	75	56	3	7	28
2d, 1st d	73	79	47	36	1	3	....
2d, 2d d	91	13	93	65	1	1	11
2d, 3d d	46	118	114	58	3	3	1
3d, 1st d	67	64	42	83	1	1	6
3d, 2d d	117	34	65	71	1	1	5
4th, 1st d	81	103	70	45	1	1	6
4th, 2d d	84	87	96	89			10
4th, 3d d	77	88	68	55	3	3	7
5th, 1st d	39	38	52	54	1	1	35
5th, 1d d	50	52	128	123			4
5th, 3d d	45	49	127	123	4	1	....
3th, 1st d	93	96	101	102	4	4	3
6th, 1d d	100	100	60	50	6	4	9
6th, 3d d	187	133	76	71	2	2	7
6th, 4th d	38	41	15	35	4	4	1
7th, 1si d	100	118	88	76	8	3	13
7th, 1d d	113	122	66	54	9	9	7
7th, 3d d	74	84	67	59	1	1	2
8th, 1st d	58	58	80	79	1		2
8th, 1d d	102	103	42	33			1
8th, 3d d	120	125	47	43	1	1	2
8th, 4th d	116	117	32	28	11	10	7
9th, 1st d	55	64	86	70	8	1	6
9th, 2d d	104	107	90	85			2
9th, 2d d	20	29	113	111			1
10th, 1st d	56	54	168	115	1	2	47
10th, 2d d	56	54	79	74			2
11th, 1st d	96	85	68	42	5	3	2
11th, 2d d	154	162	111	90	14	13	5
11th, 3d d	78	88	57	53	4	5	8
11th, 4th d	79	81	40	33	4	9	2
12th, 1st d	78	81	70	74	2	2	3
12th, 2d d	90	80	34	44	5	7	2
12th, 3d d	54	47	75	85	1	1	2
12th, 4th d	132	136	93	98	1	1	....
13th, 1st d	75	78	46	38	4	4	....
13th, 2d d	139	140	53	70	4	5	3
13th, 3d d	66	72	53	48	2	3	6
14th, 1st d	130	121	80	73	7	6	2
14th, 2d d	59	60	37	35			....
14th, 3d d	73	84	33	14	1	2	12
14th, 4th d	59	68	46	25		1	1
14th, 5th d	78	82	67	64	2	2	6
15th, 1st d	45	55	62	57	2	2	3
15th, 2d d	74	83	65	66	3	3	4
15th, 3d d	71	80	95	100			9
16th, 1st d	44	46	70	67	1	1	2

Pennsylvania Statistics.

CONTINUED.

THE LEGISLATURE, 1876.

Members of the Senate of Pennsylvania, 1875, with Postoffice address. The salary of members of the Senate is $1,000 for a session of 100 days.

Speaker—Elisha W. Davis, Philadelphia.
Chief Clerk—Russell Errett, Pittsburgh; salary, $2,500.

Philadelphia—
1st district, 1st, 2d and 26th wards—George Handy Smith, R., 1614 South 5th street.
2d district, 3d, 4th, 5th, 6th and 11th wards—David A. Nagle, D., 408 Locust street.
3d district, 16th, 17th, 18th and 20th wards—John Lamou, R., 1303 Marlboro' street.
4th district, 21st, 22d, 24th and 27th wards—Horatio Gates Jones, R., 138 S. Fifth street.
5th district, 15th, 28th and 29th wards—E. W. Davis, R., 1419 N. 16th street.
6th district, 7th, 8th and 9th wards—A. K. Dunkel, R., office *Sunday Republic.*
7th district, 10th, 12th, 13th and 14th wards—Hiram Horter, R., 2032 Vine street.
8th district, 19th, 23d and 25th wards—Jacob Crouse, R., 2d street, below Arch.
IX. Delaware—Thomas V. Cooper, R., Media.
X. Bucks—Harman Yerkes, D., Doylestown.
XI. Berks—Daniel Ermentrout, D., Reading.
XII. Montgomery—W. A. Yeakle, R., Flourtown.
XIII. Lancaster—John B. Warfel, R., Lancaster.
XIV. Lancaster—P. J. Roebuck, R., Litiz.
XV. Dauphin—A. J. Herr, R., Harrisburg.
XVI. Lehigh—Edwin Albright, D., Allentown.
XVII. Lebanon—Jacob G. Heilman, R., Jonestown.
XVIII.—Northampton—S. C. Shimer, Ind. D., Easton.
XIX. Chester—Robert L. McClellan, R., Cochranville.
XX. Luzerne—W. H. Stanton, D., Scranton.
XXI. Luzerne—H. B. Payne, R., Wilkesbarre.
XXII. Monroe, Pike and Carbon—Charlton Barrett, D., Stroudsburg, Monroe county.
XXIII. Bradford and Wyoming — Delos Rockwell, D., Troy.
XXIV. Lycoming, Montour, Sullivan and Columbia—R. P. Allen, D., Williamsport.
XXV. Tioga, Potter and McKean—Butler B. Strang, R., Westfield, Tioga county.
XXVI. Susquehanna and Wayne—W. W. Watson, R., Montrose, Susquehanna county.
XXVII. Union, Snyder and Northumberland—A. H. Dill, D., Lewisburg, Union county.
XXVIII. York—H. G. Bussey, D., Shrewsberry.
XXIX. Schuylkill—O. P. Bechtel, D., Pottsville.
XXX. Schuylkill—John P. Coolihan, D., Ashland.
XXXI. Perry, Mifflin and Juniata—Joseph B. Wearean, D., Lewistown, Mifflin county.
XXXII. Cumberland and Adams—James Chestnut, D., Shippensburg, Cumberland county.
XXXIII. Franklin and Huntingdon—Chambers McKibben, D., Chambersburg.

ELECTION RETURNS--Continued.

	B	M	I	O'	O'	H	L
16th, 2d d	40	43	45	45			1
16th, 3d d	41	45	39	37	1		3
16th, 4th d	60	62	34	30			
16th, 5th d	59	54	56	51		0	
17th, 1st d	120	127	66	59	5	5	1
17th, 2d d	117	185	91	67	3	3	13
17th, 3d d	97	106	109	100	1	2	5
17th, 4th d	79	82	75	73	4	4	1
18th	66	60	112	104	4	5	4
19th, 1st d	87	105	37	29	6	7	9
19th, 2d d	77	86	46	24	5	4	17
19th, 3d d	57	63	73	56	10	9	21
20th, 1st d	60	72	42	25	4	5	13
20th, 2d d	94	110	54	28			9
20th, 3d d	55	67	59	50	4	5	24
21st, 1st d	98	158	109	111	14	20	71
21st, 2d d	20	26	13	12	5	6	1
21st, 3d d	99	106	40	28	3	3	7
22d, 1st d	89	58	41	27	5	4	6
22d, 2d d	45	45	20	16	1	1	2
23d, 1st d	34	44	40	33			22
23d, 2d d	98	101	86	66	4	4	10
24th, 1st d	94	90	57	83			5
24th, 2d d	38	48	34	32	4	4	15
25th, 1st d	72	74	83	82	3	3	
25th, 2d d	98	103	77	81	2	2	1
25th, 3d d	88	90	83	82	1	2	2
26th, 1st d	107	106	48	54	2	2	3
26th, 2d d	110	108	184	138	1	1	1
16th, 3d d	111	111	48	41	2	2	1
26th, 4th d	99	102	71	72			3
27th, 1st d	46	44	179	189			2
27th, 2d d	51	48	48	55	2	2	1
28th, 1st d	102	100	68	65	6	6	8
28th, 2d d	66	67	67	67		0	
28th, 3d d	76	78	74	74	2	3	1
29th, 1st d	77	79	50	53	10	11	
29th, 2d d	129	130	82	86	6	6	8
30th, 1st d	91	93	28	58	3	2	8
30th, 2d d	71	74	56	72	2	2	2
31st	89	81	45	36	5	7	1
32d, 1st d	111	88	61	83	8	6	5
32d, 2d d	101	94	40	49	14	15	2
33d	26	40	40	87			8
34th	28	40	86	166	6	5	10
35th, 1st d	62	61	30	31	2	1	1
35th, 2d d	28	29	47	48	9	9	4
36th, 1st d	55	60	83	92	16	13	18
36th, 2d d	59	65	24	28	20	19	3
37th, 1st d	59	74	22	14	6	6	23
37th, 2d d	83	91	22	18	5	5	8

ALLEGHENY.
Wards.

	B	M	I	O'	O'	H	L
1st	389	432	188	145	26	27	36
2d, 1st d	109	123	67	41	20	20	17
2d, 2d d	186	210	98	72	29	32	12
2d, 3d d	207	220	83	75	26	26	60
2d, 4th d	108	118	64	59	10	12	10
3d, 1st d	134	147	56	43	14	15	15
3d, 2d d	185	200	60	53	22	26	18
3d, 3d d	123	121	45	83	5	5	18
3d, 4th d	111	115	132	128	3	2	8
3d, 5th d	127	131	115	106			1
4th, 1st d	158	168	85	57	16	15	36
4th, 2d d	112	119	61	49	14	13	5
4th, 3d d	114	119	94	88	5	5	8
4th, 4th d	169	178	152	143	2	2	2
5th, 1st d	73	81	59	25	10	11	39
5th, 2d d	200	208	113	78	11	12	12

Pennsylvania Statistics.

CONTINUED.

XXXIV. Clinton, Clearfield and Centre—
T. J. Boyer, D., Clearfield, Clearfield county.
XXXV. Blair and Cambria—John Lemon,
R., Hollidaysburg, Blair county.
XXXVI. Somerset, Bedford and Fulton—E.
D. Yutzy, R., Ursino, Somerset county.
XXXVII. Indiana and Jefferson—R. C. Win-
slow, R., Punxsutawny, Jefferson county.
XXXVIII. Cameron, Elk, Clarion and For-
est—D. P. Thomas, D., Tionesta, Forest county.
XXXIX. Westmoreland—J. C. Clark, D.,
Greensburg.
XL. Fayette and Greene—John W. Hayes,
Harvey's, Greene County.
XLI. Butler and Armstrong—S. M. Jackson,
R., Apollo, Armstrong county.
XLII. Allegheny—Hugh McNeill, R., Alle-
gheny City.
XLIII. Allegheny—George H. Anderson, R.,
Pittsburgh.
XLIV. Allegheny county.—John C. New-
myer, R., No. 89 Fifth avenue, Pittsburgh.
XLV. Allegheny.—E. A. Wood, D., South
Pittsburgh.
XLVI. Beaver and Washington.—George V.
Lawrence, R., Monongahela City, Washington
county.
XLVII. Lawrence and Mercer.—J. H. Brag-
gen, R., Mercer, Mercer county.
XLVIII. Warren and Venango.—W. S. Mc-
Mullen, R., Oil City, Venango county.
XLIX. Erie.—Henry Butlerfield, R., Erie.
L. Crawford.—George K. Anderson, Titus-
ville.

RECAPITULATION.

Republicans..29
Democrats...20
Independent Democrat.................................... 1

HOUSE OF REPRESENTATIVES.

Members of the House of Representatives,
session of 1875, with Postoffice address. The
salary of members of the House for session of
100 days is fixed at $1,009.

Chief Clerk.—Adam Woolever, Sr., Lehigh
county, $2,500.
Resident Clerk.—Eldridge M'Conkery, Harrisburg, $1,000.

Philadelphia.—

1st district, 1st ward—Wm. S. Douglass, R., 519
Moore street; John Graham, R., 1522 South
Ninth street.
2d district, 2d ward—Jno. E. Kennedy, D.,
706 Federal street; Jno. Holland, D., 936 South
Ninth street.
3d district, 3d ward—James Marshall, D., 734
Passayunk avenue.
4th district, 4th ward—Jas. T. Monagan, D.,
4th ward.
5th district, 5th ward—Emil J. Petroff, R.,
5th ward.
6th district, 6th ward—Theo. F. Miller, D.,
516 Race street.
7th district, 7th ward—Wm. H. Patterson, R.,
7th ward; J. Granville Leach, R., 733 Walnut
street.

ELECTION RETURNS--Continued.

	B	M	I	O'	O'	H	L
5th, 3d d	68	85	70	137	8	8	49
6th, 1st d	163	162	122	120	5	14	4
6th, 2d d	112	116	78	70	10	11	7
6th, 3d d	81	84	79	79	9	10	10
7th, 1st d	68	57	128	117			5
7th, 2d d	116	95	134	116			14
7th, 3d d	88	91	60	52	4	2	10
8th, 1st d	116	96	55	76			5
8th, 2d d	59	69	30	20	11	1	28
9th	49	100	156	198	1	1	22
10th	55	60	40	33	7	7	1
11th	88	133	83	70	5	4	44
BOROUGHS							
McKeesport, 1st ward	91	131	102	133	0	4	52
McKeesport, 2d w	135	46	44	64	29	16	12
McKeesport, 3d w	29	65	67	17	1	1	99
Braddocks	73	89	89	83	37	87	12
Bellevue	86	55	15	10	11	12	11
Beltzhoover	18	14	10	11	3	2	
Chartiers	69	68	39	56	4	8	3
Etna	144	168	73	56	2		6
Elizabeth	83	98	62	56	48	27	
Millvale	101	109	52	52	4	4	
Mausfield	85	102	25	21	10	8	9
Sewickley	99	153	61	17	16	20	11
Sharpsburg	149	160	173	182	19	22	5
Tarentou	58	85	42	27	48	113	1
Verona, 1st ward	45	43	8	8			
Verona, 2d ward	29	27	18	14	12	14	
West Bellevue	8	24	12	9	1	3	15
West Elizabeth	64	68	38	28	10		9
TOWNSHIPS.							
Baldwin, 1st d	30	54	109	86	4	4	
Baldwin, 2d d	48	83	64	73	4	4	79
Chartiers	101	140	101	106	12	10	27
Collier	40	59	67	57		3	14
Crescent	3	28	28	1			56
Elizabeth, 1st d	55	60	58	53	28	14	
Elizabeth, 2d d	49	50	33	32	1		2
Elizabeth, 3d d	30	34	16	15	22	21	
Elizabeth, 4th d	83	92	33	31	4	2	
East Deer, 1st d	72	102	31	33	9	27	3
East Deer, 2d d	2	65	37	24	8	15	54
Franklin	36	50	59	45	1	1	85
Fawn	40	75	11	4	5	48	
Findley	63	95	119	22	10	8	121
Forward	78	91	56	59	11	5	1
Hampton	57	66	56	53		1	4
Harrison	68	112	99	72	33	53	48
Harmar	35	68	27	22	1	3	10
Indiana	75	85	46	41	1	3	3
Jefferson	30	126	08	31	104	23	100
Kilbuck, 1st d	42	59	27	9	12	12	26
Kilbuck, 2d d	60	79	35	34	4	4	38
Leet	14	74	23	4	2	2	73
Lower St. Clair, 1st d	48	42	127	129	2	2	6
Lower St. Clair, 2d d	33	36	45	38	1	1	4
Lower St. Clair, 3d d	46	24	12	30	4	6	
Lincoln	73	79	32	28	11	8	7
Mifflin, 1st d	14	28	103	85	10	10	28
Mifflin, 2d d	65	75	78	105	9	4	20
Mifflin, 3d d	70	56	28	23	26	26	18
Moon	16	100	81	3	10	11	162
Marshall	21	42	53	47			4
McCandless	29	38	68	64			1
North Fayette	79	72	23	25	33	33	43
Neville	9	23	7				28
North Versailes	86	107	94	98	6	2	25
Ohio	6	40	59	30	4	8	2

Pennsylvania Statistics.

CONTINUED.

8th district, 8th ward—Edward A. Good, R., 8th ward.

9th district, 9th ward—J. W. Spicer, D., 9th ward

10th district, 10th ward—G. W. Hall, R., 1131 Arch street.

11th district, 11th ward—Albert Crawford, D., 139 Noble street.

12th district, 12th ward—Chas. Gentner, D., 314 Brown street.

13th district, 13th ward—Wm. H, Voxles, R., 643 North Seventh street.

14th district, 14th ward—Jas. Devereaux, R., 14th ward.

15th district, 15th ward—Jno. E. Reyburn, R., 2820 Spring Garden street; Harry Huhn, R., 802 North Sixteenth street; Edward Montgomery, R., 15th ward.

16th district, 16th ward—M. V. B. Conrad, D., 804 and 806 North Fourth street.

17th district, the 5th, 6th, 7th, 8th 9th, 10th, 11th, 12th, 13th and 14th divisions of the 17th ward—Jno. E. Faunce, D., 512 Walnut street.

18th district, the 1st, 2d, 3d and 4th divisions of the 17th ward and the 18th ward—Wm. J Roucy, R., 1319 North Front street; George A. Bakeoven, R., 18th ward.

19th district, 19th ward—Wm. Ringgold, R., 19th ward; Robt. Gillespie, D., 2448 Kensington avenue; Thos. J. Rice, R., 19th ward.

20th district, 20th ward—Jno. N. Wood, R., 1400 Mervin street; Francis W. Quirk, R., 20th ward.

21st district, 21st and 28th wards—Joseph Yeakel, R.

22d district, 22d ward—Jos. M. Hill, R., 22d ward.

23d district, 23d ward—Chas. B. Salter, R., Frankfold.

24th district, 24th ward—Jas. Newell, R., 606 Preston street.

25th district, 25th ward—Geo. L. Pallatt, D., 2553 York avenue, Rising Sun Postoffice.

26th district, 26th ward—Harry O'Neill, R., 2015 Catharine street; Jos. E. Souder, R., 26th ward.

27th district, 27th ward—John W. Leigh, R., 27th ward.

28th district, 29th ward—Frank Frederick, R., 2212 Oxford street.

Adams.—E. W. Stahle, D., Mummusburg; Daniel Geiselman, D., McSherrystown.

Allegheny.—

1st district, John Swan, D., Allegheny City; W. H. Graham, R., Allegheny City; H. M. Long, R., Allegheny City.

2d district, J. M. Irwin, D., Pittsburgh; G. C. Shidle, D., Pittsburgh.

3d district, Peter Zern, D., Pittsburg.

4th district, S. F. Patterson, D., Pittsburgh; Joseph Hayes, D., Pittsburgh; Joseph M. Carson, D., Pittsburgh; J. R. Thornton, D., Pittsburgh.

5th district, B. C. Christy, R., 160 Fourth avenue, Pittsburgh; S. P. Large, D.

6th district.—D. J. Rogers, D.; Andrew Large, D.

Armstrong.—Robert Thompson, R., Templeton; A. W. Bell, R., Brady's Bend.

ELECTION RETURNS--Continued.

.	B	M	I	O	O	H	L
O'Hara, 1st d	7	75	19	17	....	....	73
O'Hara, 2d d	24	31	31	28	2	2	7
Plum	86	103	98	80	33	48	3
Penn	135	162	90	81	16	21	1
Pine	42	51	53	48	....	....	5
Patton, 1st d	35	35	26	27	18	18	1
Patton, 2d d	59	59	59	56	13	13	....
Robinson, 1st d	6	7	1	1	....	....	....
Robinson, 2d d	7	67	38	14	10	12	78
Ross, 1st d	36	63	30	21	1	2	3
Ross, 2d d	29	60	60	37	10	5	7
Reserve	58	67	40	25	6	5	17
Richland	48	63	66	61	13	13	2
Shaler, 1st d	69	94	48	14	....	1	8
Shaler, 2d d	27	56	56	38	2	4	9
South Versailles	27	30	40	47	1	....	1
Snowden	99	116	53	45	....	18	6
South Fayette	60	95	27	11	22	19	47
Sewickley	7	30	12	4	18	....	33
Scott, 1st d	19	89	36	22	4	3	13
Scott, 2d d	20	44	31	6	1	1	45
Stowe	3	87	20	4	3	1	77
Upper St. Clair, 1st d	9	22	18	7	7	15	40
Upper St. Clair, 2d d	18	39	34	16	1	1	39
Union	114	143	61	33	7	6	22
Versailles	20	33	28	2	1	....	35
Wilkins, 1st d	88	97	13	19	7	8	5
Wilkins, 2d d	49	56	62	65	6	7	5
West Deer	111	151	40	21	22	49	5

SUNSHINE,—Did you ever notice what a different aspect everything wears in the sunshine from what it does in the shadow? And did you ever think what an analogy there was between the sunlight of the cloudless skies and the sunshine that gleams into the darkened chambers of the human soul? How bright and beautiful are the golden beams that break through the riven clouds to light up the world again after a succession of dark and stormy days! How peaceful and happy are the blessed words of hope and cheer that touch the heart and fill the soul with emotions of peace and joy after a long period of sorrow! There are none living who do not, in a greater or less degree, have an influence over the earthly happiness of others. The sense of contributing to the pleasure of others augments our own happiness. Unselfishness, Christian charity and loving kindness are sunbeams of the soul.

THAT THE FRENCH are rapidly rising to prosperity may be seen from the following figures, representing the income of Paris theatres for the last eight years:—In 1868 it amounted to 16,000,000 francs, in 1869 to 17,000,000, in 1870, (war) to 9,000,000, in 1871, (war) to 7,000,000, in 1872 to 18,000,000, in 1873 to 20,000,000, in 1874 to 23,000,000, and this year it will amount to 25,000,000 francs.

THE EXPENSES attending the entertainment of King Kalakaua, as shown by the report transmitted to the House by the Secretary of State, aggregate over $20,000. Among the items are the following:—Arlington Hotel, $8,473.50; Union Pacific Railroad Company, $8,378.87; Central Pacific Railroad Company, $8,109.30; Grand Hotel, San Francisco, $1,649.56. The majority of the items of expenses are for traveling, hotel bills, and Pullman palace-car sleepers.

Pennsylvania Statistics.

CONTINUED.

Beaver.—Joseph Graff, D., Beaver Falls; C. I. Wendt, R., New Brighton.

Bedford.—G. H. Spang, D., Bedford; Wm. Keyser, D., New Buena Vista.

Blair.—J. C. Everhart, D., Martinsburg; I. H. Rawlins, R., Hollidaysburg.

Bradford.—George Moscript, R., Windham Center; E. G. Tracy, R., Sylvania·Uriah Terry, D., Terrytown.

Bucks.—J. Miles Jamison, D., Richborough; J. W. Carver, D., Erwinna; Legrand Leauw, D., Attleborough; J. Paul Knight, R., Feasterville.

Butler.—A. L. Campbell, R., Petrolia; Jos. S. Lusk, D., Harmony.

Berks, 1st district.—Jacob Miller, D., Reading; A. B. Warner, D., Reading.
2d district.—A. Smith, D., Wernersville; B. F. Dry, D. Drysville; Joseph B. Conrad, D., Bernville; Nicholas Andre, D., Coalbrookdale.

Cambria.—John Hannan, D., Johnstown; John Buck, D., Carrolltown.

Cameron.—Jno. W. Phelps, R., Emporium.

Carbon.—James A. Harvey, D.; A. J. Durling, D.

Center.—S. T. Shugert, D.; Bellefonte; W. K. Alexander, D., Willheim Center.

Chester.—E. W. Baily, R., Penningtonville: P. G. Carey, R., Phœnixville; Geo. F. Smith, R., West Chester; John P. Edge, R., Downington.

Clarion.—Martin Williams, D., New Bethlehem; J. H. Wilson. D., Reedsburg.

Clearfield.—W. R. Hartshorn, D., Curwensville.

Clinton.—Geo. A. Achenbach, D., Lock Haven.

Columbia.—E. J. McHenry, D., Stillwater, Columbia county; S. P. Ryan. D., Ashland, Schuylkill county.

Crawford.—S. H. Findley, R., East Fallowfield; W. C. Plummer. D., Titusville; R. H. Sturtevant, D., Spring; S. J. Logan, D., Hartstown.

Cumberland.—W. B. Butler, I., Mount Holly Springs; Geo. W. Mumper, D., New. Cumberland.

Dauphin, 1st district.—R. R. Chrisman, R., Harrisburg.
2d district.—A. Fortenbaugh, R., Halifax; Jos. H. Nisley, R., Middletown.

Delaware.—W. Cooper Talley, D., Media; Wm. Worral, D., Chester.

Elk.—Sebastian Wimmer, D., St. Mary's.

Erie, 1st district.—Wm. Henry, D., Erie.
2d district.—W. W. Brown, R., Corry; F. S. Chapin, R., Wattsburg; Orlando Logan, R., Albion.

Fayette.—James Darby, D., Uniontown; T. Robb Deyarmon, D., Dawson.

Forrest.—J. B. Agnew, R., Tionesta.

Franklin.—Hastings Gehr, R., Chambersburg; M. A. Embick, D., Greencastle; Simon Lecron, D., Waynesboro.

Fulton.—H. S. Wishart, D., Harrisonville.

Greene.—Morgan R. Wise, D., Wanesburg.

Huntingdon.—W. P. McNite, D., Shirleysburg; H. M. Mateer, Ind., Mill Creek.

Indiana.—A. W. Kimmel, R., Indiana; J. K. Thompson, R., Brady.

Jefferson.—R. B. Brown, D., Summerville.

Juniata,—Jerome Hettrick, D., Mexico.

ELECTION RETURNS.

The following are the official returns of the Allegheny county election for Register, Clerk of Courts and Controller, held the first Tuesday of November, 1875.

DISTRICTS.	Gray, R.	Routh, D.	McClure, P.	McCleary, R.	O'Neil, D.	Harper, P.	Warner, R.	Mechling, D.	Grier, P.
PITTSBURGH. Wards.									
1st, 1st d	20	131		21	131		20	132	...
1st, 2d d	102	66	1	106	60	1	101	66	2
1st, 3d d	90	71	5	92	70	5	87	75	5
2d, 1st d	79	34	3	80	31	3	79	34	3
2d, 2d d	118	78	1	89	31	3	109	79	2
2d, 3d d	86	63	6	114	74	1	89	68	3
3d, 1st n	71	39	1	77	33		66	45	...
3d, 2d d	99	82	1	101	77	1	96	84	1
4th, 1st d	107	51	2	110	49	2	106	50	2
4th, 2d d	81	95		85	96		78	105	...
4th, 3d d	98	58	3	94	55	3	90	58	3
5th, 1st d	44	72	1	50	67	1	49	68	1
5th, 2d d	52	125		50	121		125	52	...
5th, 3d d	50	122	4	53	120	4	49	123	4
6th, 1st d	96	105	4	97	104	4	94	106	4
6th, 2d d	40	60	5	102	65	6	99	63	6
6th, 3d d	142	74	2	141	75	2	140	77	2
6th, 4th d	143	34	4	43	33	4	43	34	4
7th, 1st d	125	81	2	123	79	3	123	79	3
7th, 2d d	124	58	9	126	56	9	122	60	10
7th, 3d d	84	60	1	58	59	1	83	60	1
8th, 1st d	58	82	1	58	82	1	65	75	...
8th, 2d d	107	34		109	30		107	33	...
8th, 3d d	125	40	1	127	42	1	128	41	1
8th, 4th d	120	31	11	120	30	11	124	30	10
9th, 1st d	63	66	1	76	73	1	66	83	1
9th, 2d d	108	86		123	70	...	108	86	...
9th, 3d d	31	113		42	100	1	33	111	...
10th, 1st d	54	168	2	167	52		54	165	2
10th, 2d d	54	80		98	35		59	75	...
11th, 1st d	96	50	2	99	40	3	98	48	3
11th, 2d d	169	100	10	165	98	13	163	103	11
11th, 3d d	90	55	3	90	51	5	87	56	5
11th, 4th d	81	36	5	82	35	3	83	35	1
12th, 1st d	82	76	2	87	69	2	82	75	3
12th, 2d d	88	48	7	92	40	7	89	46	2
12th, 3d d	55	81	1	56	79	1	56	80	7
12th, 4th d	136	101	1	140	98	1	140	98	1
13th, 1st d	183	37	3	83	36	4	80	33	4
13th, 2d d	43	72	6	140	74	6	139	75	6
13th, 3d d	166	58	3	61	62	3	71	51	3
14th, 1st d	26	78	7	128	75	7	119	85	7
14th, 2d d	63	35		62	36		54	44	...
14th, 3d d	92	18		91	17	1	62	46	1
14th, 4th d	72	27		70	28		47	50	...
14th, 5th d	85	64	2	85	64	2	82	66	2
15th, 1st d	56	61	2	59	58	2	53	64	2
15th, 2d d	80	67	3	82	64	3	83	64	3
15th, 3d d	80	98		85	93	...	83	96	...
16th, 1st d	47	69	1	47	69	1	46	71	1
16th, 2d d	43	46		44	44	...	41	46	...
16th, 3d d	55	38		45	37	1	43	39	1
16th, 4th d	59	34		68	29	...	62	31	...
16th, 5th d	52	68		53	59	...	51	59	...

Pennsylvania Statistics.

CONTINUED.

Lancaster, 1st district.—D. P. Rosenmiller, R. Lancaster.

2d district,—Amos H. Mylin R., Lancaster; Wm. McGowan, R. Christiana.

3d district.—George H. Ettla, R., Lancaster; A. H. Summy, R., Mount Joy; J. A. Stober, R., Shoeneck.

Lawrence.—E. S. N. Morgan, R., New Castle; John Q. Stewart, R., Enon Valley.

Lebanon.—Isaac Hoffer, R., Lebanon; Wm. H. Hostetter, Myerstown.

Lehigh.—James Kimmett, R.. Catasauqua; John H. Fogel, D., Fogelsville; Geo. T. Gross, D., Allentown.

Lycoming.—Oliver H. Reighard, D., Williamsport; John Gaffey, D., Salladyburg; Geo. Steck, D., Hughesville.

Luzerne.—1st district.—C. A. Miner, R.. Wilkesbarre.

2d district.—T. H. B. Lewis, D., Kingston.

3d district.—T. J. Shook, (Pro.) R., Plymouth.

4th district.—J. C. Fincher, D., Hazelton.

5th district.—James McAsey, D., Gouldsboro.

6th district.—F. W. Gunster, D., Scranton; M. F. Lynott, D., Scranton.

7th district.—C. R. Gorman, D., Pittston.

8th district.—T. W. Loftus, Ind., Olyphant.

McKean—Byron D. Hamlin, D., Smethport.

Mercer.—E. W. Jackson, R., Mercer; H. S. Blatt, R.; G. W. Reed, R., Wheeler.

Mifflin—Joseph W. Parker, D., Lewistown.

Monroe—Wm. Kistler, D., East Strodsburg.

Montgomery—Thomas G. Rutter, D., Pottstown; Joseph B. Yerkes, D., Horsham; Francis M. Knipe, D., Frederick: John C. Richardson, D. Bridgeport; James B. Law, D., Ardmore.

Montour—James Cruikshank, R., Danville.

Northampton—Andrew Snyder D., Middaghs; John Stotzer, D., Easton; A. J. Irwin, D., Bethlehem.

Northumberland—Jesse J. John, R., Shamohin; W. P. Withington, D., Shamokin.

Perry—George N. Reutter, D., Benvenue, Dauphin county.

Pike—E. B. Eldred, D., Milford.

Potter—C. Hollenbach, D.

Schuilkill, 1st district—John W. Morgan, R., Shenandoah.

2d district—Charles J. Loudenslager, R., Sacramento.

3d district—Joshua Boyer, D., McKeansburg..

4th district—S. A. Losch, R., Schuylkill Haven; Wm. J. Lewis, R., Tremont; Fred. L. Foster, D., Pottsville.

Snyder—G. Alfred Schoch, R., Middleburg.

Somerset—Wm. Endsley, R., Somerfield; Jos. D. Miller, R., Mineral point.

Susquehanna—Samuel Faulkenbury, Susquehanna Depot; W. W. Williams, R., South Gibson.

Sullivan—Richard Bedford, D., Campbellsville; Tioga—John L. Mitchel, R., Wellsboro; Wm. T. Humphrey, R., Osceola.

Union—Charles S. Wolfe, R., Lewisburg.

Venango—Wm. Hasson, D., Oil City; J. P. Park, D., Franklin; J. M. Dickey, R., Franklin.

Warren—Geo. W. Allen, R., Tidioute.

Washington—J. K. Billingsley, R., California; W. G. Barnett, D., Canonsburg; John Birch,. D., Claysville.

ELECTION RETURNS.

(CONTINUED.)

	G	R	M	M	O	H	W	M	G
17th, 1st d	125	62	5	129	8	5	127	59	6
17th, 2d d	135	88	2	140	81	2	139	86	3
17th, 3d d	105	105	2	107	102	2	105	105	2
17th, 4th d	82	73	4	81	74	4	82	73	4
18th	60	109	4	62	106	4	61	106	4
19th, 1st d	94	42	8	101	31	6	103	33	5
19th, 2d d	80	46	5	96	31	5	87	39	5
19th, 3d d	63	78	9	74	59	10	66	68	10
20th, 1st d	71	49	4	78	41	4	76	42	4
20th, 2d d	104	46	....	119	29	....	109	40	...
20th, 3d d	56	75	3	71	58	4	67	63	3
21st, 1st d	146	129	18	162	114	20	155	124	18
21st, 2d d	28	11	3	25	11	6	24	15	2
21st 3d d	93	48	3	105	36	3	104	37	2
22d, 1st d	106	27	6	106	28	5	106	29	4
22d, 2d d	36	31	....	46	18	1	42	22	1
23d, 1st d	44	44	....	45	43	....	22	66	...
23d, 2nd d	114	71	4	113	71	5	111	72	4
24th, 1st d	98	81	....	93	85	....	105	70	...
24th, 2d d	48	38	4	48	38	4	54	30	4
25th, 1st d	71	85	3	72	84	3	73	83	3
25th, 2d d	103	78	2	104	78	2	110	71	2
25th, 3d d	91	82	2	91	83	2	97	75	2
26th, 1st d	107	54	2	108	53	2	108	53	2
26th, 2d d	108	142	1	118	132	1	108	142	1
26th, 3d d	117	42	2	117	41	2	117	42	2
26th, 4th d	102	72	....	103	71	....	105	69	...
27th, 1st d	43	191	....	44	190	....	45	189	...
27th, 2d d	51	54	2	50	55	2	51	54	2
28th, 1st d	95	75	6	101	71	6	99	72	6
28th, 2d d	64	70	....	67	66	....	66	68	...
28th, 3d d	75	79	3	78	76	3	76	78	3
29th, 1st d	79	53	10	77	54	11	77	54	11
29th, 2d d	133	87	5	131	88	6	131	89	6
30th 1st d	96	62	2	99	60	2	99	60	2
30th, 2d d	76	60	2	77	67	2	76	69	2
31st	85	41	7	85	41	7	80	38	7
32d, 1st d	124	71	7	124	71	7	122	67	7
32d, 2d d	107	43	15	108	44	15	110	42	15
33d	38	84	....	39	81	....	38	83	...
34th	38	165	5	40	164	5	39	165	5
35th, 1st d	64	20	2	64	30	2	64	30	2
35th, 2d d	40	43	4	40	44	9	29	55	9
36th, 1st d	62	97	13	62	90	13	60	98	13
36th, 2d d	66	29	19	66	29	19	66	29	19
37th, 1st d	58	41	6	78	20	7	76	23	7
37th, 2d d	80	32	5	95	19	5	95	17	7

ALLEGHENY.
Wards.

	G	R	M	M	O	H	W	M	G
1st	438	165	26	430	166	28	456	153	29
2nd, 1st d	123	56	20	127	58	20	127	53	20
2d, 2d d	214	82	33	211	80	35	210	86	30
2d, 3d d	223	78	27	222	79	27	226	77	26
2d, 4th d	119	63	10	117	60	10	123	64	5
3d, 1st d	151	50	13	147	50	14	147	51	13
3d, 2d d	198	57	24	201	58	26	198	58	22
3d, 3d d	128	45	5	120	42	6	126	48	6
3d, 4th d	120	132	2	120	131	2	120	132	2
3d, 5th d	131	115	....	138	107	....	131	115	...
4th, 1st d	175	76	16	178	76	16	180	75	16
4th, 2d d	110	59	14	125	55	13	122	56	13
4th, 3d d	121	96	6	124	92	6	127	90	6
4th, 4th d	179	146	2	186	140	2	178	146	2
5th, 1st d	81	57	11	80	56	12	93	51	7
5th, 2d d	219	94	12	218	87	13	230	87	7
5th, 3d d	86	69	3	100	54	8	96	62	8
6th, 1st d	168	124	14	172	119	14	184	111	1
6th, 2d d	117	77	10	120	73	10	134	61	9

Pennsylvania Statistics.
CONTINUED.

Wayne—Thomas Y. Boyd, R., Eldred; Wm. W. Mumford, R.

Westmoreland—H. B. Piper, D., Greensburg; James L. Toner, D., New Derry; Thompson McLean, D., Smithton.

Wyoming—Giles Roberts, R., Falls.

York—Emanuel Meyers, D., Dillsburg; Adam Stevens, D., Goldsboro; George Anstine, D. Stewartstown; John B. Gemmel, D., New Park.

RECAPITULATION.

H. of R.—Democrats 110
Republicans 88
Independent 2
Prohibition 1
Senate—Republicans 29
Democrats 20
Independent D 1

WHAT SHALL WE EAT?—Here are some of the common articles of food, showing the amount of nutriment contained, and the time required for digestion:

	Time of Digestion.	Amount of Nutriment.
Apples, raw	1 h. 50 m.	10 per cent.
Beans, boiled	2 h. 30 m.	87 per cent.
Beef, roasted	3 h. 30 m.	26 per cent.
Bread, baked	3 h. 30 m.	60 per cent.
Butter	3 h. 30 m.	96 per cent.
Cabbage, boiled	4 h. 30 m.	7 per cent.
Cucumber, raw	—	2 per cent.
Fish, boiled	2 h. 00 m.	20 per cent.
Milk, fresh	2 h. 15 m.	7 per cent.
Mutton, roasted	3 h. 15 m.	30 per cent.
Pork, roasted ed.	5 h. 15 m.	24 per cent.
Poultry, roast	2 h. 45 m.	27 per cent.
Potatoes, boiled	2 h. 30 m.	18 per cent.
Rice, boiled	1 h. 00 m.	88 per cent.
Sugar	3 h. 30 m.	96 per cent.
Turnips, boiled	2 h. 30 m.	4 per cent.
Veal, roasted	4 h. 00 m.	25 per cent.
Venison, boiled	1 h. 30 m.	22 per cent.

According to the above table, cucumbers are of very little value, and apples, cabbages, turnips, and even potatoes, at the present prices, are expensive eating. Some vegetables and fruits, should, however, enter into family consumption, even if purchased for sanitary reasons. Among those which contain the most saccharine matter, sweet potatoes, parsnips, beets and carrots are the most nourishing. Roast pork, besides being an expensive dish, requires too lengthly drain upon the forces of the stomach to be a healthy article of diet.

EDUCATION IN ENGLAND.—The average school attendance in England has been increased from 1,225,000 to 1,725,000 within the past two years. The effect of recent legislation has been to provide accomodations for 2,871,000 against 1,765,000 two years ago. There are about 4,500,000 children of school age in England, so that but little more thon one-third of the children attend, and there is room for only about nine-fifths of the whole number who should go. Still theincreased attendance argues well for the future of England's population.

ELECTION RETURNS.

(CONTINUED.)

	G	R	M	M	O	H	W	M	G
6th, 3d d.............	86	84	9	85	82	12	96	79	4
7th, 1st d.............	58	132	....	68	122	......	57	133	...
7th, 2d d..............	108	138	.....	120	127	......	107	140	...
7th, 3d d.............	90	60	3	90	60	3	90	60	3
8th, 1st d.............	97	77	......	97	77	......	97	77	...
8th, 2d d..............	72	31	1	74	28	1	69	34	1
9th.......................	100	175	1	101	171	2	100	174	1
10th......................	66	34	4	64	32	7	61	35	7
11th......................	128	83	5	135	74	6	126	77	4
BOROUGHS.									
McKeesport, 1 w..	129	153	4	135	149	4	133	150	4
McKeesport, 2 w..	144	74	16	150	67	17	147	71	16
McKeesport, 3 w..	66	74	1	66	72	1	66	73	3
Braddocks...........	81	94	35	116	55	37	89	84	37
Beltzhoover........	17	11	3	17	11	3	17	11	1
Bellevue..............	98	15	10	95	13	13	108	8	7
Chartiers	100	44	4	90	52	5	85	55	5
Etna....................	167	56	.....	108	59	.....	169	59	...
Elizabeth............	99	62	27	100	59	28	100	61	27
Millvale...............	108	48	4	109	49	4	107	51	4
Mansfield............	102	16	10	100	21	10	99	22	9
Sewickley............	158	62	20	157	58	21	162	56	20
Sharpsburg..........	160	184	19	160	180	18	162	184	17
Tarentum............	95	40	51	77	37	65	96	40	50
Verona. 1 w.........	45	8	....	45	8	.....	45	8	...
Verona, 2 w.........	26	18	13	30	14	13	29	16	12
W. Bellevue.........	22	11	3	23	10	3	23	10	3
W. Elizabeth.......	65	38	10	71	32	10	68	35	10
TOWNSHIPS.									
Baldwin, 1 d.......	42	98	5	59	81	4	59	81	4
Baldwin, 2 d.......	77	118	4	91	91	4	88	110	4
Chartiers.............	149	109	10	152	102	11	149	109	10
Collier.................	69	55	......	62	57	3	64	47	...
Crescent..............	29	31	......	35	17	.....	30	30	...
Elizabeth, 1 d.....	71	57	11	67	57	12	71	57	11
Elizabeth, 2 d.....	51	33	.....	51	33	.....	51	33	...
Elizabeth, 3 d.....	33	15	21	34	15	21	34	15	21
Elizabeth, 4 d.....	89	32	2	94	38	2	93	32	2
East Deer, 1 d.....	90	33	19	95	29	18	91	32	19
East Deer, 2 2.....	58	38	6	66	30	6	57	38	7
Franklin..............	51	57	1	50	59	1	50	59	1
Fawn...................	77	10	5	77	9	5	77	10	5
Findley................	93	121	4	93	120	4	92	121	4
Forward...............	92	56	4	90	52	5	94	54	4
Hampton	65	54	1	65	54	1	66	53	1
Harrison..............	113	88	40	128	75	39	112	89	40
Harmar................	50	27	4	37	20	19	45	32	4
Indiana................	80	45	4	79	45	4	83	91	4
Jefferson.............	140	101	22	139	98	23	139	100	23
Kilbuck, 1 2........	57	25	12	60	20	15	58	26	12
Kilbuck, 2 d........	53	39	2	83	37	3	87	34	4
Leet....................	79	16	2	79	15	3	80	15	2
L. St. Clair, 1 d....	23	157	1	44	134	2	41	137	3
L. St. Clair, 2 d....	35	43	1	28	41	1	37	42	1
L. St. Clair, 3 d....	12	44	5	45	10	6	24	32	6
Lincoln................	79	32	8	80	31	8	78	33	8
Mifflin, 1 d..........	29	106	9	30	98	9	30	107	9
Mifflin, 2 d..........	81	89	8	84	90	4	83	91	4
Mifflin, 3 d..........	47	41	37	56	41	26	71	26	26
Moon...................	102	87	8	98	86	12	99	87	11
Marshall..............	40	50	.....	36	54	.....	35	51	...
M'Candless..........	39	64	.....	39	64	.....	39	64	...
N. Fayette...........	82	66	32	80	64	33	81	67	32
Neville.................	26	6	3	27	1	3	27	6	2
N. Versailles.......	95	146	1	121	119	2	104	135	2
Ohio....................	35	35	3	35	35	3	35	35	3
O'Hara, 1 d..........	60	84	.....	62	33	.....	35	38	...
O'Hara, 2 d..........	33	29	2	31	30	2	31	81	2

BAD EFFECTS OF BEER DRINKING.—The worst results from accidents in the London hospitals are said to be draymen. Though they are apparently models of health and strength, yet, if one of them receives a serious injury, it is nearly always necessary te amputate, in order to give him the most distant chance of life. The draymen have the unlimited privilege of the brewery cellar. Sir Ashley Cooper was once called to a drayman, who was a powerful, fresh-colored, healthy-looking man, and had suffered an injury in his finger, from a small splinter of a stave. The wound, though trifling, suppurated. He opened the small abcess with his lancet. He found, on retiring, he had left his lancet. Returning for it, he found the man in a dying condition. The man died in a short time. Dr. Gordon says: "The moment beer drinkers are attacked with acute diseases, they are not able to bear depletion, and die." Dr. Edwards says of beer drinkers: "Their diseases are always of a dangerous character, and in case of accident, they can never undergo even the most trifling operation with the security of the temperate. They most invariably die under it." Dr. Buchan says: "Malt liquors render the blood sizy and unfit for circulation: hence proceeds obstructions and inflammation of the lungs. There are few great beer drinkers who are not phthisical, brought on by the glutinous and indigestible nature of ale and porter. These liquors inflame the blood and tear the tender vessels of the lungs to pieces." Dr. Maxson says : "Intoxicating drinks, whether taken in the form of fermented or distilled liquors, are a very frequent predisposing cause of disease." The hospitals of New York show an equally unfavorable record of the intemperate, and private practitioners everywhere have the same experience.—*Sanitarian for January.*

ANALYSIS OF COWS' MILK.—There is an instrument used called a lactometer, which is nothing but a hydrometer, such as is used to ascertain the strength of distilled liquors, etc.; but for use in milk it is specially graduated from 1,000° to 1,050° or thereabouts, and it indicates the specific gravity of water, in which it sinks deepest at 1,000°, and that of the heaviest milk at 1,032°. The specific gravity of milk may vary from 1,026° to 1,032°; if it is less than 1,026, it is certainly diluted with water, and if above 1,032°, it has been thinned of its cream, as the presence of cream makes the average gravity of the milk lighter. Therefore, if milk is skimmed and watered both, the lactometer gives no satisfactory indication ; and it is surprising that the instrument has not been rejected by practical persons long ago.

DR. CHALMERS beautifully says:—"The little that I have seen in the world and know of mankind teaches me to look upon their errors in sorrow, not in anger. When I take the history of one poor heart that has sinned and suffered, and represent to myself the struggles and temptations it passed through—the brief pulsations of joy, the tears of regret, the feebleness of purpose, the scorn of the world that has little charity, the desolation of the soul's sanctuary and threatening voices within, health gone, happiness gone—I would fain leave the erring soul of my fellow being with him from whose hands it came."

ELECTION RETURNS.

(CONTINUED.)

	G	R	M.	M	O	H	W	M	G
Plum	127	86	16	104	96	33	135	96	33
Penn	158	91	12	161	82	21	161	88	16
Pine	50	52	.....	49	51	.....	50	52	...
Patton; 1 d	35	42	3	35	26	18	36	27	17
Patton, 2 d	51	66	13	59	56	12	60	57	13
Robinson, 1 d	7	1	.....	7	1	.....	7	1	...
Robinson, 2 d	68	35	13	69	34	12	70	34	12
Ross, 1 d	66	21	.....	66	22	.....	64	22	...
Ross, 2 d	50	51	4	48	50	7	44	55	6
Reserve	68	34	7	71	32	6	71	31	6
Richland	61	64	13	60	55	20	62	63	14
Shaler, 1 d	84	24	1	80	22	1	49	45	1
Shaler, 2 d	53	42	3	55	40	3	54	41	2
S. Versailles	30	38	.....	30	38	.....	30	38	...
Snowden	120	47	15	118	46	17	115	47	17
S. Fayette	100	24	15	95	23	20	98	24	16
Sewickley	33	13	.....	33	13	.....	33	13	...
Scott, 1 d	43	27	3	42	28	3	39	29	3
Scott, 2 d	54	22	.....	54	13	.....	43	33	...
Stowe	40	45	2	77	6	3	39	45	3
U. St. Clair, 1 d	23	26	15	24	24	15	23	27	15
U. St. Clair, 2 d	40	33	2	41	30	3	40	33	2
Union	152	36	6	152	35	6	150	40	6
Versailles	33	30	.....	30	26	.....	33	29	...
Wilkins, 1 d	88	38	6	102	29	7	101	24	7
Wilkins, 2 d	64	70	4	56	64	7	57	65	7
West Deer	132	43	29	132	32	38	131	45	28

THE GRAPE CURE.—Since the chemical constituants of grapes have been found similar to that of some celebrated medicinal waters, establishments have been set up in some parts of Europe to cure invalids, by feeding them copiously with this fruit. Among the matters contained in the grape are mentioned tartaric acid, potash, soda, oxide of iron and manganese, &c. Grapes have more soluble matter than perhaps any other fruit, and we know from experience that they are good in some instances of derangement of the digestive system. We also know that they are much more agreeable to take than some other medicines. At the grape-cures, the patients are not allowed to eat much else than the fruit, commencing with three or four pounds daily, and gradually increasing to more than twice this amount. Such delicious sorts as the Chasselas are employed for this purpose

NEEDLESS SICKNESS.—Prevention is better than cure, and in most small ailments there cannot be a safer physic than abstinence—abstinence from overfood, overwork. How persistently we shut our eyes to the beginners of disease, beginnings so trifling that we hardly notice them, until they end in that premature decay which seems only too common among our best and greatest men, and those whom the world can least spare! People rush to doctors to cure them; they never think of curing themselves by putting a stop to the exciting causes of ill health. The selfishness of people who will not stop, and go on indulging their luxurious, careless, or studious habits until they make themselves confirmed invalids, an anxiety and a torment to those about them, can not be too strongly reprobated; ay, even though it takes the form of a noble indifference to self, in pursuit of knowledge, wealth, ambition, any of the pretty disguises in which we wrap up the thing we like to do, and make believe to other people, often almost to ourselves, that it is the very thing we ought to do.

SOUND MADE VISIBLE.—A sound writer, called an epeidoscope, is a new invention. On the end of a two inch tube is passed a piece of thin rubber or tissue paper, in the centre of this is fastened a piece of looking-glass, one-eighth of an inch square. Hold this end in the sun and the other end in the mouth, and sing or speak in it. The ray of light reflected from the mirror falling a white surface describes curves and patterns differing for every pitch and intensity, while the same conditions give uniform results.

HOW HENRY CLAY WAS SOLD.—Some time ago before the introduction of railroads, Governor Metcalfe represented in Congress a district of Kentucky of which Nicholas county was a part. Mr. Clay was Secretary of State under President Quincy Adams. The two distinguished Politicians agreed to travel to Washington in Governor Metcalfe's carriage. While passing through the State of Pennsylvania, Mr. Clay told Governor Metcalfe that he had received intimation that in a certain town they were approaching he would be honored with an ovation by the citizens. Just before coming to the town, Governor Metcalfe, who had all along been driving, suggested to Mr. Clay that he take the lines and drive, as he himself was tired. Mr. Clay readily consented, whereupon the Governor took the back seat in the carriage. Mr. Clay drove the team successfully into the town, and they were met by a large concourse of people. Governor Metcalfe alighted from the carriage, and being asked whether he was Mr. Clay, answered yes, that he was glad to meet them, &c., and at this the crowd fairly hoisted him upon their shoulders and triumphantly started with him to the place of reception. Looking back at Mr. Clay, who still sat in the carriage somewhat nonplussed, the Governor cried: "Driver, take the horses to the stable and feed them." The merriment of the crowd, when the joke was discovered, can better be imagined then described—Mr. Clay himself as heartily entering into it as the rest.

JUDICIARY.

SUPREME COURT OF PENNSYLVANIA.

OFFICE.	NAME.	RESIDENCE.	TERM ENDS.	SALARY.
Chief Justice,	Daniel Agnew,	Beaver County,	December, 1878,	$7,000 00
Associate Judge,	George Sharswood,	Philadelphia,	do 1882,	7,000 00
do	Henry W. Williams,	Pittsburgh,	do 1884,	7,000 00
do	Ulysses Mercur,	Towanda,	do 1887,	7,000 00
do	Isaac G. Gordon,	Brookville,	do 1888,	7,000 00
do	Warren J. Woodward,	Berks,	do 1890,	7,000 00
do	Edward M. Paxson,	Philadelphia,	do 1890,	7,000 00
Prothonotary, E. Dist.	Benj. E. Fletcher,	do	At Pleasure of Court.	
do W. do.	J. B. Sweitzer,	Pittsburgh,	do do	
do M. do.	Robert Snodgrass,	Harrisburg,	do do	
do N. do.	C. J. Cummings,	Williamsport,	do do	
Reporter,	P. Frazer Smith,	West Chester,	December, 1875.	

PLACES AND TIME FOR HOLDING COURT.

At Philadelphia, commencing 1st Monday of January.
At Harrisburg, commencing 1st Monday of May.
At Pittsburgh, commencing 1st Monday of October.
At Williamsport, commencing 3d Monday of September.

QUALIFICATION OF VOTERS.

In elections, every citizen of the United States, of the age of twenty-one years, having resided in the state one year, and in the election district where he offers to vote ten days preceeding the election, and within two years paid a state or county tax, which shall have been assessed at least ten days before the election, shall be qualified to vote; but if he has previously been a qualified voter of this state, and removed therefrom and returned, who shall have resided in the election district and paid taxes as aforesaid, shall be entitled to vote, after residing in the state for six months.

Those citizens, however, between the ages of twenty-one and twenty-two, having resided in the state one year, and in the election district ten days, as aforesaid, shall be entitled to vote, although they shall not have paid any taxes.

An alien can become a citizen by declaring, on oath or affirmation before a circuit or district court of the United States, or any state court of record, at least two years before his admission, that was *bona fide* his intention to become a citizen, and his renouncing forever all allegiance, etc., to any foreign state. In addition he must have been five consecutive years a resident of the United States, one year of which immediately preceding his naturalization, must be in the state wherein the court applied to his jurisdiction.

Any alien who shall have resided in the United States the three years next preceding his arriving at the age of twenty-one, and after he shall have resided five years therein, and one year in the state wherein the application is made, is entitled to naturalization without being required to make the declaration two years before his admission. The declaration in this case is made at the time of admission to citizenship.

The minor children of persons naturalized under any law of the United Strtes are considered citizens, and are not required to take out papers.

An alien dying after declaring his intentions and before his final papers are due, his widow and children may become citizens by taking the oath prescribed by law.

Aliens have rights as follows, in acquiring and holding real estate in this state. [See Purdon's Digest, paragraph 7, page 37.]

It shall and may be lawful for all and every foreigner and foreigners, alien or aliens, not being the subject or subjects of some sovereign, state or power which is or shall be at the time or times of such purchase or purchases, at war with the United States of America, to purchase lands, tenements, or hereditaments within this Commonwealth, not exceeding 5,000 acres, and to have and to hold the same to them and their heirs and assigns forever, as fully, to all intents and purposes, as any natural born citizen may or can do.

CHURCH DAYS.

Epiphany	January 6.
Septuagesima Sunday	January 24.
Sexagesima Sunday	January 31.
Quinquagesima Sunday	February 7.
Ash Wednesday	February 10.
Quadragesima Sunday	February 14.
Mid Lent Sunday	March 7.
Palm Sunday	March 21.
Good Friday	March 26.
Easter Sunday	March 28.
Low Sunday	April 4.
Rogation Sunday	—May 2.
Ascension Day	May 6.
Whit Sunday	May 16.
Trinity Sunday	May 23.
Corpus Christi	May 27.
Sunday before Advent	November 21.
Advent Sunday	November 28.
Christmas Day	December 25.

UNITED STATES.

BOUNDARIES.

The United States is bounded on the North by British America and the Canadas; on the East by Nova Scotia and the Atlantic Ocean; South by the Gulf of Mexico and Mexico; West by the Pacific Ocean. Area, 3,400,000 square miles.

PRINCIPAL OFFICERS OF THE U. S. GOVERNMENT, January 1, 1876.

President.

ULYSSES S. GRANT, Illinois.

Vice President.

*HENRY WILSON, Massachusetts.

Secretary of State—Hamilton Fish, New York.
Secretary of Treasury—B. H. Bristow, Kentucky.
Secretary of War—William W. Belknap, Iowa.
Secretary of Navy—George Maxwell Robeson, New Jersey.

Secretary of Interior—Zach. O. Chandler, Mich.
Postmaster General—Marshall Jewell, Connecticut.
Attorney General—Edwards Pierrepont, New York.

Supreme Court of the United States.

Name.	State.	Age.	App'd.
M. F. Waite	Ohio,	—	1874
Nathan Clifford,	Maine,	68	1858
D. H. Swayne	Ohio,	62	1862
David Davis	Illinois,	57	1862
Samuel F. Miller	Iowa,	56	1862
Stephen J. Field	California,	55	1863
Joseph P. Bradley	New Jersey,	59	1870
William Strong	Pennsylvania,	63	1870
Ward Hunt	New York,	52	1872

UNITED STATES CIRCUIT JUDGES, 1875.

1st Circuit, George F. Shepley, Maine; 2d Lewis B. Woodruf, New York; 3d, William McKennan, Pennsylvania; 4th, Hugh L. Bond, Maryland; 5th, Wm. B. Wood, Alabama; 6th, Palmer H. Emmons, Michigan; 7th, Thomas Drummond, New York; 8th, John F. Dillon, Iowa; 9th, Lorenzo Sawyer, California.

MINISTERS TO FOREIGN COUNTRIES.

Envoys Extraordinary and Ministers Plenipotentiary.

Country.	Capital.	Ministers.	Salary.	Appointed
Austra	Vienna	John Jay, New York	$12,000	1868
Brazil	Rio Janeiro	James R. Patridge, Maryland	12,000	1871
Chili	Santiago	Cornelius A. Logan	10,000	1869
China	Pekin	Benjamin B. Avery	12,000	1869
France	Paris	Elihu B. Washburne, Illinois	17,500	1869
Great Britain	London	Robert C. Schenck, Ohio	17,500	1870
Italy	Florence	George P. Marsh, Vermont	12,000	1861
Mexico	City of Mexico	John W. Foster	12,000	1869
Peru	Lima	Francis Thomas, Maryland	10,000	1872
Germany	Berlin	J. C. Bancroft Davis	17,500	1867
Russia	St. Petersburg	Eugene Schuyler		
Spain	Madrid	Caleb Cushing	12,000	1873
Japan	Yedo	John A. Bingham, Ohio	12,000	1873

FORTY-FOURTH CONGRESS.

A LIST OF THE SENATORS AND REPRESENTATIVES OFFICIALLY CORRECTED BY THE CHIEF CLERK.

The regular session of the National Legislature will begin on Monday, December 6. Except the Pinchback matter, all is settled in the Senate. In the House there is a vacancy in the Fourth Tennessee district, caused by the death of the Hon. John W. Head. The Hon. Samuel M. Fife, who was then elected to the seat, died at Little Rock, Arkansas, since, and there is still a vacancy.

THE SENATE.

Republicans, 44; Democrats, 28; Independents, 2.

States.	Begin.	End.	Names.	Politics.
Alabama	1871	1877	Geo. Goldthwaite,	Dem.
	1868	1879	Geo. E. Spencer...	Rep.
Arkansas	1871	1877	Powell Clayton...	Rep.
	1873	1879	S. W. Dorsey	Rep.
California	1875	1881	Newton Booth	Ind.
	1873	1879	Aaron A. Sargent	Rep.
Connecticut	1876	1881	Wm. W. Eaton	Dem.
	1875	1879	James E. English	Dem.
Delaware	1869	1881	Thos. F. Bayard	Dem.
	1871	1877	Eli Salisbury	Rep.
Florida	1875	1881	Chas. W. Jones	Rep.
	1873	1879	S. B. Conover	Rep.
Georgia	1871	1877	Thos. M. Norwood	Dem.
	1871	1879	John B. Gordon	Dem.
Illinois	1871	1877	John A. Logan	Rep.
	1873	1879	Rich'd A. Oglesby	Rep.
Indiana	1875	1881	Jos. E. McDonald	Dem.
	1867	1879	Oliver P. Morton	Rep.
Iowa	1871	1877	George G. Wright,	Rep.
	1873	1879	Wm. B. Allison	Rep.
Kansas	1873	1877	J. M. Harvey	Rep.
	1873	1879	John J. Ingalls	Rep.
Kentucky	1871	1877	J. W. Stevenson	Dem.
	1868	1879	T. C. McCreery	Dem.
Louisiana	1871	1877	J. Rodman West	Rep.
	1873	1879	Vacancy	
Maine	1848	1881	Hannibal Hamlin,	Rep.
	1861	1877	Lot M. Morrill	Rep.
Massa'h's'tts	1873	1877	G. S. Boutwell	Rep.
	1874	1881	Henry L. Dawes...	Rep.

UNITED STATES—Continued.

Maryland.....1875 1881 Wm. P. Whyte..... Dem.
         1873 1879 Geo. R. Dennis..... Dem.
Michigan.....1875 1881 I. P. Christiancy.. Rep.
         1871 1877 Thos. W. Ferry.... Rep.
Minnesota...1875 1881 S. J. R. McMillan.. Rep.
         1871 1877 Wm. Windom...... Rep.
Mississippi...1875 1881 B. K. Bruce.......... Rep.
         1861 1877 James L. Alcorn... Rep.
Missouri......1875 1881 F. M. Cockrell...... Dem.
         1873 1879 L. V. Bogy........... Dem.
Nebraska.....1875 1881 A. S. Paddock...... Rep.
         1871 1877 P. W. Hitchcock... Rep.
Nevada........1875 1881 Wm. Sharon......... Rep.
         1873 1879 John P. Jones....... Rep.
N.Ham'shire1865 1877 A. H. Cragin........ Rep.
         1873 1879 B. Wadleigh......... Rep.
New Jersey..1875 1881 T. F. Randolph..... Dem.
         1866 1877 F. T. Fleighuysen Rep.
New York....1875 1881 Francis Kernan... Dem.
         1867 1879 Roscoe Conkling.. Rep.
N. Carolina..1872 1877 M. H. Ransom...... Dem.
         1873 1879 A. S. Merrimon...... Dem.
Ohio............1869 1881 A. G. Thurman.... Dem.
         1861 1870 John Sherman..... Rep.
Oregon.........1871 1877 James K. Kelly.... Dem.
         1873 1879 John H. Mitchell, Rep.
Pennsyl'ia...1875 1881 Wm. A. Wallace... Dem.
         1845 1879 Simon Cameron... Rep.
RhodeIsland1875 1881 A. E.Burnside...... Rep.
         1859 1877 H.B. Anthony...... Rep.
S. Carolina...1868 1879 T. J. Robertson..... Rep.
         1873 1879 John J. Patterson Rep.
Tennessee...1875 1881 D. M. Key.......... Dem.
         1871 1877 Henry Cooper...... Dem.
Texas...........1875 1881 S. B. Maxey......... Dem.
         1870 1877 M. C. Hamilton... Ind.
Vermont......1866 1881 Geo. F. Edmunds Rep.
         1867 1879 Justin S. Morrill, Rep.
Virginia......1875 1881 R. E. Withers...... Dem.
         1870 1877 JohnW. Johnston Dem.
W. Virginia.1875 1881 A. T. Caperton... Dem.
         1871 1877 Henry G. Davis... Dem.
Wisconsin....1875 1881 Angus Cameron... Rep.
         1861 1879 Timothy O. Howe Rep.

Republicans...44
Democrats...28
Independents.. 2

Total Senate...74
Republican majority.......................................14

ACTIVITY NOT ALWAYS ENERGY.—There are some men whose failure to succeed in life is a problem to others, as well as to themselves. They are industrious, prudent and economical; yet after a long life of striving, old age finds them still poor. They complain of ill luck. They say fate is always against them. But the fact is that they miscarry because they have mistaken mere activity for energy. Confounding two things essentially different, they have supposed that, if they were always busy, they would be certain to be advancing their fortunes. They have forgotten that misdirected labor is but a waste of activity. The person who would succeed in life is like a marksman firing at a target; if his shots miss the mark, they are a waste of powder. So in the great game of life, what a man does must be made to count, or it might almost as well have been left undone. Everybody knows some one in his circle of friends, who, though always active, has this want of energy.

THE HOUSE.

Republicans (marked R.), 107; Democrats (marked D.), 778; Independents (marked I.), 6. One vacancy exists in Tennessee, caused by death. The asterisk (*) indicates members of Congress re-elected. The C. stands for colored.

Alabama—8.

1 J. Haralson, C. R.
2 J. N. Williams, D.
3 T. Bradford, D.
4 *C. Hays, R.
5 *J. H. Caldwell, D.
6 G. W. Hewitt, D.
At Large—
  B. B. Lewis, D.
  W. H. Forney, D.

Arkansas—4.

1 L. C. Gause, D.
2 W. F. Slemons, D.
3 W. II. Wilshire, D.
4 *T. M. Gunter, D.

California—4.

1 W. A. Piper, D.
2 *H. F. Page, R.
3 *J. K. Luttrell, D.
4 P. R. Wigginton D.

Connecticut—4.

1 G. M. Landers, D.
2 J. Phelps, D.
3 H.H. Starkweather R.
4 *W. H. Barnum, D

Delaware—1.

1 J. D. Williams, D.

Florida—2.

1 *W. J. Puman, R.
2 *J. T. Walls, C. R.

Georgia—9.

1 J. Hartridge, D.
2 W. E. Smith, D.
3 *P. Cook, D.
4 *H. R. Harris. D.
5 M. A. Candler, D.
6 *J. H. Blount, D.
7 W. H. Felton, D.
8 *A. H. Stephens, D.
9 B. H. Hill, D.

Illinois—19.

1 B. G. Caulfield, D.
2 C. H. Harrison, D.
3 *C. B. Farwell, R.

4 S. A. Hurlbut, R.
5*H. C. Burchard, R.
6 T, J. Henderson, R
7 A. Campbell, I.
8 *G. L. Fort, R.
9 R. H. Whiting, R.
10 J. C. Bagby, I.
11 S. Wike, D.
12 W. M. Springer, D.
13 A. E. Stevenson, D.
14 *J. G. Cannon, R.
15 *J. R. Eden, D.
16 W. A. J. Sparks, D.
17 *W. R. Morrison,D
18 W. Hartzell, D.
19 W. B. Anderson, I.

Indiana—13.

1 B. S. Fuller, D.
2 J. D. Williams, D.
3 * M. C. Kerr, D.
4 J. D. New, D.
5 *W. S. Holman, D.
6 M. L. Robinson, R.
7 F. Landers, D.
8 *M. C. Hunter, R.
9 *T. J. Cason, R.
10 W. S. Haymond, D
11 J. L. Evans, R.
12 A. H. Hamilton, D.
13 J. H. Baker, R.

Iowa—9.

1 *G. W. McCrary, R
2 J. Q. Tufts, R.
3 L. L.Ainsworth, D.
4 H. O. Pratt, R.
5 *J. Wilson, R.
6 E. S. Sampson, R.
7 *J. A. Kasson, E.
8 *J. W. McDill, R.
9 A. Oliver, R.

Kansas.—3.

1 *W. A. Phillips, R.
2 J. R. Goodin, D.
3 W. R. Brown, R.

Kentucky—10

1 A. R. Boone, D.
2 *J. Y. Brown, D.
3 C. W. Milliken, D.
4 J. P. Knott, D.
5 E. Y. Parsons, D.
6 T. L. Jones, D.
7 J.S.C. Blackburn D
8 *M. J. Durham, D.
9 J. D. White, R.
10 J. B. Clarke, D.

UNITED STATES—Continued.

Louisiana—6.

1 R. L. Gibson, D.
2 E. J. Ellis, D.
3 *C. B. Darrell, R.
4 W. M. Levy, D.
5 *F. Morey, R.
6 *C. E. Nash, C. R.

Maine—5.

1 *J. H. Burleigh, R.
2 *W. P. Frye, R.
3 *J. G. Blaine, R.
4 H. M. Plaisted, R.
5 *E. Hale, R.

Maryland—6.

1 P. F. Thomas, D.
2 C. B. Roberts, D.
3 *W. J. O'Brien, D.
4 *T. Swann, D.
5 E. J. Henkle, D.
6 W. Walsh, D.

Massachusetts—11

1 W. W. Crapo, R.
2 *B. W. Harris, R.
3 *H. L. Pierce, R.
4 R. S. Frost, R.
5 N. P. Banks, I.
6 C. P. Thompson, D.
7 J. K. Tarbox, D.
8 W. W. Warren, D.
9 *G. F. Hoar, R.
10 J. H. Seelye, I.
11 C. W. Chapin, D.

Michigan—9.

1 A. S. Williams, D.
2 *H. Waldron, R.
3 *G. Willard, R.
4 A. Potter, D.
5 W. B. Williams, R.
6 G. H. Durand, D.
7 *O. D. Conger, R.
8 *N. H. Bradley, R.
9 *Jay A. Hubbel, R.

Minnesota—3.

1 *M. H. Dunnell, R.
2 *H. B. Strait, R.
3 W. S. King, R.

Mississippi—6

1 *L. Q. C. Lamar, D.
2 G. W. Wells, R.
3 H. B. Money, D.
4 O. R. Singleton, R.
5 C. E. Hooker, D.
6 R. Seal, D.

Missouri—13

1 E. C. Kehr, D.

2 *E. Wells, D.
3 *W. A. Stone, D.
4 *R. A. Hatcher, D.
5 *R. P. Bland, D.
6 C. H. Morgan, D.
7 J. F. Philips, D.
8 B. J. Franklin, D.
9 D. Rea, D.
10 R. A. DeBolt, D.
11 *J. B. Clark, Jr., D
12 *J. M. Glover, D.
13 *A. H. Beckner, D.

Nebraska—1.

1 *L. Crouse, R.

Nevada—1.

1 W. Woodburn, R.

New Hampshire—3

1 S. N. Bell, D.
2 F. Jones, D.
3 H. W. Blair, R.

New Jersey—7.

1 C. H. Sinniekson, R.
2 *S. A. Dobbins, R.
3 M. Ross, D.
4 *R. Hamilton, D.
5 A. W. Cutler, D.
6 F. H. Teese, D.
7 A. A. Hardenbergh, D.

New York—33.

1 H. B. Metcalfe, D.
2 J. G. Schumaker, D
3 S. B. Chittenden, I.
4 A. M. Bliss, D.
5 E. R. Meade, D.
6 *S. S. Cox, D.
7 S. Ely, Jr. D.
8 E. Ward, D.
9 *F. Wood, D.
10 A. S. Hewitt, D.
11 B. A. Willis, D.
12 N. H. Odell, D.
13 *J. O. Whitehouse D
14 G. M. Beebe, D.
15 J. H. Bagley, Jr. D
16 C. H. Adams, R.
17 M. I. Townsend, R.
18 A. Williams, R.
19 *W. A. Wheeler, R.
20 *H. H. Hathorn, R
21 S. F. Miller, R.
22 G. A. Bagley, R.
23 S. Lord, D.
24 W. H. Baker, R.
25 E. W. Leavenworth R.
26 *C. D. McDougall, R
27 E. G. Lapham, R.
28 *T. C. Platt, R.
29 C. C. B. Walker, R.
30 J. M. Davy, D.

31 *G. G. Hoskins, R.
32 *L. K. Bass, R.
33 N. I. Norton, R.

North Carolina—8.

1 J. Y. Yeates, D.
2 J. A. Hyman, C. R.
3 *A. M. Waddell, D.
4 J. J. Davis, D.
5 A. M. Scales, D.
6 *T. S. Ashe, D.
7 *W. M. Robbins, D.
8 *R. B. Vance, D.

Ohio—20.

1 *M. Sayler, D.
2 *H. B. Banning, D.
3 J. A. Savage, D.
4 J. A. McMahon, D.
5 A. V. Rice, D.
6 F. H. Hurd, D.
7 *L. T. T. Neal, D.
8 *W. Lawrence, R.
9 E. F. Poppleton, D.
10 *C. Foster, R.
11 J. L. Vance, D.
12 A. T. Walling, D.
13 *M. I. Southard, D.
14 J. P. Cowen, D.
15 N. H. Van Vorhes R.
16 *L. Danford, R.
17 *L. L. Woodward R
18 *J. Monroe, R.
19 J. A. Garfield, R.
20 H. B. Payne, D.

Oregon—1.

1 L. Lane, D.

Pennsylvania—27.

1 C. Freeman, R,
2 *C. O'Neill, R.
3 *S. J. Randall, D.
4 *W. D. Kelley, R.
5 J. Robbins, D.
6 *W. Townsend, R.
7 A. Wood, Jr. R.
8 *H. Clymer, D.
9 *A. H. Smith, R.
10 W. Mutchler, D.
11 F. O. Collins, D.
12 W. W. Ketchum R
13 J. B. Reilley, D.
14 *J. B. Packer, R.
15 J. Powell, D.
16 *S. Ross, K.
17 J. Reilly, D.
18 W. S. Stenger, D.
19 L. Maish, D.
20 L. A. Mackey, D.
21 J. Turney, D.
22 J. M. Hopkins, D.
23 A. G. Cochrane, D.
24 J. W. Wallace, R.
25 G. A. Jencks, D.
26 J. Sheakley, D.
27 A. G. Egbert, D.

Rhode Island—2.

1 *B. T. Eames, C.
2 L. W. Ballou, R.

South Carolina—5.

1 *J. H. Rainey, C. R.
2 E. W. M. Mackey, D
3 S. L. Hoge, R.
4 *A. S. Wallace, R.
5 R. Smalls, C. R.

Tennessee—10.

1 W. McFarland, D.
2 *J. M. Thornburg, R
3 G. G. Dibrell, D.
4 Vacancy.
5 *J. M. Bright, D.
6 J. F. House, D.
7 *W. C. Whitthorne, D.
8 *J. D. C. Atkins, D.
9 W. P. Caldwell. D.
10 H. C. Young, D.

Texas—6.

1 J. H. Reagan, D.
2 D. B. Culberson, D.
3 J. W. Throckmorton, D.
4 *R. Q. Mills, D.
5 *J. Hancock, D.
6 G. Schleicher, D.

Vermont—3.

1 C. H. Joyce, R.
2 D. C. Denison, R.
3 *G. W. Hendee, R.

Virginia—9.

1 B. B. Douglas, D.
2 *J. Goode, Jr. D.
3 G. C. Walker, D.
4 *W. H. H. Stowell, R
5 G. C. Cabell, D.
6 J. R. Tucker, D.
7 *J. T. Harris, D.
8 *E. Hunton, D.
9 W. Terry, D.

West Virginia—3.

1 B. Wilson, D.
2 C. J. Faulkner, D.
3 *F. Hereford, D.

Wisconsin—8.

1 *C. G. Williams, R.
2 L. B. Caswell, R.
3 H. S. Magoon, R.
4 W. P. Lynde, D.
5 S. D. Burchard, D.
6 A. M. Kimball, R.
7 *J. M. Rusk, R.
8 G. W. Cato, D.

·UNITED STATES—Continued.

TERRITORIAL DELEGATES.

Arizona—Hiram S. Stephens.
Colorado—Thomas M. Patterson, D.
Dakota—Jefferson P. Kidder, R.
Idaho—Thomas W. Bennett, R.
Montana—*Martin Maginnis, D.
New Mexico—Stephen B. Elkins, R.
Utah—*Georfie Q. Cannon, I.
Washington—Orange Jacobs, R.
Wyoming—*William R. Steele, D.

CONTESTED SEATS IN THE HOUSE.

State.	Seat.	Contested by
Alabama...Haralston, R.	....	F. G, Bromberg, D.
Florida......Walls, col., R.	....	J. J. Finley, D.
Illinois......Farwell, R.	....	J. V. LeMoyne, D.
Louisiana { Morey, R.	....	W. D. Spencer, D.
{ Darrall, R.	....	—— Breux, D.
Mass........Frost, R.	....	J. G. Abbott, D.
Minnesota..Strait, R.	....	E. St. J. Cox, D.
Virginia.....Goode, D.	....	J. H. Platt, Jr., D.

PATRONAGE—OFFICERS OF THE HOUSE, WITH
THE SALARIES ATTACHED.

The Speaker	$8,000
Clerk	4,896
Sergeant-at-Arms	4,320
Chief Clerk.	*3,600
Journal Clerk	*3,600
Door Keeper	2,592
Postmaster	2,592
Assistant Journal clerk	3,000
Two reading clerks, each	3,000
Tally clerk	3,000
Four assistant clerks, each	2,592
One assistant clerk	2,520
Six assistant clerks, each	2,160
Librarian of the House	2,160
Assistant Librarian of the House	2,160
Sup't document room of House	2,160
Ass't Sup't document room of House	2,160
Superintendent folding room	2,160
Sup't document room clerk's office	1,800
Doorkeeper in charge of hall	2,592
Assistant postmaster	2,088
File clerk document room	1,800
Clerk to Speaker	2,102
Private Secretary to Speaker	2,102
Five official reporters, each	5,000
Two stenographers, for committees	4,290
Chaplain	900
Engineer of ventilator	1,800
Three ass't engineers of ventilator, each.	1,440
Six firemen of ventilator, each	1,095
Chief Messenger of House	2,098
Three Assistant Messengers of house	1,440
Clerk to Sergeat-at-Arms	2,500
Paying teller to Sergeant-at-Arms	1,800
Messenger to Sergeant-at-Arms	1,440
Seven messengers for P. O	1,500
Seven messengers for P. O	1,200
Five messengers for D. K	1,800
Six messengers for D. K	1,440
Twelve mes. (during session) for D. K	1,440
One telegraph operator	1,200
Clerk to Appropriations Committee	2,592
Clerk to Ways and Means Committee	2,592
Clerk to Claims Committee	2.160
Clerk to War Claims Committee	2.160

Clerk to Public Lands Committee	2,160
Messenger to Ways and Means	1,214
Messenger to Appropriations	1,314
Fifteen laborers, each	720
Seven laborers (during the session,) each	720
One laborer	820
One laborer	920
One female at'dnt, ladies retiring room..	600

*Only when filled by present officer.·

There are some fifty employees paid per diem, including most of the committee clerks and the pages, twenty-eight id number of the latter, who receive $2.50 day. The clerks to the following committees are also paid a per diem ranging from $4.80 to $6.50, viz: Accounts, Agriculture, Banking and Currency, Commerce, District of Columbia, Education, Elections, Foreign Affairs, Indian Affairs, Invalid Pensions, Judiciary, Military Affairs, Mines, Naval Affairs, Pacific Railroads, Patents, Postoffices, Printing, Private Land Claims, Public Buildings, Railways and Canals, Revision of the Laws, and Territories. The total expenditure per year for the above officers amounts to $249,-500.29. The total pay of members $1,550,000. Their mileage is $100,000 additional.

POST OFFICE REGULATIONS.

Letters, Postal Cards, Newspapers, etc.

Letters must be stamped with three cents for first half ounce, and the same for each additional half ounce or fraction thereof.

Newspapers, excepting weeklies, periodicals and circulars deposited in a letter carrter office for delivery by the office or its carriers, are subject to postage at the following rates: On newspapers, regular or transient, not exceeding two ounces in weight, one cent each; on periodicals, other than newspapers, regular or transient, not exceeding two ounces in weight, one cent each; on periodicals, other than newspapers, regular or transient, exceeding two ounces in weight, two cents each; circulars unsealed, one cent each; weekly newspapers to transient persons. one cent for each two ounces or fraction thereof. These rates must be prepaid by postage stamps affixed; weekly newspapers to regular subscribers, two cents per pound, to be weighed in bulk and paid at the office of mailing.

Under this section county papers pass any mail free to subscribers actually living within the county, but when delivered at letter-carrier offices or by letters they are subject to the rates of postage fixed in the laws and regulations, page 67, section 158, namely : On publications not exceeding four ounces in weight, issued less frequently than once a week, one cent for each copy, and when issued once a week, five cents per quarter, and five cents additional per quarter for each issue more frequent than once a week. An additional rate shall be charged for each additional four ounces or fraction thereof. These rates must be paid quarterly before the delivery of such matter either at the office of mailing or delivery. When not so paid, postage must be collected on the delivery of each copy at transient tates, viz: One cent for each two ounces or fraction thereof.

UNITED STATES—Continued.

The foregoing instructions took effect on the first day of January, 1875, and are to continue in force until modified or superseded by the Department.

Postal cards to any part of the United States, one cent; to the Canadas, 2 cents. The exchange of postal cards between countries of the United States and Germany went into effect on the 15th of December, 1873. The postage to Germany, including Austria, Hungary and the Grand Duchy of Luxemburg, is 2 cents each, pre-payment to be made by affixing an ordinary one cent United States postage stamp in addition to the stamp printed on the card.

Liquids, glass, poisons, chemicals, or any other article likely to injure the mails, are prohibited.

Books not exceeding four ounces, 4 cents; additional four or fractions, 4 cents.

Daily newspapers, 35 cents per quarter; six times a week, 30 cents; tri-weekly, 15 cents; semi-weekly, 10 cents; weekly, 5 cents.

Quarterly postage on publications — semi-monthly, four ounces and less, 6 cents; over four and less than eight ounces, 12 cents; over eight and less than twelve ounces, 18 cents; monthly, four ounces, 3 cents; to eight, 6 cents; to twelve, 9 cents; quarterly, four ounces, one cent; eight ounces, 2 cents; twelve ounces, 3 cents.

Postage on printed matter can only be prepaid to the Canada line.

Unsealed circular, not more than two ounces in weight, to one address, 1 cent.

United States Money Orders.

Fifty dollars is the greatest amount allowed to one money order, and the issue to a single applicant, in one day, of more than three orders, payable at the same office and to the same payee, is positively forbidden. Rates: On orders not exceeding $15, 10 cents; over $15 and not exceeding $30, 15 cents; over $30 and not exceeding $40, 20 cents; over $40 and not exceeding $50, 25 cents.

Rates of charge for exchange (to be deducted by the postmaster at New York from the value in United States gold, or international order on Switzerland), on orders not exceeding $20, 20 cents, gold; on orders over $20 and not exceeding $30, 40 cents, gold; on orders over $30 and not exceeding $40, 40 cents, gold; on orders over $40 and not exceeding $50, 50 cents, gold.

Advertised Letters.

Request letters, and letters bearing the name and address of the writer on the outside, when not delivered within the time specified, are returned direct, without being sent to the dead-letter office. They are not advertised.

All letters remaining in the office are advertised on Tuesday and Friday of each week. If not called for in one month thereafter, they are sent to Washington. City letters are not advertised unless prepaid by a 3 cent stamp.

Prepaid and free letters are forwarded at the request of the party addressed from one post-office to another without additional postage. A letter delivered by the postoffice to an authorized person, and by him redirected to another postoffice, cannot be forwarded to a new address without the pre-payment of postage. Drop letters can be so forwarded, but are charged 3 cents for each half ounce or fraction thereof. These provisions do not apply to any mail matter except letters.

Registered Letters.

Letters may be registered by paying postage in full, and without registry fee, for any part of the United States; for Canada, Nova Scotia, New Brunswick, and Prince Edward's Island, 5 cents; West Indies, Island of Jamaica and Panama, 8 cents; Burmah, China, East Indies, Siam and Japan, 17 cents; Cape of Good Hope, Ceylon, Constantinople, East Indies, Falkland Islands, Gambia, Gibraltar, Gold Cost, Hong Kong, Java, Lagos, Labaun, Liberia, Malta, Mauritius, Natal, New South Wales, Queensland, St. Helena, Sierra Leone, South Australia, Tasmania, Victoria and Western Australia, 16 cts.; Egypt, (Alexandria, Cairo and Suez only), 8 cents; Great Britain and Ireland, Belgium, the Netherlands, Italy, Switzerland and the North German Union, (including all the countries and places reached via the North German mails, except Alexandretta, Latakia, Mersina, Retimo and Tripoli, in Turkey), 8 cents.

Registered letters must always be indorsed on the back with the name and address of the writer, and should be deposited fifteen minutes prior to closing the mails.

HOUSE PLANTS.—Do best in rather cool rooms, or at a temperature not so high as 60°. This is the reason that we often see finer plants in the cottages of the mechanic and laboring man, than in the warm, furnace-heated mansions of the rich. In the latter, however, much improvement may be made by keeping the air-chamber of the furnace abundantly and constantly supplied with evaporating water—at least eight or ten gallons daily for a medium-sized furnace; and if the plants still appear to suffer from dry air, hang wet napkins over them. If this attention cannot be given, the plants should be selected from such sorts as grow naturally in dry climates, such as the cactus, sedum, &c. House plants are often injured by the accumulation of dust in sweeping, which may be partly remedied by syringing, but more easily by placing large funnels of tissue paper inverted over the plants till the dust settles. Tissue paper is best, on account of its little weight on the plants.

THE SEA MOUSE.—This is one of the prettiest things that live under water. Although living in the mud at the bottom of the ocean, it sparkles like a diamond. It should not be called a mouse, however, for it is larger than a big rat and is covered with scales that move up and down as it breathes, and glitter like gold

CRANBERRIES IN NEW JERSEY, are said to cover about 7,000 acres,—5.000 in bearing and 2,000 new. There are also about 10,000 acres of cranberry land not occupied. In 1875, about 125,000 bushels were raised in the country.

ON NOVEMBER 15, 90 miles of new railways were opened in Italy, including that from Tuoro to Chiusi.

FOREIGN POSTAGE.

Countries, &c., and routes by which correspodence may be forwarded.	Letters, per half oz.	Registration fee on each letter.	Newspaper, each, if not exceeding 4 oz.	Book Packets and other printed matter. Not over 1 oz. in weight.	Over 1, but not over 3 oz.
	cts.	cts.	cts.	cts.	cts.
Austria, including Hungary, German mail direct....................	†5	8	3	2	4
Azore Islands, British mail.........................:...................	5	16	6	4	8
Belgium, by direct steamers..........................	†5	8	3	2	4
Belize, British Honduras, via St. Thomas...................	13	8	......	......	......
British Columbia,* (letters unpaid 10 cents per half oz.)............	†3	5	......	b	b
Canada,* (letters, *if unpaid*, 10 cents per half oz.)........	6	5	b	b	b
Cape of Good Hope, British mail...................	28	16	4	4	8
Cape de Verdo Islands, British mail...........................	16	16	6	4	8
Central America*...	21	......	......	2	2
Ceylon, British mail, via Southampton (a)....................	22	16	6	4	8
Constantinople, German mail direct..............................	15	8	6	3	6
Costa Rica*...................................	10	......	......	2	2
Cuba, U. S. packet*............ ....:...................	10	......	......	2	2.
Denmark*...	†7	10	4	3	6
East Indies, British, via San Francisco.......................	†10	......	......	......	......
France, direct*..	10	......	......	2	2
Germany, via Hamburg or Bremen direct.......................	†6	8	3	2	4
Gibraltar, British mail via Southampton......................	16	16	4	4	8
Gold Coast, British mail via Southampton.....................	16	16	6	4	8
Great Britain and Ireland (a)................................	†5	8	2	4	4
Greece, German mail direct (a)..............................	†14	8	9	8	10
Greenland, Danish mail..	7	10	4	4	6
Havana, U. S. packet*............	10	......	......	2	2
Hawaiian Islands, U. S. packet, (newspapers 1 cent per oz.)................	6	......	......	......	......
Heligoland, German mail direct...............	†12	8	8	......	......
Holland...	†10	8	4	......	......
Italy*...	5	8	4	......	......
Jamaica, U. S. packet*..	10	8	......	2	2
Japan, U. S. packet..	10	8	......	2	2
Java, British mail via Southampton.............................	28	16	6	4	8
Jerusalem, German mail direct.................................	†11	8	7	6	8
Mexico, U. S. packet (by sea)...................................	10	......	3	2	3
Panama, U. S. packet*..	10	8	......	2	2
Paraguay, U. S. packet (c).....................................	18	......	......	......	......
Russia, German mail direct......................................	10	8	6	3	6
Spain, German mail direct.......................................	11	8	6	3	6
St. Helena, British mail via Southampton......................	28	16	4	4	8
Sweden and Norway, by direct steamer from U. S'..............	†5	8	2	2	4
Switzerland, via England..	†5	8	4	2	4

* Denotes that the postage is the United States postage only, which must be prepaid, or sent and collected on matter received.

† Denotes that the prepayment of postage is optional; in all other cases it is compulsory.

(a) Printed matter is subject to the same rates of postage and same conditions of prepaid printed matter exchanged with Mexico by sea.

(b) Denotes that the postage is the domestic rate on correspondence of the the third class.

(c) Newspapers, irrespective of weight, 4 cents.

REMARKS.

Great Britain and Ireland—Letters wholly unpaid, or insufficiently pre-paid, are, on delivery, in addition to the deficient postage, subject to a fine of 6 cents in the United States and in Great Britain. Book manuscript and corrected proof may be sent at book-packet postage.

Germany—Letters wholly unpaid are charged, on delivery, double the postage of prepaid letters, and insufficiently prepaid letters, double the postage on prepaid letters, deducting the amount prepaid.

Canada and Prince Edward's Island—The Dominion of Canada comprises the Provinces of Ontaaio and Quebec, Nova Scotia, New Brunswick, Manitoba and British Columbia.

LEADING LOCAL EVENTS, 1875.

JANUARY.

1st. Sixteenth annual feast of the newsboys and bootblacks given by Mr. John W. Pittock at old City Hall. Total indebtedness of Allegheny City, $1,547,500; total deposits, $576 02.

2d. Common Pleas Court issues an alternative writ of mandamus on Mayor Blackmore, commanding him to issue a proclamation for a new election or show cause why he should not.

4th. District Court changed to Common Pleas No. 2 in accordance with provisions of the new State Constitution.

5th. Supreme Court affirms the judgment of the court below in the case of Ernest Orcwein, the convicted murderer of the Hammett family.

6th. Judge John Farrar, of Washington county, dies.

7th. Business men of the two cities meet at. Lafayette hall to devise a means of remedy sor the prostrated condition of the country's industries.

8th. The Allegheny Trust Co. Suspends. Commissioner-elect Lashell applies for a writ of quo warranto on Commissioner Stuckrath to show by what warrant he holds office beyond his regular term. Court considers the case and decides in favor of Mr. Lashell.

12th. The Grand Lodge of the American Order of United Workingmen holds a convention at Lafayette Hall.

13. The Chamber of Commerce memorializes the Legislature in the matter of the oil refining interests.

18th. Signor Alonza Viti, Italian Vice Consul at Philrdelphia, visits the city to enquire into the form of procedure to be taken by the courts in the matter of the American miners' riots at Buena Vista.

19th. Alderman Louis Hagar dies. The deceased served through the late war attained the rank of Major. Was at the time of his death a member of the Duquesne Grays, and held a Colonel's commission.

20th. John Ross, former Secretary of the City Water Commission, dies.

25th. Major Wm. Wade dies at his residence Allegheny.

26th. Great destruction by ice gorge in the Ohio river at Cincinnati. A number of Pittsburgh coal fleets lost.

28th. Non-official copy of the proclamation for a new municipal election published. The mayoralty matter was, at this juncture, in a perplexing shape. Wm. C. McCarthy, the Republican nominee, was elected to succeed Mayor Blackmore on the third Tuesday of February, 1874. The Democrats, who were defeated, raised a question as to the proper time, under the new State Constitution, for electing. An investigation together with legal opinions from members of the city bar brought them to the conclusion that the election had been premature—that it should have been held on the third Tuesday of February, 1875. The Republicans, representing the McCarthy faction, also prrcured opinions, one from the State Attorney-General pronouncing the election legal. When the proper time came Mr. McCarthy took his

seat. Meanwhile the Democrats had been arranging for a new election and nominated Chrisoopher Magee for the office of Mayor. A mandamus on Mayor Blackmore, requests, petition and legal notifications, the issuing of an unofficial proclamation, were all resorted to before Mayor B. was induced to proclaim for the new election. This he did finally, and Mr. Magee was elected without opposition, the Republicans standing aloof from the proceeding.

80th. Edward Carr, for the murder of Thos. Dolan, sentenced six years and ten months to the penitentiary.

FEBRUARY.

1st. Mayor-elect McCarthy takes his seat.

2d. The County Grand Jury fails lo make out an indictment in the Buena Vista riot cases. The Westmoreland County Grand Jury takes the matter in hand. Ex-Mayor Blackmore applie s to court for a writ of quo warranto on Mayor McCarthy to show by what warrant he holds office.

4th. Forty employes of the Columbia Conduit Co. arrested at Powers' run at the instance of the Pennsylvania Railroad Company on a charge of promoting a riot. They were discharged on their own recognizances.

6th. Annual report of the County Workhouse Superintendent shows 2,236 prisoners confined in the institution during the year.

7th. Captain Dempsey's stable at Milvalle, with twenty-five race and draught horses burned.

8th. Ex-Mayor Blackmore dies.

10th. The Chamber of Commerce meets and takes measures toward raising funds for the relief of the Kansas and Nebraska Grasshopper sufferers.

11th. South Side residents take measures toward seceding from the city. Democrats of the city nominate Christopher Magee for Mayor.

13th. East End residents petition for a separation from the city on account of excessive taxation.

15th. Hon. Webster Craig, of Cross Creek, Washington county, dies.

16th. The Refiners' Association and the Chamber of Commerce advise the passage by the Legislature of a Free Pipe bill.

18th. The jury in the case of Max Schamberg, indicted for libelling Col. Bayne, renders a verdict of not guilty.

23d. Ernest Ortwein, the murderer of the Hammett family, hanged. The Grand Jury of Westmoreland county iudicts Charles H. Armstrong and Frederick Gussetti for inciting the Buena Vista riots.

24th. State Supreme Court affirms the judgment of the court below in the case of Kitty Roup vs. the City of Pittsburgh, involving the right of the city to collect more than two-thirds of the taxes assessed in the rural wards, decision being in favor of Miss Roup. $3,867 16 raised in the two cities and forwarded to the Kansas and Nebraska grasshopper sufferers. Will of Ortwein, the murderer, filed in the Register's office, bequeathing certain of his interest in the paternal estate in Germany to his counsel as fees.

25th. $25,090 worth of property destroyed by fire at Irwin station. Dr. A. G. McCandless dies.

LEADING LOCAL EVENTS, 1875.

CONTINUED.

27th. Legislative Appropriation Committee visits the city to inspect the several State institutions which have called for enlargement and improvement.

28th. Autopsy on the body of Orwein, the Hammett murderer. The brain weighs 52½ ounces.

MARCH.

1st. Grand Jury of Westmoreland county indict John H. Watson, Ferd Thompson, James Boon, Larimer Douglass and Michael Pecci, as principals in the murder of the Italians in the miners' riot at Buena Vista.

2d. Puddlers meet in Old City Hall and determine to continue the strike. No funds in the city treasury.

3d. Colored puddlers, from Virginia, take the place of the strikers at the Pittsburgh Bolt works.

7th. First death of the season from Small-pox takes place in Allegheny.

8th. City Controller's annual report shows a city debt of 813,500,000.

16th. Survivors of the Pittsburgh and California Enterprise Co., (Forty-niners) reunite. Councils authorize a loan of $125,000 to pay interest on bonds issued under the Penn Avenue act.

17th. St. Patrick's Day, Grand parade of Irish citizens.

18th. Thirty-seventh ward, by decree of court, withdraws from the city. The residents of this ward, anxious to free themselves from the burden of city taxation, employed counsel to examine the petition, which had caused the ward to be created, to see if it was up to the requirements of the law. It was fund to lack the necessary number of signatures, on which grounds the above decree was made.

22. Christopher Magee applies to court for a mandamus to compel Councils to swear him in as Mayor.

24th. Board of Revision rescinds the ten per cent. reduction on property valuation.

29th. Alexander Chambers, a well-known glass manufacturer, dies. Joseph Lansbury, the murderer of Col. Black, U. S. Provost Marshal of Clearfield county, in 1864, arrested and brought to the city for trial.

APRIL.

2d. County valuation placed at $305,000,000.

3d. William Murray and Frederick Myers sentenced to be hanged for the murder of Gotthardt Wahl.

7th. Centennial Tea Party held at Library Hall. Striking puddlers resume work at the Keystone Iron mills.

12th. Allegheny Councils pass ordinances requiring Street and Police Committees to find employment for tramps.

14th. Public outlays of the city for educational purposes for the year 1874, $284,820 00.

15th. The puddler's strike ends, Iron Association agreeing to pay $5.50 per ton. First prosecution under the Civil Rights bill, entered in the Circuit Court by Boston Laney, (colored) vs. the proprietor of the St. Cloud hotel, for refusing Laney the accommodations of his establishment.

16th. The Ohio river Improvement Commission decides to construct a series of moveable dams, commencing at Davis' Island, at an estimated cost of $750,000.

17th. Philip Murray convicted in the Oyer and Terminer Court of the murder of James White, at Zug's mill.

19th. Old U. S. Marine Hospital property sold for $33,000.

20th. Ann Eliza, nineteenth wife of Brigham Young, lectures at Sloan's station, on the Pan Handle railroad.

22d. Ex-Mayor's clerk, James S. Patterson, dies.

23d. The Taxpayers' Union recommends the sale of the water works to a corporation. The steamer Exporter, of Pittsburgh, burned at New Orleans. Mrs. Musgrave, daughter of Jas. Rees, captain and owner of the boat, lost.

25th. The county workhouse partially destroyed by fire.

30th. The Grand Lodge, Knights of Pythias, hold a special session in the city. The "Bond of Friendship" case, involving a question as to the legality of a document, purporting to have been signed by James Cully, deceased, which bequeathes $75,000 to Robert D. Clark, decided in the latter's favor.

MAY.

1st. Martin Ammon, of the South Side, killed in a row in Sorg's saloon.

4th. Messrs. Lucky, Davis and Dickson elected superintendents of the public schools of Pittsburgh, Allegheny and Allegheny county, respectively.

6th. Rody Patterson, a well-known liveryman, dies at his residence in Chartiers township.

7th. G. H. Price, Adams express messenger, shoots and kills a robber, who attempted to rob the safe in his care on the Ft. Wayne road.

12th. National Temperance convention meets in the second Presbyterian church.

13. John Hamill elected Chief Engineer of the city Fire department, and Henry Evans Assistant Chief. Westmoreland county Centennial held at Greensburg.

22d. A committee from the Woman's Temperance Alliance calls on the Mayor, and requests that Sunday liquor selling be stopped.

26th. Capt. Theodore Bogaley, a well-known coal merchant, dies. Republican State convention, in session at Lancaster, re-nominates Hartranft for Governor and Henry Rawle, of Erie, for State Treasurer.

28th. Steamers Mollie Ebbert and Juniata destroyed by fire at the Monongahela wharf. The Buena Vista rioters tried at Greensburg and found guilty.

29th. Decoration Day. Military, in small force, turns out and aids in decorating soldiers' graves in Allegheny cemetery.

31st. Nation Trust Co. stockholders make a proposition to the city to compromise their indebtedness at 40 per cent; Edward O'Connor, a Washington county farmer, killed by his insane son.

JUNE.

1st. Democrats hold conventions to elect delegates to the State convention at Erie, resulting in favor of the Hopkins faction.

LEADING LOCAL EVENTS, 1875.

CONTINUED

4th. Thomas Slavin, the alleged murderer of Benjamin Lynch, at West Elizabeth, in January, 1874, arrested at Wilkesbarre and brought to the city. Tried and adjudged not guilty,

8th. American Society of Civil Engineers holds its seventh annual convention in the city.

9th. Alex. McIlwaine, a well-known auctioneer dies of injuries received by a fall from a moving train.

11th. Beltzhoover borough, in Lower St. Clair township, incorporated.

12th. W. D. Moore, attorney, recovers $10,000 from the Pittsburgh Post, for alleged libel. The verdict was appealed to the Supreme Court. The Brilliant oil works, at Negley's run, destroyed by fire. Loss, $218,000.

15th. Republican county convention nominates Joseph H. Gray for Register and Clerk of Orphans' court, Ralph Richardson for Recorder and Wm. C. McCleary for Clerk of Quarter Sessions court.

17th. The prize fight, proposed between Tom Allen and George Rooke, ends in a failure on the part of the principals to come together.

18th. The Messenger of the German American bank decamps with $3,000 of the bank funds.

19th. Bowen's hardware manufactory, on Wood street. destroyed by fire, occasioning a loss of $75,000.

22d. Democratic county convention nominates R. H. Patterson for Sheriff, Alex. McFarland for Register and Clerk of Orphans' court, Wm. Giles for Recorder and J. P. O'Niell for Clerk of the court of Quarter Sessions.

23d. The steel works of Hussey, Dravo & Co. destroyed by fire. Finance committee agree to allow the Nation Bank Co. four years to cancel their indebtedness with the city at 40 per cent.

24th. Information made against the Pittsburgh and Oakland and the South Side Street railways for nuisance in obstructing Fourth avenue. Mrs. Elizabeth Swisshelm, one of the oldest residents of the county, dies, at her residence at Swissvale.

25th. School children's jubilee in West Park, Allegheny.

30th. Two little daughters of Mrs. Mitchell, of Saltsburg, accidentally ignite their clothing and are burned alive in their mother's absence.

JULY.

2d. The Anti-Treating Society, an organization having for its motto "every man pay for his own drink," holds its first meeting in Municipal hall.

5th. The anniversary of the Declaration of Independence celebrated.

7th. Indignation in the temperance element at the action of the county Grand Jury, which ignores nine-tenths of the liquor cases brought before it, and puts the costs on the prosecutors.

8th. Richard H. Fife nominated by the Republicans for Sheriff. An unknown tramp shot dead at Braddock's Fields by a resident while attempting to break into his dwelling.

10th. The Mayor refuses to license Ben Hogan to give sparring exhibitions in the city. The annual review of the City Fire Department had on the Monongahela wharf.

11th. James Geist, a convict in the penitentiary, attempts to cut his throat. The orangemen parade the streets. The Pittsburgh Boltworks suspends and makes an assignment.

12th. Mr. A. W. Black committed to jail for unpaid costs on liquor cases, ignored by the Grand Jury, in which he was prosecutor. After languishing in confinement over night the costs were paid, and he was released.

13th. A terrible storm of wind and rain causes great damage to property in the city and vicinity.

15th. Seven hundred and fifty Mormons pass through the city en route to Utah.

16th. Property holders on the line of Washington and Brownsville avenues protest against the city issuing more bonds for the avenues' improvement.

19th. Corner-stone of the new German Evangelical Lutheran church laid.

23d. Four dwellings destroyed by incendiary fires at Braddock's Fields.

24. Mr. T. S. Baird, shoe dealer of Allegheny, charges four of the deputy Sheriffs with having purloined some of his goods during the progress of a sale of his stock by the Sheriff. The cases were ignored by the Grand Jury.

26th. Anniversary of the great Butcher's Run flood in 1874.

28th. Re-union of the Ninth Reserves held at M'Keesport.

29th. Mr. Edward Rahm, a well-known banker, dies.

30th. Robert S. Gatchell, a well-known printer, jumps from the suspension bridge and is drowned.

AUGUST.

1st. Heavy freshet in the Monongahela. The steamer Elector carried against the Smithfield street bridge and badly damaged.

7th. The O'Connel Centennary celebrated by citizens of Irish nationality. The Penn'a railroad decides to furnish its conductors with pocketless uniforms, substituting satchels as receptacles for money and tickets, instead of pockets. The sentence of Ambrose E. Lynch, the murderer of Hatfield, commuted from hanging to imprisonment for life.

2d. The Phœnix rolling-mill destroyed by fire.

13th. The police make a raid on the Shakspeare house, East Liberty, a place of questionable resort, and arrests forty-three persons, who are fined by the mayor.

18th. Dr. Arnold Hurtz found dead in bed.

21st. Dave Hall, an Allegheny saloon-keeper, shoots and severely wounds constable J. J. Hays, in the county jail yard.

23. —— Beynon —— Watson, engineer and fireman at Painter's mill, killed by the explosion of a boiler.

26th. Alexander Gibson, a twelve year old lad, abducted from his home in Allegheny, by a tramp, and after a lapse of two days escapes and returns.

27th. Jessie York, a servant girl in the employ of Mr. Bausman, at Hazelwood, burned to death while using carbon oil for kindling purposes.

LEADING LOCAL EVENTS, 1875.

CONTINUED.

28th. Rev. John A. Peck, a well-known colored minister, dies.

31st. Cimiotti's pawn shop entered and robbed of all its contents.

SEPTEMBER.

1st. Rev. Dr. Noble, of the Third Presbyterian Church, receives a call from New Haven, Con., and decides to resign.

2d. Wm. Green, colored, shoots and kills his half brother Thomas Marshall, at Mansfield. He is captured near Freedom, Beaver Co.

9th. Democratic State Convention meets at Erie, and nominates Cyrus L. Pershing for Governor and Victor E. Piolett for State Treasurer. Colored citizens hold camp meeting at Castle Shannon.

11th. The sculling contest between Morris and Coulter, on the Allegheny river. Won by the former by four boat lengths.

14th. The Westmoreland County court acquits Douglass, Watson and Ford, indited for implication in the Beuua Vista miners' riot.

15th. Jacob Ewart, a well-known merchant, dies.

20th. Miss Mary Jones, of the South Side, shot and fatally injured by the accidental discharge of a revolver in the hands of a companion.

21st. Rev. Dr. Strong inaugurated president of the Pennsylvania Female College.

23d. Senator Morton, of Indiana, speaks at Lafayette Hall.

24th. Twenty prisoners in the Washington County jail overpower the Sheriff and make an ineffectual attempt to escape.

OCTOBER.

4th. An injunction is served on McKee Rankin, actor, by judge Ewing, at the instance of Shook & Palmer, of New York, restraining him from playing the "Two Orphans," at the Academy of Music. Two thousand dollars worth of plate stolen from the Nickel establishment of Walter Hogne. The Pittsburgh bolt works are sold to Gerry, Tilton & Caldwell.

5th. Slaven indited for the murder of Daniel Lynch, is tried and acquitted, having proved an *alibi*.

6th. The opening of the Exposition postponed till Saturday. The horse disease in a mild form again appears.

8th. Puddlers in some of the mills notified that a reduction of their wages will be in order.

9th. The Exposition opens. Bell punch placed on Wylie avenue car line.

10th. Rev. F. A. Noble preaches his farewell sermon in the Third Presbyterian Church.

11th. The managers of the Exposition oust beer sellers from the basement.

13th. The steel rail manufacturers close a lengthy conference session at the Monongahela House. Stedeford & Eicbeis' planing mill in Manchester destroyed by fire. Loss, $12,000.

14th. The Chippewa Indians leave the city for Washington to hold a conference with President Grant.

15th. The funeral of W. H. Brown, coal king, takes place from the Union depot.

16th. A second race between Morris and Coulter ever the Allegheny river course at Hulton, is won by the former.

18th. Prof. Grimly ascends in a baloon, and after a dangerous voyage lands in Beck's Run.

19th. Dr. Fronk, the leader of a gang of counterfeiters, is found guilty on six indictments.

20th. Fred. Swett and Joseph McClurg, of this city, were drowned on the Kankakee river, in Illinois.

22d. Senator Wallace and Victor E. Piolette address Democratic meeting at Lafayette Hall.

23d. The Republican torch light procession attended by riot. No one seriously injured.

25th. Governor Allen, of Ohio, and Governor Hartranft arrive in the city.

26th. Joseph Sotto, a saloon keeper, enters suit against the Exposition managers for alleged violation of an agreement to allow him to sell beer in the building. The Evangelical Conference holds its opening session.

27th. In the Hopkins McIlroy sculling contest the former won.

30th. A temporary compromise at $5 a ton is made by the manufacturers and puddlers.

NOVEMBER.

1st. The application for a new trial in the cases of Murray and Meyers refused by the Supreme Court.

2d. Election for Governor, State Treasurer and county officers held.

4th. A number of produce merchants swindled by the representations of a man giving his name as John Collins, and purporting to be a shipper in the interests of commission merchants.

8th. The stermer Tigress No. 2 exploded boiler near Sewickley, and kills two men. Prof. De Long is convicted in the U. S. Court of using the mails for circulating immoral matter, and is sentenced to pay $500 fine and to two years imprisonment in the penitentiary.

6th. Rolling mill proprietors at Etna make a successful transfer of gas from Millerstown, Butler County, to their furnaces.

8th. The house of G. F. Ebbert, at Dawson station, burglarized of $1,800.

9th. Dr. Hugo Schilling, a druggist on Mt. Oliver, commits suicide by shooting. John Newell, a convicted gamester, pardoned by Governor Hartranft.

11th. The Coroner's jury on the investigation of the causes of the fatal explosion on the steamer Tigress No. 2, implicate the engineer, on grounds of incompetency.

13th. Lansburry on trial in the U. S. Court for the murder of provost marshall Butler, in Clearfield County, in 1864, is acquitted. The Exposition closes after a successful run of five weeks.

14th. Mrs. Woodhull lectures at the Academy of Music.

15th. Colored prisoners revolt in the penitentiary. They are quelled by the Deputy Warden.

16th. Fire occasions a damage of $75,000 at Irwin's Station.

17th. A pickpocket on the Philadelphia express, name unknown, dropped dead shortly after stealing a lady's pocket book

LEADING LOCAL EVENTS, 1875.

CONTINUED.

18th. The B. & O. Railway compromises with the county the indebtedness of the Connellsville branch.

19th. Governor Hartranft signs the death warrants of Murray and Myers. The time for their execution is fixed at January 6th.

20th. The judges on the competitive exhibition of plans for the improvement of the Ohio river award in favor of Felix R. Brunot. Jenkins, indited for the murder of Thomas, was found guilty of murder in the second degree.

22d. The National Trust Company effects a compromise with the county, wherein its indebtedness is to be liquadated in four years.

24th. A fire at McKeesport occasions a loss of $15,000. Thomas Gatewood, a post office clerk, (colored) is charged with purloining a letter, and after a hearing committed for trial.

25th. Thanksgiving Day. Lizzie Johnston, aged four years, is burned to death at her home on North street, 17th Ward.

26th. The Supreme Court adjournes.

27th. Miss Elizabeth Scott, of Penn Township, was accidently shot, and died of her injuries.

29th. Application made to the board of pardons for a commutation of the sentence of Frederick Myers, convicted of the murder of Gotthardt Wahl.

30th. Allegheny Common Council votes down a resolution to provide labor for tramps.

DECEMBER.

1st. Two men by the names of Williams and Robinson are arrested at Foxburg on a charge of robbing Adams Express Company of $1,000. Sheriff elect Fife files his bonds of office.

2d. A meeting of Dairymen to regulate the price of milk, held at the Union Depot Hotel.

3d. The business returns of the county for the year amount to $20,265,530.

4th. Gatewood, colored clerk in the post office, who was charged with purloining a money letter, is acquitted of the charge by U. S. Commissioner Gamble.

5th. A report to the effect that Charlie Ross, the abducted boy, was living in the vicinity of Kittanning. Armstrong county is investigated and found to be without foundation.

6th. Mrs. Stoner, of Allegheny, is burned to death by a lamp explosion.

8th. Centennial of the Estalishment of Presbyterianism in Western Pennsylvania is celebrated by the Presbyterian Church.

9th. The Board of Pardons recommends the pardon of Dr. Hunter, confined in the Workhouse for an assault upon Dr. Floyd.

10th. Allegheny Councils extend the time for the removal of the stock-yards to a more isolated locality.

11th. The Lawrenceville and Evergreen Railway purchased by the Pittsburgh and Northwestern Railroad Company. Manufacturers and puddlers compromise on $4 75 per per ton for one month.

13th. The ministers of the two cities, with others, meet and appoint a committee to organize a general society of all churches to relieve destitution. Charles Armstrong and Frederick Guscetti convicted of aggravated riot are sentenced by the Westmoreland county court to pay $5 each and costs.

14th. The Sheriff called upon to protect laboring miners at Keilling's coal works from the violence of strikers. No demonstration made.

15th. The Allegheny Presbytery resolves to transmit to the Presbytery of Cayuga, New York, a copy of the address of Dr. Hopkins at the Biennial Conference here, with a disapproval of its context.

16th. A delegation of twenty laboring men visit the Allegheny Mayor's office and petition him to provide them with work. A citizens' meeting to devise means of relief was the result.

17th. Organization of the "Lord Lytton Bulwer Literary Association." W. F. Hanrahan, Secretary and Treasurer.

18th. A colored woman and a man, name unknown, killed on the Ft. Wayne road at Jack's run, in the same instant, by the fast mail. Messrs. Heath & White, coal operators, announce their desire to deliver coal to the poor of both cities, through the winter, free of charge.

20th. A million dollars estimated as necessary to complete the new water works. The Annual Institute of Teachers of Allegheny City and county open,

21st. Suit entered by the Allegheny Valley Railroad against the estate of Col. Phillips to recover $357,527 40.

22d. Mrs. Marian Love of Edgeworth station had both legs taken off by a train and died of her injuries.

23d. The Committee on the Ohio river improvement makes its report, condemning all moveable dams and recommending wing dams (chutes) and the dredging plans.

24th. A committee of fifty citizens of Allegheny, appointed by Mayor Phillips to improvise an entertainment for means to relieve the poor. Edward Everson, a Pittsburgh riverman, killed on the boat Mary Ann by Charles Wilson.

25. Christmas. Church festivals the order of the day.

27th. Chief-of-Government Engineer Humphreys recommends "draws" on the bridges of the Allegheny river, which are said to interfere with navigation.

28th. Isaac Mills, Sr., of Braddocksfields, was assaulted and dangerously injured by two men, names unknown.

30th. The $100,000 endowment fund, contribution to the Western University by Wm. Thaw, conditional that a like amount be secured on outside contributions, is secued, the condition having been complied with.

Leading Events of the World.

JANUARY.

1st. Mrs. J. Lothrop Motley, wife of the historian, died.

4th. The Select Committee on the Condition of the South arrived in New Orleans. The Louisiana Legislature organized. Gen. Sheridan assumed command of the Department of the Gulf.

7th. Congress passed the Senate bill for the resumption of specie payment.

12th. Ex-Governor Bramlette, of Kentucky, died.

19th. The House Committee on Elections reported in favor of the expulsion of George Q. Carrion, delegate from Utah.

FEBRUARY.

22d. Sir Charles Lyle, an eminent English geologist, died.

25th. The falling of the roof of St. Andrews' church, New York, kills five persons and injures three others.

MARCH.

1st. M. Buffet elected President of the French Assembly.

2d Gen. Lorenzo Thomas died at Washington.

3d. The Senate bill for the admission of Colorado as a State passed by Congress.

4th. News in London of the wreck of the steamer Gothenburg in Bass' Straits, between Van Dieman's Land and Australia; eighty-eight persons lost.

5th. The Senate of the 44th Congress met in extra session and postponed action on the admission of Pinchback, Senator from Louisiana. Godlove S. Orth was confirmed as Minister to Austria, and Horace Maynard as Minister to Turkey. The Convention between Spain and the United States for the settlement of the Virginius affair was signed.

7th. Sir Arthur Helps, author of "Friends in Council" died in London.

10th. The new treaty with Belgium was ratified.

16th. A new Ecclesiastical bill was introduced into the Prussian Diet. It withdraws State grants from the Roman Catholic Bishops, and deprives the priests of any share in the administration of local church property.

20th. John Mitchell, representative in Parliament from Tipperary, Ireland, died.

APRIL.

23d. Three steamers burned at the New Orleans levee. Fifty lives lost.

28th. Destructive fire at Oshkosh, Wisconsin. A square mile of the city laid in ruins. Loss over $2,000,000.

MAY.

1st. Explosion at Bunker Hill colliery, North Staffordshire, England. Forty-one lives lost.

5th. News in London of a mutiny on board the schooner Jefferson Borman from New Orleans. First and second mrtes killed. Four of the mutineers severely wounded; afterwards placed in irons.

7th. Wreck of the steamship Schiller in a fog on the Retarriere Ledge, near Bishop's Rock, Scilly Island, off the Cornwall Coast. She was bound from Hamburg to New York. Three hundred and eleven persons were drowned, including the captain, John G. Thomas. A bill was passed by the New York Legislature providing for the suspension of delinquent State officers by the government, and for their removal upon conviction by a majority of the Senate.

10th. Ehe centennial anniversary of Fort Tieoderoga by Col. Ethan Allen was celebrated.

18th. Earthquake in New Granada. Six cities destroyed. Sixteen thousand lives lost.

20th. Fire at Osceola, Pa. Two hundred and fifty houses destroyed. Loss, $2,000,000. The centenary of the Mecklinburg Independence was celebrated at Charlotte, North Carolina.

15th. Attorney General of the United States Williams' resignation took effect. Judge Edwards Pierrepoint was appointed his successor.

24th. Intelligence in London of the sinking of an Austrian ferry boat in the Tyrol, with Catholic pilgrims aboard.

26th. The Pennsylvania Republican Convention at Lancaster, re-nominated General Hartranft for Governor, and passed resolutions disapproving of the election of President Grant for a third term. Explosion of a drug store in Boston. Six persons killed and three seriously injured.

27th. The French Catholic church at Holyoke, Mass., during the celebration of the feast of Corpus Christi, was burned. Seventy-five lives lost.

30th. The steamer Vicksburg, bound for Liverpool from Montreal, went down in a field of ice. Eighty-three lives lost.

JUNE.

2d. The Ohio Republican Convention, at Columbus, nominated ex-Governor R. B. Hayes for Governor, and in its platform opposed a division of the school fund.

3d. Sixty persons drowned by the capsizing of a lighter on the Tagus, in Portugal.

6th. M. Charles de Remusat, author and statesman, died in France.

14th. Samuel G. Drake, historian and antiquarian, died in Boston.

16th. Explosion of a manufactory of fireworks in Boston. Six persons killed and three seriously injured. Gen. Garribaldi's bill for the improvement of the Tiber passed the Italian Chamber of Deputies.

17th. The Ohio Democratic Convention, at Columbus, re-nominated Gov. Wm. Allen.

24. Rear Admiral DeCamp died at New Jersey. The British House of Lords passed the Canadian Copy-right bill to a second reading.

25. Mortimer Thompson, "Q. K. Philander Doesticks," died in New York.

Leading Events of the World.

CONTINUED.

29th. Ferdinand I, ex-Emperor of Austria, died, aged 82 years. The American rifle team won the rifle match at Dollymount, Ireland, the score for the Americans being 968 against 929 for the Irish. Count Von Arnim was convicted by the Prussian Court of intentionally abstracting state papers, of the character of public deeds intrusted to him, and sentenced to nine months imprisonment. Immense destruction of life and property was caused by the floods in France. Two hundred and sixteen persons were drowned at Toulouse. The damage to that city and to Ager was estimated at $20,000,000.

JULY.

5th. Collision on South Side Rail road between two trains near Kor Rockaway, Long Island. Seven persons killed, six fatally and twenty-two seriously injured. The steamer Lumberman, while returning from Fortress Monroe with a pleasure party of eighteen aboard, was run down by the steamship Isaac Bell, off Sewell's point, and sank in fifty feet of water. Nine of the company were drowned.

7th. J. E. Caines, professor of political economy in the London University, died in London.

8th. Gen. Frank P. Blair died in St. Louis.

18th. Lady Jane Franklin, widow of Sir John Franklin, the Artic Explorer, died in England, aged 70 years.

OCTOBER.

21—23d. Heavy gales off the Scottish coast. Five vessels lost with their crews.

26th. Great fire in Virginia City, Nevada. Business portion of the city completely destroyed. Estimated loss $4,000,000.

27th. The German Parliament opened. The Emperor was absent on account of an indisposition. His speech, read by the Minister of State, declared that peace was now more assured than at any time preceding the reconstruction of the Empire.

29th. Hon, Amasa Walker, of Brookfield, Mass., died.

NOVEMBER.

4th. The steamship Pacific founded between San Francisco and Portland. Nearly two hundred lives lost. The French Assembly reassembled and adopted M. Buffet's motion to discuss the Electoral bill. On the 11th the Ministorial party gained a triumph in the vote relating to the method of voting. Gambetta unsuccessfully urged the adoption of universal suffrage.

7th. Wreck of the British ship Calcutta, from Quebec to Liverpool, on Grosse Isle. Twenty-three lives lost.

9th. The steamship City of Waco burned off Galveston bar. Nearly seventy lives lost.

8th. The Prince of Wales, who is visiting India, was accorded a grand reception on landing at Bombay. Over 200,000 spectators witnessed the procession which escorted him to the Government house.

11th. Explosion of fire damp in a Belgian colliery. Over forty lives lost.

15th. News in London of the wreck of the British ship Astrida near Boulogne, France. Nine lives lost.

18th. Railway disaster between Stockholm and Malmo, Denmark. Sixty passengers killed or severely wounded.

21st. U. S. Senator Orris S. Terry died in Norwalk, Connecticut.

22. Vice President Henry Wilson died, aged 64 years.

MISCELLANEOUS.

HOW TO COUNT INTEREST.—Four per cent. Multiply the principal by the number of days, separate the right hand figure from the product and divide by nine.

Five per cent—Multiply number of days and divide by seventy-two.

Six per cent—Multiply by number of days, separate right hand figure and divide by six.

Eight per cent—Multiply by number of days and divide by forty-five.

Nine per cent—Multiply by number of days, separate right hand figure and divide by four.

Ten per cent—Multiply by number of days and divide by thirty-six.

Twelve per cent—Multiply by number of days, separate right hand figure and divide by three.

Fifteen per cent—Multiply by number of days and divide by twenty-four.

LEAP YEAR.—Every year the number of which is divisible by four without a remainder is a leap-year, except the last year of the century, which is a leap year only when divisible by four without a remainder. The year 1900 will not be leap-year.

JOSEPH GUIBORD was buried in the Catholic cemetery, Cote des Neiges, in Montreal, November 16. The coffin was laid in a bed of cement, to preclude the possibility of its removal. Guibord died in 1869. He was a printer, and as a member of the Institut Canadien had been excommunicated from the church. His remains were refused admission to consecrated ground. His wife applied to the Superior court for an order to compel the church to allow his burial in his own lot in the above cemetery. The order was granted by the Queen's Privy council, November 28, 1874. Previous to the final execution of the order (November 16) an attempt was made to bury him, but it occasioned a riot and was postponed.

IT HAS been until lately a rule of the British House of Commons that when attention was drawn by any member to the presence of strangers, the latter should be expelled. This rule was so far modified last May as to cause a division of the House on the question of expulsion.

MISCELLANEOUS—Continued.

PUTRIFACTION ARRESTED BY PRESSURE.—A communication to the Paris Academy of Science, by M. Paul Bert, on the "Influence of Air-Pressure on Fermentation," a summary of which appears in the *Academy*, states that a piece of meat placed in oxygen, with a pressure of twenty-three atmospheres, remained from July 26th to August 3d without putrescence or bad odor. It consumed in that time 380 cubic centimetres of the gas. A similar piece, suspended in a bell-glass full of air at the ordinary pressure, acquired a bad smell, consumed all the oxygen, amounting to 1.185 centimetres, and was covered with mould. Another trial was made with oxygen at a pressure of forty-four atmospheres; no oxygen was absorbed between December 19th and January 8th, and no bad odor was exhaled. M. Bert could eat cutlets preserved in this way for a month, and found them only a little stale in flavor. After being exposed to the air at this pressure, allowing an escape so that only normal pressure remained, the meat suffered no damage, provided the bottle was well corked, so that no external germs could enter. Thus it appears that the microferments which cause fermentation can be killed, when they are moist, by a sufficient tension of oxygen. Fermentations of milk and wine are arrested by high pressure, and fruits keep sound. Distaste continues to act as a ferment, and bodies of this description preserve their properties indifinitely if retained under pressure.

INTENSITY OF SOLAR RADIATION.—In a letter to Ste.-Claire Deville, Soret alludes incidentally to some recent optical observations which show the great intensity of solar radiation. If we look at an ordinary flame through plates of glass colored blue with cobalt, we observe that with a certain thickness of glass the flame presents a purple color, as the glass transmits the extreme red rays, and the highly-refrangible blue and violet rays, while it intercepts the rays of intermediate refrangibility. If the source of light have a high temperature, and therefore emit highly-refrangible rays, the flame appears blue, and it requires a number of superposed plates in order to develop the purple tint. Thus it was found that, at the temperature at which platinum fuses, two plates would give a purple color; at the fusion of iridium three plates were required, and on observing the sun the purple color was not developed even with half a dozen plates.

ON comparing the statistics of the German universities for the summer semester of 1874 with those of the same semester of 1875, the *Allgemeine Zeitung* finds a decrease in the number of medical students; it has fallen from 6,190 to 6,039. One of the causes of this is the fact that now Jewish students devote themselves, in great numbers, to the study of jurisprudence. Until lately, the legal career could hardly be said to be open to Jews in Germany, and hence a great number of them studied medicine.

THE THREAD on a ⅜ inch gas pipe will sustain a weight of 5,000 lbs., ½ inch, 7,000 lbs., and ¾ inch, 9,000 lbs., so that chandeliers cannot be readily shaken from their supports.

LUTHER'S HOUSE AND WIFE.—The house at Eisenach, says Dr. Stoughton, bears Luther's name; part of it has been turned into a shop, where is sold a little pamphlet, containing a rude woodcut, with a curious history of the building. It appears to have been occupied by an order of German knights since Luther's time, memorials of which circumstance remain in rude bas-reliefs and Biblical inscriptions. Two or three years ago Luther's name had not been placed over the door; I was told no relics of him were preserved within. But on my last visit I found it had become a show house, and a party of us were conducted up a dark old staircase on the left-hand side round the corner, to a room leading into another apartment through a door of lattice-work. The woman who showed the house maintained that Luther slept in the inner room when a boy. In answer to inquiries as to the authority for such a statement, she averred that the Grand Duke supported it, and approved of the room being shown, which he would not do, she naively remarked, if the tradition were not correct. There was no resisting this. But more interesting to readers will be the description of Luther's wife in her burial attire. Of this lady Dr. Stoughton writes: "Some say she was not attractive in appearance, and certain portraits to be seen in Germany might confirm that notion; but other portraits, when carefully examined, suggest a different idea, and make me think she must have been a pleasant looking person. I have just discovered a passage in the 'Venetian Correspondence,' which supports the favorable view. Francesco Contarini, writing on the 2d of November, 1535, describes his visit to Wittenberg, and an interview he had with Agricola, Spalatin, and others. He observes that Luther remained at home with his wife, who was a nun, and, according to their account, a very handsome and virtuous young woman." The finger and thumb rings, and the profusion of chains and embroidery, shown in her portrait, are hardly in accordance with the asceticism of some of Luther's followers.

DISPROPORTION OF THE SEXES IN GERMANY —The proportion of males to females in the population of the German Empire appears to be steadily declining In 1855 the excess of females over males in what is now the German Empire was 348,631, which declined in the following nine years of peace to 313,383 in 1864. At the end of 1866, that is, after the Schleswig-Holstein and Austrian Wars, the excess was 471,885. In December, 1871, the effects of the war with France was shown in an ascertained surplus female population of 755,875. Thus in the seven years, from 1864 to 1871, the excess of females over males in the German population had increased by no less than 14 per cent. Although no inconsiderable portion of this loss to the German male population is due to actual slaughter on the battle field, it is undoubtedly caused principally by emigration. Even if emigration could now be checked, it would take more than one generation to restore the proportion between the two sexes in Germany to what it was ten years ago.

MISCELLANEOUS—Continued.

Is CONSUMPTION CONTAGIOUS?—Some experiments and observations recently made, on the transmission of tuberculosis or phthisis from one animal to another, are worthy of note, as indicating one fruitful source of pulmonary disease. Thus it has been found that when an animal with tuberculated lungs is made the yoke-fellow of a perfectly healthy animal, and the two are housed and fed together, so as to inhale one another's breath, the one which at first was sound, before long exhibits the symptoms of tuberculosis. Again, Krebs has produced tuberculosis by giving animals milk from those which were diseased. In addition to rabbits and Guinea-pigs (which animals are very suceptible to the artificial production of the malady), he accidentally induced the disease in a dog by feeding it with milk of a cow in the last stage of phthisis. As a result of his observations, he asserts that tubercle virus is present in the milk of phthisical cows, whether they are slightly or gravely affected. On vigorous subjects such milk may produce no injurious effects, but the case is likely to be different with children, and those of enfeebled constitution. Similar effects may result from eating the flesh of animals affected with tubercle, and by inoculation with the virus. Thorough cooking of milk and flesh meat neutralizes their injurious action.

THE DRAFT of the Spanish constitution provides that the Senate shall be composed of three hundred members of the classes, viz: first, Senators by hereditary title; second, Senators elected by popular corporations; third, Senators nominated by the crown. All grandees of Spain receiving incomes of $10,000 and over, are included in the first class. For the Lower Chamber the Deputies are to be chosen for five years, one representative to every 5,000 voters. The king has the right to dissolve the Chamber and the elective portion of the Senate simultaneously, or separately, but must convoke new Chambers within three months. He appoints the President and vice President of the Senate, and has the right to veto bills. Any person arrested must be brought before a tribunal or released within seventy-two hours. Either the Cortes or the government may decree the suspension of the constitutional guarantees, but banishment of a Spaniard from his country is prohibited.

THERE IS A firm doing business in San Francisco who purchase the thousands of dogs slaughtered by the poundmaster of that city, or that may have been otherwise killed, for which they pay forty cents each. The carcasses are conveyed to their manufactory at South San Francisco, where the skins are removed and sold to the tanneries, the hair taken off and resold to plasterers, the hide tanned, made into gloves and sold in market. The denuded carcass is then thrown into a huge caldron and boiled until the bones are easily separated from the flesh, when they are removed and sold to sugar refineries, where they are ground to a fine powder and used to clarify sugar. The oil that rises to the surface of the boiling mass is skimmed off and manufactured into cod liver oil, and the remainder is used for the fattening hogs.

THIS TABLE shows the mean time at different places when it is "mean noon" at Washington, D. C. The sign (X) signifies forenoon, and (—) afternoon:

	H.	M.	S.
Albany, New York	—0	13	13
Alexandria, Egypt	—7	7	44
Berlin, Prussia	—6	1	46
Bremen, Germany	—5	43	24
Canton, China	x 0	41	48
Charleston, South Carolina	x11	48	30
Chicago, Illinois	x11	17	41
Cincinnati, Ohio	x11	30	13
Constantinople, Turkey	—7	4	8
Detroit, Michigan	x11	36	0
Dublin, Ireland	—4	42	49
Edinburg, Scotland	—4	55	28
Geneva, Switzerland	—5	32	49
Gibraltar, Spain	—4	46	48
Halifax, Nova Scotia	—0	53	47
Havana, Cuba	x11	38	47
Jeddo, Japan	x 2	28	12
Lima, Peru	x11	59	41
London, England	—5	7	34
Louisville, Kentucky	x11	26	12
Mobile, Alabama	x11	16	6
Moscow, Russia	—7	38	28
New Orleans, Louisiana	x11	8	12
Newport, Rhode Island	—0	22	58
New York City, New York	—0	12	12
Norfolk, Virginia	—0	2	58
Paris, France	—5	17	33
Pittsburgh, Pennsylvania,	x11	48	4
Quebec, Canada	—0	23	23
Richmond, Virginia	x11	58	22
Rio Janeiro, Brazil	—2	15	36
Rome, Italy	—5	53	6
Salt Lake City, Utah	x 9	39	48
San Francisco, California——	x 8	58	25
Savannah, Georgia	x11	43	51
St. Louis, Missouri	x11	7	23
St. Petersburgh, Russia	—7	9	25

AGRICULTURAL RESOURCES OF CALIFORNIA.— From the report of the Surveyor General of California, among other items of interest we find that, of the 3,254,900 acres cultivated, 2,156,000 are in wheat; 492,000 in barley; 65,000 in oats, and 40,000 acres in Indian corn. They have 25,500 acres of common potatoes, and 1,300 acres of sweet potatoes are raised. There are 580,000 acres in grass for hay. Other products are—peas, 3,000 acres; beans, 6,800; flax, 1,730; hops, 1,125; tobacco, 967; cotton, 586; onions, 860; buckwheat, 560, and peanuts 155 acres. Among the products of the year were 752,000 tons of hay; 75,000 of cotton; 16,080 of sugar beets; 10,000 of wool; 3,463 of butter; 1,700 of cheese; 673 of hops; 621 of tobacco, and 448 tons of honey produced. The State has 5,464,000 sheep; 844,000 neat cattle; 242,000 hogs; 230,000 horses; 44,000 Angora goats, and 23,000 mules. There are 144 grist mills, and 323 saw mills in the State.

POSTAL AND TELEGRAPH SERVICE.—The twenty-first annual report of the British post office has just been issued, giving the postal and telegraphic statistics for 1874. It appears that the letters sent through the post during the year was 967,000,000, besides about 79,000,000 post cards, and 259,000,000 newspapers and book packets. On an average there were 30 letters to each head of the population in the United Kingdom.

MISCELLANEOUS—Continued.

THOSE WHO HAVE TRAVELED in Spain have remarked the dirty stripes on the necks of the lovely senoras: No devout Spanish woman dares to bathe without the permission of her confessor. This aversion to cleanliness comes forward from the time of the anchorites, Sabinus Pachomimus, Beraoion and other saints of the desert, and, indeed, whole sects of that epoch condemned all ablutions as heathenish, and were lauded because they wore their clothes so long that they rotted to pieces and fell off them, or because their skins became as "pumice-stone" from the crust of dirt on it. The superstition that cleansing the body soils the soul exists, to-day, among the women of those Christian nations who have long carried on conflicts with the Mohammedans, on whom the Koran enjoins frequent ablutions. A female Bulgarian is permitted to wash only once in her life—on the day before her wedding · and in most South Sclavonian families the girls are rarely allowed a bath, the woman never. I recall with a shudder the interior of the Montenegrin huts. When a woman offered me wine she always dipped her fingers into it, the same fingers which had just been engaged in the chase, on her children's heads, or which had been gently scratching the pig, the pet of the family, which is addressed by endearing names. The adults squat or lie down, the children tumble about in the liquid manure which covers the door of the hut, and many women are blear-eyed in consequence of the creosote caused by the smoke, which can only escape through the door. The Princess Milena, as I have said, forms an exception.

AMERICAN INVENTION ABROAD.—The great American inventions, which have been adopted all over the world, are the following:

1. The cotton gin, without which, the machine, spinner, and the power loom, would be helpless.
2. The planing machine.
3. The grass mower and grain reaper.
4. The rotary printing press.
5. Navigation by steam.
6. The hot air (caloric) engine.
7. The sewing machine.
8. India rubber industry.
9. The machine manufacture of horseshoes.
10. The sand blast (for blasting.)
11. The gauge lathe.
12. The grain elevator.
13. The artificial manufacture of ice on a large scale.
14. The electro-magnet, and its practical application, by Henry and Morse.
15. The only successful composing machine for printers.

THE LIQUOR BILL of Pennsylvania during 1870 was more than sixty-five millions of dollars, a sum equal to one-third of the entire agricultural product of the State. Illinois paid more than forty-two millions, and Ohio more than fifty-eight millions. Massachusetts paid more than twenty-five millions, a sum equal to five-sixths of her agricultural products, while the liquor bill of Maine was only about four millions and a quarter.

LEAF PHOTOGRAPHY.—A very pretty amusement, especially for those who have just completed the study of botany, is the taking of leaf photographs. One very simple process is this : At any druggist's get a dime's worth of bichromate of potash. Put this in a two-ounce bottle of salt water. When the solution becomes saturated—that is, the water has dissolved as much as it will—pour off some of the clear liquid into a shallow dish; on this float a piece of ordinary writing paper till it is thoroughly moistened. Let it become nearly dry, in the dark. It should be of a bright yellow. On this put the leaf; under it a piece of soft black cloth and several sheets of newspaper. Put these between two pieces of glass (all the pieces should be of the same size), and with spring clothespins fasten them together. Expose, to a bright sun, placing the leaf so that the rays will fall upon it as nearly perpendicular as possible. In a few minutes it will begin to turn brown, but it requires from half an hour to several hours to produce a perfect print. When it has become dark enough, take it from the frame and put it in clear water, which must be changed every few minutes, till the yellow part becomes perfectly white. Sometimes the venation of the leaves will be quite distinct. By following these directions it is scarcely possible to fail, and a little practice will make perfect. The photographs, if well taken, are very pretty as well as interesting.

STATE FINANCES.—The report of · Auditor General Temple for the year ending November 30, 1875, shows the total revenues of Pennsylvania from all sources during the fiscal year to be $6,480,099 02. Balance in Treasury November 30, 1874, $1,054,551 65. Total, $7,534,650 67.

INCOME.

Among the larger items of revenue are the following:

Tax on corporation stock	$2,135,587 45
Tax on coal companies	521,729 47
Commutation of tonnage tax (Pennsvania Railroad Company)	460,000 00
Collateral inheritance tax	443,753 97
Tavern licenses	423,763 97
Retailers licenses	422,602 91
Tax on bank stock	285,671 92
Foreign insurance companies	156,460 23
Tax on loans	176,458 61
Tax on gross receipts	124,214 27
Tax on whts, wills, deeds, etc	152,133 19

Of the smaller items, there are the following:

Fines and penalties	$ 24 00
Cases of conscience	100 00

SHRUBS FROM JAPAN.—No country in the world has supplied the American want for ornamental shrubs so fully as has Japan. Within the past quarter of a century, the whole aspect of our yards and gardens has been entirely changed on this account alone. Florists, ever on the alert for novelties, have, in a great measure, dropped the old-time lilacs, snowballs, burning-bush, and Missouri currants; their places are now filled with wiegelas, forsythias, spireas, tree pæonias, duetzias, etc. We must acknowledge that the change has been for the better, for, by this radical innovation, we have flowers of every hue, with a longer season of bloom, entire hardiness, with very few exceptions, and a more compact habit of growth.

MISCELLANEOUS—Continued.

HEBREW CALENDAR FOR 1876.

5636. 1876

Tebeth, 4—January 1, Sabbath.
Shebat 1—January 27, new moon.
Shebat 15—January 10, Chamisha Assar.
Adar 1—Feb 6, new moon and Sabbath.
Adar 13—March 9, Fast of Esther.
Adar 14—March 10, Fast of Purim.
Nisan 1—March 26, new moon.
Nisan 14—April 8, Sabbath Haggadol.
Nisan 15—April 9, Passover.
Nisan 21—April 15, 7th Day of Passover.
Iyar 1—April 25, new moon.
Iyar 18—May 12, Lag B'Omer [33d day of Omer.]
Sivan 1—May 24, new moon.
Sivan 6—June 29, Shabuoth.
Tamuz 1—July 9, new moon.
Tamuz 17—July 20, Feast of Tamuz.
Ab 1—July 22, new moon.
Ab 9—July 30, Feast of Ab.
Elul 1—August 1, new moon.
Tishri 1—September 19, new year.
Tishri 3—Sept. 21, Fast of Guedaliah,
Tishri 10—Sept. 28, Day of Atonement.
Tishri 15—Oct. 3, Feast of the Tabernacles.
Tishri 21—Oct. 9, Hoshaana Rabba.
Tishri 22—Oct. 10, Shomini Azereth.
Heshvan 1—Oct. 19, new moon.
Kisler 1—November 17, new moon.
Kisler 25—December 1, Chanucca [Feast of of the Temple Dedication by the Asmoneans.
Tebeth 1—December 17, new moon.

MACCARONI is the principal food of the poorer classes of the Neapolitans. It is made of wheaten flour and the small, hard-grained wheat grown on the Black Sea, and shipped from Odessa, is considered to make the best flour for the purpose. The best maccaroni is made entirely of this hard-grained wheat; the inferior sorts are mixed with soft wheat. The wheat is ground into flour rather coarser than that intended for bread, and is kneaded for a long time in water, the object being to make a tough paste of it. After being sufficiently kneaded it is forced through a series of small holes in a plate of iron or tin. A wire passes through these holes, so that when the paste is forced through the holes it comes out in the form of a hollow tube. The kneading having made the paste very tough, the tubes retain their shape until they become dry. Different sizes of tubes are made, the smallest being called vermicelli. The Neapolitans are extremely fond of this food, especially if they can eat it with the addition of graded cheese.

TO PREVENT GLUE FROM CRACKING.—Glue frequently cracks because of the dryness of the air in rooms warmed by stoves. An Austrian contemporary recommends the addition of a little chloride of calcium to glue to prevent this disagreeable property of cracking. Chloride of calcium is such a delinquescent salt that it attracts enough moisture to prevent the glue from cracking. Glue thus prepared will adhere to glass, metal, etc., and can be used for putting on labels without danger of their dropping off.

RESUSCITATION OF THE DROWNED.—The Massachusetts Humane Society has published the following plain directions for saving the lives of persons rescued from drowning after they have become insensible.

1. Lose no time. Carry out these directions on the spot. 2. Remove the froth and mucus from the mouth and nostrils. 3. Hold the body, for a few seconds, only with the head hanging down, so that the water may run out of the lungs and windpipe. 4. Loosen all tight articles of clothing about the neck and chest. 6. See that the tongue is pulled forward if it falls back into the throat. By taking hold of it with a handkerchief, it will not slip. 6. If the breathing has ceased, or nearly so, it must be stimulated by pressure of the chest with the hands, in imitation of the natural breathing, forcibly expelling the air from the lungs, and allowing it to re-enter and expand them to the full capacity of the chest. Remember that this is the most important step of all. To do it readily, lay the person on his back, with a cushion, pillow or some firm substance, under his shoulders; then press with the flat of the hands over the lower part of the breastbone and the upper part of the abdomen, keeping up a regular repetition and relaxation of pressure twenty or thirty times a minute. A pressure of thirty pounds may be applied with safety to a grown person. 7. Rub the limbs with the hands or with dry cloths constantly, to aid the circulation and keep the body warm. 8. As soon as the person can swallow, give a tablespoonful of spirits in hot water, or some warm coffee or tea. 9. Work deliberately. Do not give up too quickly. Success has rewarded the efforts of hours.

THE FOLLOWING is a list of the race horses which have won $5,000 or upwards in races run in America during the year 1875:

	Am't Won.
Aristides, by Lexington	$16,700
Tom Ochiltree, by Lexington	11,000
Olitipa, by Leamington	10,500
Calvin, by Tipperary	9,150
Aaron Pennington, by Tipperary	8,480
Ozark, by Pat Malloy	8,150
Ballenkeel, by Asteroid	7,800
Wildidle, by Lexington	7,600
Grinstead, by Gilroy	7,390
Dearolo, by Jonesboro	6,435
Countess, by Kentucky	6,200
Faithless, by Leamington	5,800
King Alphonso, by Phæton	5,660
Nannie Norton, by Leamington	5,460
Parroll, by Leamington	5,400
Ascension, by Australian	5,375

A CHINESE PAPER.—The Pekin *Gazette* has been established over one thousand years, and probably its present numbers are exact counterparts of the first it issued. It covers over ten pages, 4x8 inches, and has a yellow cover, on which its name is printed. It is the only native paper circulating in a kingdom of 414,-000,000 souls, among a people who have a literature which is vaster in its influence than that of any other nation. It is exclusively confined to official notices. The Chinese, slow, proud and conservative, have made no progress in a thousand years.

MISCELLANEOUS—Continued.

A NORWAY MAELSTROM.—Nearly midway in Lofoden strait, a huge naked rock, which might be fairly called an island, lifts itself above the waters, breasting the conflicting currents, caused by the winds and tides. Between this rock and the cape on Muskenoe is the famous maelstrom which fertile imaginations have clothed with many terrors. Its geographical position is such as to expose it to fierce tidal currents, and, when these are assisted by high western winds, they are, no doubt, terrific. The bottom of the strait is strewn with immense bowlders, which are so arranged as to give the current a spiral motion, directed toward the isolated rock from the northern side, which is so much increased in times of high tides and storms, when it whirls quite around the island rock. Then it is that it becomes really difficult for boats and vessels, without steam power, to keep clear of the rocks against which the wayward currents would dash them. While there are at times vast and powerful eddies, which give objects floating upon them a fearful spiral motion, there is nothing like a vortex produced by a subterranean discharge of the water, although the tumbling and boiling character of the spiral currents may submerge temporarily objects drifting on the surface. No doubt in the course of time the action of the waters has tended to level down the bed-rocks, some of which, we may presume, showed themselves above the surface. This may have made the maelstrom much more terrific than it is now, and better justified the ancient fables. As it is, in ordinary times and favorable weather, the fishermen do not hesitate to seek for fares throughout these waters, which to strangers are suggestive of the most terrible dangers.

A GAS SHADOW.—A striking and curious experiment, showing the superior weight of carbonic acid gas over air, may be made by projecting the shadow of the gas, as it is poured from its containing vessel, upon a screen. The latter should be of white paper, and bright sunlight should fall on the stream of gas, which should be poured from the spout of a pitcher held within ten inches of the screen. The curious result, of a shadow produced by apparently nothing, will be seen, the former resembling descending smoke, quite black at the spout of the vessel, but brightly illuminated whenever the sunlight is concentrated by passing through the gas.

EXPANSION OF HEAT.—A cold glass stopper put into a warm bottle, will become set so hard that no force can remove it, the glass contracting about it. The only way to remove such a stopper, or one made tight in any way, is to heat rather suddenly the neck of the bottle by a hot wet cloth, or by holding and turning it over a lamp; this will loosen the stopper. A warm nut was put on a cold screw, and when cold no man with a wrench could move it, till a red-hot iron, applied to the nut, loosened it. In another case, three men tried to unscrew a cast-iron pump tube, without success; but after heating the outer one, the application of the strength of a child unscrewed it.

AN OPTICAL ILLUSION.—St. Simon, in his famous "Memoirs," describing the personal appearance of the twelfth Duke of Albuquerque characterizes his hair as "coarse and green." The question here arises, Was the Duke's hair really of this color, or was St. Simon the victim of an optical illusion? That the latter was in all probability the fact, is shown in a communication made to the Paris Academy of Sciences by the venerable M. Chevreul, "the oldest student in France." On the day when the Duke de St. Simon saw Albuquerque, the latter wore a bullock's blood coat of coarse cloth, with buttons of the same, and his hair hung down on his shoulders. "Now" says Chevreul, "if we take hairs of a certain color, and arrange them on a red ground in parallel lines, making a small ribbon of them, and place beside them exactly similar hair on on a white ground, the former relatively to the latter will appear green. If for white we substitute orange, the red ground will assume a bluish tint; if violet a yellow tint; if green, a ruddy tint; if blue, an orange tint; if violet, a greenish yellow; and finally, if we substitute black for the white ground, the hairs on the red ground will become whitened. In short, if we look at a broad surface of one simple color, we see it and appreciate it absolutely. If we see it in juxtaposition with another color, or, still better, at the centre of a broad surface of another color, we see it relatively, and the sensation produced by it will be quite different."

REDUCTION OF OBESITY.—As a means of counteracting a tendency to obesity, and for reducing that habit after it has been established, Philbert recommends a mode of treatment somewhat different from that proposed by Banting. He interdicts the use of corbonaceous food as far as possible, and would augment the amount of oxygen. Hence the food must be nitrogenous, varied with a few vegetables containing no starch, and some raw fruit. The temperament, however, must be taken account of; the lymphatic should have a "red" diet—beef, mutton, venison, pheasant, etc.; the sanguine a "white" diet—veal, fowl, oysters, etc. Vegetables not sweet or farinaceous may be taken. Coffee without cream, and tea with little sugar, may be used. Sugar, butter, cheese, potatoes, beans, ets., are forbidden. In addition to these dietetic precepts, Philbert recommends favoring the action of the skin, supporting the wall of the abdomen by the use of a tight roller, and taking exercise freely. As a purgative, intended to promote the success of the treatment, the author recommends water containing sulphate of soda.

THE FOUR SEASONS.

			D.	H.	M.	
Winter begins,	1875,	December	22	0	8	mo
Spring	"	1876, March	20	1	2	mo
Summer	"	1876, June	20	9	23	ev
Autumn	"	1876, September	22	11	33	mo
Winter	"	1876, December	21	5	46	mo
Winter lasts			89	0	54	
Spring lasts			92	20	21	
Summer lasts			93	14	10	
Autumn lasts			89	18	13	
Tropical year			365	5	38	

MISCELLANEOUS—Continued.

THE CENSUS OF 1870.—The following statistics, from full returns of the ninth census, are interesting:

	1870		1860	
	Pop'n	Rank.	Pop'n	R'k
Alabama	996,992	16	964,201	13
Arkansas	484,471	23	435,450	25
California	560,247	24	379,094	26
Connecticut	537,454	25	460,147	24
Delaware	125,015	34	112,216	32
Florida	187,748	33	840,124	31
Georgia	1,184,109	12	1,057,286	11
Illinois	2,539,891	4	1,711,951	4
Indiana	1,680,637	6	1,350,428	6
Iowa	1,194,020	11	674,913	20
Kansas	364,399	29	107,206	33
Kentucky	1,321,011	8	1,155,684	9
Louisiana	726,915	31	708,002	17
Maine	626,915	23	628,279	22
Maryland	780,894	20	687,049	19
Massachusetts	1,457,351	7	1,231,066	7
Michigan	1,184,059	13	749,113	16
Minnesota	439,706	28	172,023	30
Mississippi	827,922	18	791,305	14
Missouri	1,721,295	5	1,182,012	8
Nebraska	122,993	35	28,841	36
Nevada	42,491	37	6,857	37
New Hampshire	318,300	31	326,073	27
New Jersey	906,096	17	672,035	21
New York	4,382,759	1	3,880,735	2
North Carolina	1,071,361	14	992,622	13
Ohio	2,665,260	3	2,339,511	4
Oregon	90,923	36	52,045	31
Pennsylvania	3,521,951	2	2,906,215	2
Rhode Island	217,353	32	174,028	29
South Carolina	705,606	22	703,707	18
Tennessee	1,248,520	9	1,109,801	10
Texas	818,579	19	604,215	23
Vermont	330,551	30	315,098	28
Virginia	1,223,163	10	1,219,630	5
Wisconsin	1,054,670	15	775,881	15
West Virginia	441,814	27	376,688	
Arizona	9,658	...	6,482	....
Colorado	39,864	....	34,277	....
Columbia	131,700	....	75,080	....
Dakota	14,181	....	4,837	....
Idaho	14,999	...	....	....
Montana	20,595	...	....	....
New Mexico	91,874	...	87,034	...
Utah	86,786	...	30,273	...
Washington	23,955	...	11,594	...
Wyoming	9,118	..	....	...
Total	38,558,371		31,443,321	

TO PREPARE tin for tinning brass, copper and iron. Melt the metal in a crucible which has previously been slightly warmed; and at the moment the metal begins to set, and when it is very brittle, pound it up rapidly, and sift when cold to remove any large particles.

AT BONN, GERMANY, headaches, dyspepsia, etc., affecting several patients, have been traced to evening studies pursued under the baleful influence of a green lamp shade, from which arsenic was set free by the heat of the flame.

A GERMAN astronomer has discovered two new small planets, not visible with the naked eye, in the constellation *Aries*. This makes the number of the lesser planets one hundred and fifty-three.

CHANCES OF MARRIAGE.—The following curious statement, by Dr. Granville, is drawn up from the registered cases of 876 married women in France. It is the first ever constructed to exhibit to ladies their chances of marriages at various ages. Of the 876 tabulated there were married

Years of age.	Years of age.	Years of age.
3 at 13	59 at 23	7 at 33
11 at 14	53 at 24	5 at 34
16 at 15	36 at 25	3 at 35
43 at 16	24 at 26	0 at 36
45 at 17	28 at 27	2 at 37
77 at 18	22 at 28	0 at 38
115 at 19	17 at 29	1 at 39
118 at 20	9 at 30	0 at 40
86 at 21	7 at 31	
85 at 22	5 at 32	

In considering this record it should be remembered that women, and men, too, mature somewhat earlier in France than in England, or in the northern or middle states of America. Our girls are no older at 20 than French girls are at 18. In the South, toward the tropics, girls mature as in France and Italy, and the rate of development is correspondingly the same with men.

LEGAL RATES OF INTEREST.—The following are the rates of interest allowed by the several States and Territories:

Five per cent. is legal rate in Louisiana.

Six per cent. is legal interest in Arkansas, Delaware, District of Columbia, Illinois, Indiana, Iowa, Kentucky, Maine, Maryland, Mississippi, Missouri, New Hampshire, New Mexico, North Carolina, Ohio, Pennsylvania, Rhode Island, Tennessee, Vermont, Virginia and West Virginia. In most of these States, however, written contracts for a higher rate are admissible in law.

Seven per cent. is legal in Connecticut, Dekota, Georgia, Kansas, Michigan, Minnesota, New Jersey, New York, South Carolina and Wisconsin.

Eight per cent. is legal rate in Alabama, Florida and Texas.

Ten per cent. is legal rate in Colorado, Idaho, Nebraska, Nevada, Oregon, Utah and Washington Territories.

Twelve per cent. is legal rate in Wyoming Territory, and in Montana parties may stipulate for any rate of interest.

A KING SOLOMON WANTED.—A mysterious basket, addressed to the station-master at Clayham Junction, on being opened, was found to contain a living child. The station-master declining the gift, a porter volunteered to accept it, and took the basket and child. On lifting the child, £800 was found in the basket. The story goes that the station-master then demanded the basket and its contents, which the porter very properly refused to give up. One can hardly doubt to which of the two the mother would entrust her child.

VEGETABLES do not ordinarily form as large a part of the ordinary subsistence of an American as they should. Whether cooked alone, or jointly with the cheaper pieces of meat in the form of a ragout, they will always serve as a substantial means of nutrition and tend to diminish the cost of household consuption.

INDEX.

EVERY BOTTLE WARRANTED. NO CURE, NO PAY.

Dr. Radcliffe's Great Remedy,

FOR INTERNAL AND EXTERNAL USE.

We challenge the world to produce a remedy which will prove by actual test a more speedy, certain and effectual cure for all Pains, of whatever form, external or internal, acute or chronic, deep-seated or otherwise, than

SEVEN SEALS OR GOLDEN WONDER.

It will effect a speedy cure in all cases of headache, Neuralgia, Toothache, Sprains, Cholera-Morbus, Diarrhœa, &c., and especially Rheumatism. It cures Pain almost instantly, and this is the grand secret of its success, for in hundreds of cases where this preparation has been used it has saved life, after science and skill had been completely baffled, all hope abandoned, and the patient's life despaired of. Try a bottle. If it does not cure you we will return you your money. Our motto: NO CURE, NO PAY.

Sold by all Druggists.

KENNEDY & CO., Sole Proprietors,
PITTSBURGH, PA.

☞ We want one good Agent in every county in the United States. Rare inducements offered Send for Circular.

www.ingramcontent.com/pod-product-compliance
Lightning Source LLC
Chambersburg PA
CBHW030018030726
47499CB00008B/3045